Indra Station

Joseph R. Lallo

ISBN: 9780999708170

Table of Contents

ACKNOWLEDGMENTS

I would like to acknowledge, as I so often do, the brilliant cover produced by Nick Deligaris and the skillful editing of Tammy Salyer.

Intro

Adrenaline is a dangerous high. Any addiction can ruin a life. The junkie on the street corner spending his last credits for something to burn his veins and fog his mind faces terrible risks and terrible consequences. But a thrill seeker's addiction is the risk itself. The high doesn't come in a bottle or a vial. It comes in a free fall. It comes in hairpin turns. Or in Lex's case, it came in a tightly packed cluster of overpowered hoversleds.

Lex snapped his gum and listened to the symphony of his sled's operation. He gripped the steering stick with one hand and cycled through a half-dozen other controls with the other hand as the throbbing power plant roared in an angry rhythm. More engines joined the chorus. The nearest of them wasn't five meters away from his flimsy cockpit. He didn't bother looking at the galaxy of meters and gauges reading out pressures and temperatures. If they weren't pegged against the redline, he wasn't doing his job. And the speedometer may as well have only two settings, "as fast as possible" and "loser."

The most incessant and irritating alarm was the proximity alarm. It was a remnant of more-civilized racing leagues where minimum distances were tightly enforced so as to at least marginally decrease the chances of fatal wrecks. The alarm hadn't stopped beeping at him since the start of the race. As wide as the track was, the optimal racing line was razor thin, so no one was interested in being anywhere else.

Pebbles the size of grapes clattered and blasted at his cockpit windscreen as he drew near enough to the lead sled to get into its backwash.

"I'm reading major collisions on your windscreen," barked a voice over the sled's radio.

"Yeah? Well, keep reading, because here come some major ones."

He danced his fingers over three controls that a sane man would never be tweaking during a race. The modules that kept his sled aloft sputtered and stuttered. His whole sled dropped until it was a whisper away from grinding against the ground. At the same time, he punched the throttle.

The lead sled hopped a mound of gravel. Lex plowed directly through the mound. It cost him some speed, but at the rate he was traveling, all that meant was he was knocked down to the speed at which he *should* have been taking the turn. The bouncing sled that had been ahead of him came down on top of him. He juiced the hover repulsors to keep from bottoming out. The sled smashed into his and spun madly toward the edge of the track.

"The goal is to *win* the race. Not to kill the other drivers," growled his pit man.

He took a sharp turn. One of the trailing racers seized the opportunity to ram him at full speed, forcing him off the smoothed-out track and into the jagged, sunbaked stone of the strip-mined former mountain they'd carved the track out of.

"Tell *them* that, would you?" he said, his eyes gleaming with demented glee as he wrestled his sled back onto the track.

A spiderweb of fine cracks were spreading across his left window as he glanced aside to see whom he was about to swap paint with. Another tooth-rattling smash kicked the bleeping alarm tones to a new level of intensity. He glanced at the nav screen and his rank indicator. It rolled from *Off Track* to *3rd Place*. Then he glanced at a flashing red blob on his diagnostic screen just below it. One of his repulsors was on the verge of failing.

Four turns left. A tenth of a second separating first from tenth. It was anyone's race. Or, at least, that was what the announcers would be barking. They didn't know what Lex knew. It was all over but the gloating.

He wrenched the controls hard, and his much-abused sled lurched up onto two of its repulsors. The damaged one sparked and physically dropped away, pushed past its limit. Lex feathered the controls to keep himself from coming down too early. Digging a damaged strut into the gravel of the track at this speed would turn his sled into a cross between a centrifuge and a rock tumbler in the blink of an eye.

The sled ahead was slowing up for another turn. He didn't bother, keeping his speed steady and waiting for his opportunity. Just as the sled came into range and that pesky proximity alert became more urgent, he flipped the controls. The tipped-up end of his sled came down like a guillotine. His suspension locked with that of the second-place sled.

Now effectively a sidecar for one of his opponents, he pushed his engines for all they were worth and did his best to keep from being shaken free. Something between fear and uncertainty kept the other driver from trying too hard to lose him. The joined-at-the-hip sleds navigated two more turns without losing any ground. They accelerated down the straightaway, perilously close to the first-place sled. What Lex had in mind had a window of opportunity that could probably be measured in nanoseconds, but that was true of most of the maneuvers in a race like this. The tricky part would be making sure his conjoined partner of the moment didn't mess things up.

The almost imperceptible shift in hue of the thrusters on the first-place sled signaled that the driver had down-shifted. A puff of additional gravel marked the firing of his retrothrusters. He was slowing for the final turn. Now was the moment.

Lex heaved the controls to one side, then the other. The other racer tried to compensate. Having to react meant he was correcting Lex's hard right with a hard left, but Lex was already turning left again. The combined shifts sent the pair of sleds into a wild spin. One final yank of the controls tore Lex free. The complex maneuver sent him twirling forward with all the precision of a drunken discus toss.

For two seconds that seemed more like two minutes, even Lex's vaunted powers of perception couldn't make heads or tails of what was happening. Then a distinctive tone sounded off and slid down into a register almost below the limits of hearing. The blur of debris and dislodged sled parts slowed until the flakes of metal and fragments of pulverized stone looked like leaves drifting in the wind. A bright light flashed lazily on and off. The TymFlex safety system had engaged. This came with the minor effect of shutting off all control systems and the major effect of slowing the passage of time within his cockpit to a crawl. Now he couldn't correct his flight even if he wanted to. But a quick glance at his trajectory told him there was no need.

A slow revolution brought him around to face the first-place sled. The driver within had his eyes locked on the finish line. With molasses slowness, he began to flick his eyes toward the spinning sled "piloted" by Lex. Lex grinned and gave a thumbs-up as his out-of-control trajectory took him past. In real time, it would be nothing but a flicker, but when they slowed it down for the replay, it'd make for one heck of a highlight.

Lex glanced down to his navigation screen. It was updating so slowly he could see the individual pixels shifting colors. The glowing *2nd* gradually gave way to a smoldering *1st*.

Ahead, the flickering wall of the finish line awaited him. He bounced once off the ground, which added a second axis to his spin and gave his journey the rock-tumbler quality he'd been hoping to avoid. It cost him a lot of speed as well, but not quite enough to give his opponent the lead before he crossed the finish line and cemented his victory.

A crash and tumble that lasted all of fifteen seconds outside of the influence of the safety system took several dizzying minutes within it. That didn't matter. The system did its job, and when the wadded-up pile of roll cages and impact dampeners wrapped around his cockpit came to rest, time resumed its natural flow. Out of habit, he shut his eyes and covered his ears. He knew what would come next.

Earsplitting bleeps started to blare from a canister affixed to the inside of the cockpit. The terrible sound was accompanied by a blinding strobe that was still almost painful even through tightly shut eyelids. Of all the safety equipment that was mandatory on these hoversleds, this was the only thing he genuinely hated. Because the tracks were so enormous and the hoversleds moved so fast, there was the very real chance that a wreck might be difficult to locate. Thus, this torture device was present on every racer. When it detected a crash, it would flash and bleep until its power was expended or an emergency key was inserted. The thing was entirely self-contained, so he couldn't even yank the power on it. He had no choice but to wait for the safety crew to cut him out of the wreckage and end his torment.

Torches flared, tools found their way to designated weak points, and finally the cockpit cracked open like an egg to let in the searing heat of the Operlo sun. The emergency workers hauled Lex out and silenced the device. When he was clear of the wreck, he shook the last of the dizziness away and gave another thumbs-up. The crowd roared.

While the medics applied various sensors and took assorted readings, Lex drank it all in. This is what he had been missing. Pushing his mind and body to the absolute limit. Pulling victory from the jaws of defeat. And having a crowd of people who knew just how impossible it had all been reward him with their adulation and adoration. He squinted at the stands, sweeping across them to see the distant faces of the crowd in a climate-controlled grandstand. He checked the big board to see his time. Not a track record, but fast enough to win. Off to the side he saw the other hoversleds, most of them far more intact than his, securing their own times and pulling aside. The second-place finisher was glaring at him. As well he should be.

Finally, he turned to the second crew cart approaching. The first had carried the medics and track techs. Now that the track was cleared of danger, the second cart carried people with a more personal investment in the crash. Foremost were Preethy Misra and Michella Modane. The former was COO of Operlo Entertainment Enterprises and commissioner of the Operlo Racing Intersystem Circuit. The latter was GolanaNet's top investigative reporter. They were Lex's boss and girlfriend respectively. Both managed to achieve the look of combined concern and fury that so often seemed to grace the faces of the women in his life.

Lex spat out his gum.

"I don't suppose any of you guys can give me a doctor's note, can you?" he said as the medics packed their things up. "Something tells me Michella's not going to go easy on me after this one."

Chapter 1

Lex and Michella stepped out of a hovercar in front of the gleaming new apartment building the league had set up as housing for its racers during the season. It was not clear if it was an oversight or intentional, but this meant the local press knew exactly where to find any racers they felt like hounding, and more often than not, this meant Lex.

A crush of bodies and a swarm of drifting camera modules pressed in around them as they made their way to the front door, sheltered from the punishing sun and enjoying the runoff of the building's air-conditioning.

"Lex! Lex, how do you feel after your fourth crash of the year?" barked a man holding a slidepad in record mode.

"Hey, hey. This was crash number three. That last one was a fender bender at *best*," he said with a grin.

"This brings your preseason record to 4-2," said another person straddling the roles of reporter and paparazzi.

"That's not how they keep track of the standings in league racing, pal. You're thinking of *lesser* sports," Lex jabbed. "But yeah, this puts a fourth first-place finish under my belt."

"Is there any truth to the rumor that you've got a personal vendetta against Mars Washington?"

"'Vendetta' is a pretty strong word. The guy's placed ahead of me twice. It's a little early to be declaring rivalries."

"But unofficially?"

"Let's just say he shouldn't get too used to spending time in that winner's circle."

More questions flowed and the rapid click and flicker of video and stills recorded his responses, but Lex's patience gave out long before their thirst for answers was satisfied. He slipped into the building and gave them a final wave as the building security kept them at bay.

"You're a little too comfortable with fame," Michella said.

"You're just upset this was a racing crowd so you didn't get many questions," Lex jabbed.

"I'm not in it for the fame," Michella said.

"Me neither. I'm in it because this is one of the only careers that pays me to go fast *and* pairs me up with decent competition. The fame is just a nice little bonus."

The doors to the building's elevator slid open, and the pair stepped inside.

"Man," Lex said, gazing about at the sprawling, carpeted conveyance. "I still can't get over it. This elevator is bigger than my old dorm room."

"Yeah. Mobsters do like to make a point of flaunting their blood money at every opportunity."

"Hey. Race promoters, not mobsters."

"Oh? Are we just *pretending* Nick Patel isn't a notorious crime lord?"

"No. I'm just pointing out that he's not the one behind all this; his niece is."

Michella crossed her arms. "There's a reason why they call them crime *families*, Lex. You're playing a dangerous game."

He shrugged and let the comment hang for a moment. They'd had this conversation enough times that he didn't feel obligated to rush through it. Instead, he gazed at an advertising screen showing a shallow holographic promo for the first official race of the season. The high-impact nature of the exhibition races had not been lost on the marketing team. The ad was practically a nonstop montage of the bumps, crashes, and wrecks that had happened thus far.

"I'll grant you things are a little more full-contact in ORIC than back in the old days. But, you know. Racing was never without risks."

"That's not what I'm talking about."

"In that case, why aren't you talking about that?" He pointed dramatically at the crash footage. "Look at those maniacs smashing into each other. Aren't you worried about me getting mangled?"

"I know you, Trev. You're safe as a baby in his mother's arms so long as you've got a vehicle to manhandle. But you're a tad too trusting to be wrapped up in organized crime. Remember what happened last time?"

"Last time? Let's see…"

The doors opened and they stepped out onto his apartment's floor, which was just shy of penthouse level.

"I'm having trouble recalling. Oh, right. I remember. That's when I took a bribe to take a dive, because I was up to my neck in debt and needed a way out. That got me kicked out of the sport for a few years and reduced me to driving a limo, delivering packages, and otherwise squandering my talents. Funny how that slipped my mind."

"I don't appreciate your tone, Trev."

"I don't appreciate your inability to conceive that I might have learned from my mistakes."

"Well, here we are, you racing in a sport that's completely entrenched in organized crime."

"No. Here we are, me racing in a sport that is completely *separate* from organized crime."

"Allegedly," she muttered.

They approached a turn in the hallway and paused as the excited tapping of toenails on the polished tile floors approached.

"Sounds like *someone* let herself out of the room again," he said in an accusatory tone.

The tapping nails stopped. Lex crouched down low and crept up to the corner. When he was nearly there, he poked his head out and was immediately assaulted by a bundle of black-and-white fur, who lavished his face and neck with licks and nibbles.

It was Squee. While genetic tinkering was responsible for producing the fox-skunk hybrid, Squee was unique in her capacity to overcome any and all attempts to electronically wrangle her, thanks to the side effects of some rather significant modifications.

She curled happily about his shoulders and rode him back up. When Michella's face came into range, Squee gave her a pity lick. It was clear the creature was far more excited to see Lex than her.

"What was I saying?" Michella asked.

"We were talking about how it is supposed to be a *beautiful* day tomorrow and we should make the best of it."

"It's supposed to be sixty degrees Celsius tomorrow with a severe sandstorm watch," she said.

"But I am fresh off a win, and I'm here with my two best girls. That makes *every* day a beautiful day." He waved his slidepad at the lock for his apartment and happily stepped inside. "I know. Let's hit Sarafa tonight."

"Sarafa is way too expensive and exclusive."

He pulled open the fridge and grabbed a container of beans and rice. Squee practically vibrated with glee at its appearance.

"Sometimes you've got to treat yourself. I won the race today." He popped the beans in the cooker to reheat. "And as for exclusivity, I know someone who can pull some strings."

He waggled his eyebrows. She smirked, but the moment of weakness passed quickly.

"*That's* what we were talking about. Mob connections. You might be ready and willing to fall in with that crowd again and get mixed up in their schemes, but I'm not willing to stand idle while you do it."

He gritted his teeth as the cooker bleeped. Squee sprang to the ground and commenced hopping up and down, practically to shoulder height, in anticipation of the meal.

"So let me get this straight. Ripping across the landscape at super-sonic speeds, no problem. But the possibility that I might have to say no to someone offering to pay me to do the thing I *least* want to do—lose a race—and suddenly I'm this wide-eyed rube who can't be trusted to make the right decision."

"You did it before."

"Yes! We've established that! I just—" He shut his eyes and took a breath before setting the beans down for Squee to dig into. "Look. We can discuss this if you want to. Over dinner. At Sarafa. Tonight at six p.m. I've already got reservations."

"Tonight at six?" she said.

"Yep! Come on. It's supposed to be the most authentic Indian cuisine outside of Earth."

"I can't make it. Not tonight."

He tapped out the warmed beans and rice, which Squee promptly shoved her face into.

"You have plans?" he said, eyebrow raised.

"I do. Should run until seven."

"What *sort* of plans?"

"Work stuff."

"But you are on sabbatical."

"Yeah. That means time off work for study."

"And you've got studying to do here." He glared at her. "Haven't we already learned what happens when you do that?"

"For your information, it *isn't* here." She glanced aside. "Which is another thing. I'm going to need to borrow your ship tomorrow."

"My ship. The *SOB*. You need to borrow the *SOB*," he said, like a parent who was asked for the keys to the family grocery hauler right before spring break.

"Yeah. You've been teaching me how to fly it. It's a short trip. I can probably do ninety percent of it on autopilot."

"You can probably do one hundred percent in a rental."

"You won't let your own *girlfriend* borrow your precious ship for a few hours?"

"Where are you taking it?"

"That's… private."

"Then no, I'm not letting you borrow my ship."

"*Please…*" she said with a calculated shift in tone. She ran her fingers through his hair and pulled him close. "I know you like the thought of me at the controls of a ship."

He winced at the words.

"Is something wrong?" she asked.

"It's nothing. I was reminded of something. I didn't—" He shook the rest of the sentence away. "Listen, I'll make you a deal. You can borrow the *SOB* on three conditions. First, you promise to have it back by 8 p.m. tomorrow."

"Done."

"Second, you deliver it to me at Sarafa right before we have *dinner* at 8 p.m. tomorrow."

"I thought the reservation was for tonight."

"You let me worry about that."

"Okay, fine. Done. And the third?"

He pulled her just a bit closer. "We stop with the arguing for the rest of the night and just enjoy ourselves."

"I think I can manage that."

He gave her a kiss. "Okay. The ship's yours for tomorrow."

"Great!" She pulled away and checked the fridge. "Are there any leftovers?"

Squee, having made short work of her meal, bounced back to Lex's shoulder and immediately left a smear of beans on his cheek in her eagerness to lavish some more affection on him.

"We were going to go shopping, but the press conference ran long. I figured we could order in."

"No time," she said, snatching a hummus. "I've got an appointment in twenty minutes."

Lex tried to deliver a withering glare, but his intensity was somewhat diffused by Squee industriously licking his ear.

"More 'study'?"

"What else would I allow to take me away from a night in with you two?" she said.

"You're finding an awful lot of journalism to do on a planet that has exactly three industries," he rumbled.

"Uh-uh-uh! *You're* the one who said no more fighting."

"That's dirty pool, Michella Modane."

Squee finally settled down and went into "scarf mode," flopping down on one shoulder and curling her enormous fluffy tail around his neck. Lex grabbed a beer from the fridge.

"When will you be back?"

"Maybe ten?"

"Okay. Now I'm not telling you how to live your life, but I'm just giving you fair warning. At 10 p.m., there will be a chocolate cake sitting on that table. And if you're not here by 10:15, me and Squee are splitting it and you're not getting a piece."

She offered a wry grin. "How dare you threaten me like that."

He raised his hands. "Hey, don't blame me. This little cutie's sweet tooth will *not* be denied."

She grabbed some carrot sticks and checked the time.

"I'd better get going. Maybe next time don't finish in the top three and we'll get out of the press event quick enough to have dinner together," she joked.

Michella tousled Squee's hair, then Lex's, and hurried out the door.

Lex took a sip of his beer and looked wearily at Squee. "Just you and me for the night. Again…"

He stood and paced through the apartment. The living room alone could probably fit two of his apartment back on Golana. The furniture was sleek and modern. More impressively, thanks to the housekeeping the building provided, the cushions and carpets were still pristine white. How they managed to keep everything free of hair despite Squee's best efforts was as near to a genuine miracle as Lex had ever witnessed.

The amount of time Lex and Michella spent on the road meant the bedroom was virtually unused. Despite having been living on Operlo for the eight weeks that had passed since the league's preseason, they still had bags and boxes waiting to be unpacked. He shifted them around and popped the lid off a plastic crate near the bottom of the stack.

Squee peered down into the box from her perch on his shoulder as he rummaged through it. Eventually, he turned up a small white box of a distinctive size and shape. He opened it and gazed at its contents.

"Going on three months and I still haven't gotten a chance to give it to her. I'm not going to lie, Squee. Ignoring these red flags is starting to be a full-time job." He snapped it shut. "But enough about that. I've got another first-place finish under my belt. My first official race season is just a week away, and one way or another, I'm going to execute Operation Romantic Surprise. Things are finally going my way. What do you say we go for a ride?"

Squee's eyes lit up, and she sprang about the room happily before trotting for the door.

"Just let me get cleaned up and we'll—"

He was cut off by the sound of the door hissing open and Squee trotting out into the hall. Lex sighed.

"Someday I'm sure one of the women in my life will actually care about the sounds that are coming out of my mouth."

#

Michella tapped open the door of the autocab that had dropped her off. The sun had slid from the sky already, casting the dry desert landscape into a surprisingly brisk night. That was something that always came as a shock to newcomers, just how quickly and sharply the cold could descend once the sun was gone from the sky. Fortunately, she'd been here long enough to bring her long coat. Today, that coat would serve a dual purpose. Not only would it keep her teeth from chattering, but its upturned collar and her wide-brimmed hat would keep her from being recognized, too. Success as a reporter had brought fame, which helped give her more latitude with the stories she could investigate. That fame also made it harder for her to actually do the investigation. People with something to hide weren't likely to open up to a woman renowned around the galaxy for revealing secrets.

She paced through the cool streets of what would soon be a new neighborhood. Operlo was growing quickly, with lots of fresh construction springing up to house the crews associated with Nick Patel's venture into sports and entertainment. Lots of new construction meant lots of new employees. Lots of new employees meant security stretched ever thinner. That was a golden opportunity for someone in her business. All it took was a single new hire who'd skipped the section in the employee manual about nondisclosure agreements and she had her next scoop.

A large, freshly applied sign on a chain-link fence labeled the construction site ahead as a project under the oversight of Technic Infrastructure Solutions. A wry smile came to her face.

"It must burn at him to have someone else doing construction on his home turf," Michella said. "I'll bet he never thought he'd see the day that there'd be a worksite on Operlo that didn't bear the Patel Construction logo."

She continued along the fence until she came to a flimsy metal trailer with a huge air-conditioning unit hanging off the side. Doors on either side of the trailer made it clear this was some sort of access control point. Workers must have had to pass through it to reach the worksite. Though it was well after hours, the small window on the door showed that a light was burning within.

Michella climbed the wobbly aluminum steps and knocked on the door. After a moment, a sunbaked fellow in TIS overalls opened it a crack.

"Yeah?" he said.

"Hello, we spoke earlier. About the interview?"

"Huh?"

"The interview. About these new construction projects."

"Oh, oh. Right. Yeah. I remember. I remember there was… uh… some criteria for the interview."

She casually slipped her hand into her purse and pulled out a short stack of casino chips.

"I don't know *what* you're talking about," she said with a straight face as she dropped the chips into his waiting palm. "This was just an interview."

"Right. Right. I must've been thinking about someone else. Come on in."

He held the door, and she stepped into the trailer. The inside wasn't much to look at. It was all one big room with some desks, some chairs, and a strange chain-link fence with an extra gate blocking off the door that would lead into the construction site. The metal walls were unpainted. They got hot enough to scald anyone foolish enough to touch them during the day. The whole trailer had the lingering funk of sweat-drenched workers popping inside to cool off a few times a day.

Her host wiped a layer of caked dust off a folding chair and invited Michella to sit. He took a seat opposite.

He leaned down to get a better look at her face as she removed her hat.

"Heh. I figured it was you. Michella Modane." He reached out a hand. "Pleased to meet you. I got this job because of you."

"I don't know that I really deserve the credit," she said.

"Too bad this meeting is all hush-hush," he said. "A bunch of the crew is from Golana. I remember when you were just doing financial news on GolanaNet Local. You were the hottest of the money honeys."

"Well thank you," she said with an expertly crafted false smile.

"Hey, you think maybe we could get a picture together? Not to show anybody."

"Let's talk about that later," she said quickly, fetching a pad and pen from her bag. "I don't have a lot of time, so I wonder if we could get straight to business."

"Sure, sure. Ground rules, though. No recording. And if I tell you to put the pen away, put the pen away. I don't want my name or any me-specific info getting out there and losing me my job."

"That's fair."

"Good. So, what do you want to know?"

"Let's start with what exactly your role is."

"Security. I'm the jobsite security tech for this project. The, uh…" He leaned aside and tapped a datapad sitting on a nearby desk. "The Workers Housing Project, Unit 5. I'm only a temp here, though."

"I see. When did you get started?"

"Heh. You know that. I got started about six weeks ago, when you went on the newsfeed talking about how all the construction on the planet was Patel Construction projects and how that seemed like a perfect chance to do money laundering. TIS got the contract for the overflow work when Patel agreed to subcontract some stuff, and that's when I got brought in."

"They subcontracted security?"

"Uh, no. They subcontracted construction, but every site handles its own security." He shrugged. "Nothing much to secure here, anyway."

"What *is* being built here?"

"Down south of here, they're putting the finishing touches on a racetrack. I guess they expect there to be a ton of upkeep on it, because this place is supposed to house like a two-hundred-member crew to keep it running in tip-top shape. So it's nothing but some housing and some workshops and garages. I don't even know why they need security in the first place."

"How are you liking the work?"

"It sucks. I'm just working the office and it sucks. I can't even imagine how the workers handle it."

"Patel doesn't treat you well?"

He shrugged again. "He doesn't. Patel's not in charge of us. Running this little operation is all on TIS. You ask me, I don't think the eggheads handing out assignments even checked the climate of Operlo before they took the contract. From what I hear, Patel's guys have plenty of shade and drinks and stuff out there in the worksite. We've got the same setup we had when we were doing a job on Movi. And if you ask me, they don't have half as many people down here as they should to get the job done. Seriously understaffed. I've been working a double assignment. Lucky for me, I'm fully reassigned to a cushier part of my job starting tomorrow."

Michella jotted down some notes, then flipped back in her pad. "Yes, you mentioned something about an orbital job."

He glanced aside, as though the room that they'd had to themselves since she'd arrived might suddenly have eavesdroppers.

"You put that pen away, and we'll talk about it. This is one of the super hush-hush things."

She stowed the pad and pen.

"Yeah. They've had me on the low-level security staff on this big orbital project for almost as long as I've been here. Same stuff as in here. Access control. Some scheduling. They've got a mandatory security bulk-up on the station around the same time every week. That's why I'm due up there tomorrow. But now I'll be staying up there until the project is done, apparently. Sweet gig, as long as you can handle a little zero-g."

"So there is a large space-station construction project going on?"

"Yeah. I guess they've been saying it was just building up the communication system."

"There have been an awful lot of network outages and slowdowns lately."

"Right, yeah. That's what this is *supposedly* about. You ask me, I think it's more than that."

"You think it's more than that? You don't know what the station is for?"

"Not really. I mean, I'm only doing access control and some camera monitoring and stuff. It's not like they gave me the operating manual."

"How close to completion is it?"

"It's pretty much done. They've had some of us TIS guys up there working on it round the clock."

"But you don't know what it is."

"No idea."

Michella's mind clicked through some possibilities. "Would you agree it is fair to say Mr. Patel and Ms. Misra are going to reveal it when it is complete?"

"Who knows what the C-level people are thinking?"

"You've got me intrigued, sir. I smell the opportunity for an exclusive." She delivered the line with dramatic flair, expertly masking the fact that she'd been planning the next little exchange since before she's left her apartment.

"Oh yeah?"

"I don't suppose you could find some time for me to visit the station while you're on duty tomorrow."

"What for? Why not just ask what you want to ask down here?"

"There's no substitute for a hands-on tour."

He whistled. "That's a tall order, Miss."

She reached into her bag and jingled some casino chips. "How tall of an order are we talking about?"

His jaw tightened and his brow furrowed slightly. From the looks of him, it was all he could do to keep from salivating at the potential palm-greasing another favor would earn.

"You'd have to get up there without anyone knowing."

"That shouldn't be a problem."

"If you do this wrong, I'm going to ignore your hail and pretend like you're not there."

"I've handled far more harrowing situations than this. I'm confident I can slide in without anyone noticing."

"Let's call it… fifty thousand credits? Half now, half when I come through with it?"

"That sounds fair to me."

"And I want the full 'top secret source' treatment. No one can know I'm the one who let you up there."

"Absolutely. I've covered the work of spies who would be killed if their identity was known, and they remain safe and sound."

"Good, good. Then let's see the down payment."

She retrieved five 5K chips from her bag and dropped them into his hand.

"Pleasure doing business with you."

"And with you."

"Here. Gimme that pad of yours. I'll write down the coordinates."

She obliged. When he returned it and her pen, a geostationary orbital position was jotted down in shuttle notation. Below it was a user ID for a messaging service. When she looked back up to him, he winked. "In case you ever want to ditch that racer of yours and get with a real man."

Michella flipped the pad shut and stowed it. "As you said," she said, standing and extending a hand, "it has been a pleasure doing *business* with you."

She emphasized the word "business" in order to underscore that pleasure was not on the menu. After a few more bits of idle chitchat about the way TIS did business on Operlo, she excused herself and went off on her way.

Most of what she'd learned in the meeting had been just the song and dance on the way to the bribe for access to the station. She'd had a feeling there was something major going on in orbit. All the signs pointed to it if you knew where to look for them. From the constant network interruptions to various orbital traffic rerouting announcements. The key things she'd learned were where to find the station, how to get onto the station, and when the station was intended to be the most secure. Just as she'd suspected, the times of highest security coincided with uncharacteristically large sections blocked out on the schedule of some of the higher-ranking members of both Operlo Entertainment and Patel Construction.

This station had Nick Patel's fingerprints all over it, just like everything else on this planet. And that he wanted it to be a secret meant it was downright *tantalizing*. She'd be putting Lex's ship to *excellent* use tomorrow.

Chapter 2

Early the next morning, Lex brought his personal hoversled to a stop outside a headquarters building so pristine and grand it was physically painful to view it in the sun.

He popped open the gullwing door and stepped into the blast furnace of a morning. Squee hopped down to the ground, yelped, and immediately abandoned the searing surface for the safety of Lex's shoulder. There were two things that made a planet worth colonizing. The first was an environment that either was similar to or could quickly be *made* similar to Earth in one way or another. That's how places like Tessera or Golana became so populous so quickly. Less than a generation of massaging the atmospheric balance or seeding the soil with the appropriate vegetation and they were more or less identical to Earth. Operlo *technically* fulfilled this requirement. There was enough oxygen and enough pressure to keep a human alive. Gravity was quite near one g. The temperature ranges in the habitable zones were just barely survivable if exposure was kept to a minimum. Much closer to the equator and human life required protective suits. Much farther north and the temperature swings made permanent settlement inadvisable. In an earlier stage in space exploration, it would have been a miracle to find something so well suited to human colonization, but advanced terraforming and increased superluminal speeds meant finding a better planet would have been the proper course of action, barring something on Operlo that made up for the mediocre habitability.

Fortunately for those who laid claim to the smoldering little rock, Operlo handily satisfied the *other* big reason to settle a planet. Resources. Solar collectors made energy effectively free, and the veins of elements crucial for everything from superconductors to high-temperature fusion regulators meant virtually everyone who set foot there in its earliest days had gotten filthy rich.

Like any other gold rush, only the first to arrive and the first to leave actually *stayed* rich. Latecomers missed out on the better land,

and people who stayed too long saw prices drop and mines run dry. This left the scrappy and the crazy to fight over the leftovers. Couple that with the off-the-beaten-track position with respect to travel corridors and Operlo may as well have been a designated mob planet from the start.

But the glorious new headquarters sheltered beneath its roof-mounted solar array wasn't some sort of mafia don's pleasure palace or a relic of the mining barons. Against all odds, this shining jewel was a brand-new one in Operlo's crown. League headquarters for the Operlo Racing Intersystem Circuit, or ORIC.

A humming drone darted out from the entryway and deployed a silvered parasol to shield Lex and Squee from the sun. "Welcome, Lex," came a voice from a speaker installed in the base of the drone as it hovered over his head.

"Preethy?" he said.

"Yes. What do you think of the escort drones? Uncle insists on race days we use actual parasol bearers, but for less overtly glamorous occasions I thought these would be more efficient."

"It certainly beats getting sunstroke."

"You should see the bioluminescent lampposts. Cost-free, self-maintaining lighting. But that is a discussion for a later time. You are a bit early. I'm due back in a meeting. In a moment we will be discussing something you should have some insight into, if you'd care to sit in."

"Sure. I'll be right up."

He hurried to the entryway. As he slipped inside, the drone clicked its parasol shut and drifted over to a grid of identical devices to mount itself like a wall sconce until it would be needed again.

Despite the fact that they'd yet to have their first official race of the first official season, the lobby of the ORIC HQ looked like it belonged to an organization with a decades-long history. Columns housing holographic emitters displayed slickly produced videos of everything from track tours to racer interviews. They'd gotten a fair amount of press already, thanks in no small part to Lex's involvement. His past celebrity in racing combined with his more recent fame as a "hero of the day" was enough to put the league on the radar of some of the better-established news sources in the area, so they were spoiled for choice when it came to showing footage of sharp-dressed talking heads reading from press releases.

Indra Station

One of the larger holoscreens looped around to the beginning of a video package that had been shown so frequently, Lex was *certain* the public must be sick of it.

"The rebel that started it all, Trevor 'Lex' Alexander," proclaimed a silky-voiced narrator. "Fresh out of college, Lex was already burning up the tracks. He was one of the youngest racers to become a household name on the bustling planet of Golana. By earning his way to the Tremor Grand Prix, Lex's place in history was all but assured. But a poor decision and a zero-tolerance policy cost him not only his place in the winner's circle, but his entire career. Lex wasn't one to let destiny pass him by, though. For years he sharpened his talents, dancing on the ragged edge of any and all jobs that could push the limits of speed. When an act of heroism during the now infamous Westin University Terror Attack spared the lives of countless citizens, Preethy Misra felt the time had come for a chance at redemption. And so, ORIC was born. ORIC is a rebel league, a place of second chances. ORIC racers don't let limits define them."

The video switched to a shot of Lex.

"We push the limits until they break," he said in unison with his recording.

The advertisement continued on to list off the prospective schedule and to encourage fans to view, visit, like, favorite, thumbs-up, and otherwise lavish engagement upon ORIC in the weeks to come.

He trotted up the glossy black steps to the executive offices on the second-floor landing and scanned across the glass-walled conference rooms. He found the one where Preethy stood before a table of investors, pointing out this figure or that on a chart displayed behind her.

Preethy's Indian descent was plainly obvious at first glance, but her poise and diction screamed "expensive business school." Any trace of an accent of any kind had been ruthlessly drilled out of her. It produced an almost mechanical tone and delivery as she worked through dizzying gauntlets of business terminology. It was the sort of sterile homogenization of executives that made investors feel more comfortable, even if it left the average boardroom rather flavorless.

Lex had first met Preethy when her role had still been limited to the secretarial requirements of her uncle, Nicholas Patel. In those days she'd tended toward a wardrobe that teetered on the precipice of risqué, a rare bit of rebellion that did a remarkable job of destabilizing the largely male clientele she did her day-to-day dealings with. Something about being elevated to the chief executive level of her own organization had persuaded her to temper her fashion decisions just a bit.

She buzzed the door open and Lex slipped inside.

"We'll discuss the countermeasures in greater detail later, but I'm sure you'll all be quite satisfied," Preethy said, concluding the current point of business. "But, gentlemen, I'm sure you know Trevor Alexander, one of our premier racers and advisers."

"Fellas," he said with a wave.

"Ah," Preethy said, a warm smile coming to a face that until that moment had been nothing but serious. "I see you've brought our mascot."

Lex gave Squee a scratch. "She can't be trusted by herself," he said, pulling out an expensive mesh-backed office chair. "And frankly, I'd feel like a heel leaving her alone besides."

"I take it Ms. Modane is not in your apartment then."

"She found some work to do," he said.

The warmth faded from her expression. "Lovely. Well, since you are here, I was just about to discuss the safety measures in our vehicles. As you know them better than anyone, would you care to give your summary and assessment?"

"Um, sure," he said. "Do you have any slides you want to put up?"

An exploded diagram of the hoversled appeared on the main display. Lex stood and paced past Preethy. Along the way, Squee eyed up the boss's shoulder an made ready to jump to it. With reflexes that suggested considerable experience with the funk's proclivities, Preethy caught her out of the air and carried her over to the doorway. A young man stepped into view as if magically conjured. He was carrying a crystal bowl and a bottle of spring water. As Lex got started, she filled the bowl for Squee.

"As I hope most of you know, this is my second professional league. I've been at or near the top of this sport twice, and I can say without a shadow of a doubt that the sort of commitment to safety you see in this sled design is unprecedented. And trust me, I've put it to the test…"

#

Lex oozed charisma during the meeting in a way that only someone who lived and breathed racing could. He worked his way through dry topics like the very same TymFlex safety system that had saved his life. He talked up the crumple zones, reactive repulsors, and other little details that allowed him to push the performance of the sled well past the point of sanity without risking his life. Each time interest drifted, he wrapped this feature or that into an anecdote that started with screeching metal and ended with him without a scratch on him. He did an impressive job illustrating how making the sleds safer for the drivers gave the drivers the freedom to, if they had the intestinal fortitude, make the races much more exciting.

"… And that's what it really comes down to, isn't it? More excitement means more butts in seats. More butts in seats means more money," he said.

"But, surely, all of this comes at a cost," opined one of the business types at the far corner of the table.

"For budget, you talk to Preethy. But in my biased opinion, the most valuable part of a hoversled is the person at the controls."

Preethy stepped up. "Price, at this stage, is no object. We have had six exhibition races. In other leagues these are lightly attended and lightly viewed. In our case the ticket and on-demand revenue alone has recouped nearly seventy-five percent of the cost outlay per race. Advertisers are lining up for air time, product placement, and logo placement. We can guarantee you that the very first official race will be fully solvent, and as the season progresses, that income will only grow."

"But the official races will have more racers," countered the naysayer as he glanced at a datapad. "In these six races alone, six sleds have been totaled, and a further four have been damaged enough to be removed from rotation. Multiply that by the proportionate increase in racers, and equipment costs alone will be ruinous."

Lex rolled his eyes. "Speaking as the guy who was piloting half of those totaled sleds, let me make one thing clear. Those crashes? Those are the things people pay to see. Sure, we all love to see good racing done right, but every last person in those stands is secretly hoping to see a wreck. It's human nature," Lex said.

Preethy clicked to a complex chart. "Lex is correct. We have found that audience attention spikes considerably during crashes. Our drivers are more aggressive than in other leagues, and if we can give people this sort of excitement while simultaneously guaranteeing the safety of the drivers, the increase in viewership and the loyalty of the fanbase will more than offset the equipment costs." She clicked to another slide. "We are even preparing Quarry 6 to serve as a demolition derby track to reuse damaged sleds that cannot be made safe to move at racing speeds."

The potential investor seemed reluctantly mollified.

"If there are no more questions, I think that will conclude our meeting for today. I will be unavailable for calls between 4 and 10 p.m., but if you have any questions, contact my staff and we'll be sure to have answers for you by the next meeting."

One by one, the suit-wearing executives stood. Lex quickly snagged Squee, who was already waggling her butt in preparation to cover some very expensive suits with her fur. He tucked her under his arm while shaking hands with the procession of investors. When they were gone, Preethy led the way from the conference room toward her office.

"You are a natural salesman, Lex," she said. "Yet another entry on a long list of your talents."

"It helps that I'm the product," he said. "It really lights a fire under you to get people excited about something when, if they don't, you're out of a job."

"Indeed. And may I say I was pleased, though confused, to see you draw the attention so swiftly to the danger aspect of our league. As you saw, I had the data to suggest our audience is, in a word, bloodthirsty. But I was reluctant to emphasize this aspect out of respect for you. It hardly seems appropriate to underscore those parts of the sport that put your life in danger."

"Heh, trust me. *This* isn't putting my life in danger. I've been through stuff that makes this look like a walk in the park."

"I am well aware," she said.

"And you don't know the half of it. Honestly, while we're on the subject of safety, is there any way we can drop the safety locator requirement? Or at least make it a radio thing instead of a siren? My ears are still ringing."

"I'm afraid it's non-negotiable. If you'd like to avoid having your ears assaulted by our safety features, I would recommend you stop crashing hoversleds."

He stopped walking for a moment and tapped his chest. Squee took the moment of distraction to wriggle free and climb to his shoulder.

"Are you not feeling well?" she asked.

He blew out a breath. "I spite-ate most of a cake last night," he said. "It's repeating on me."

"How you spend your off time is your own business, but you have some curious habits, Lex," she said.

Her slidepad bleeped. She slid it from her pocket and clucked her tongue before dismissing the notification.

"Something bad?" he asked.

"Sandstorm watch. The weather service sends them out at the drop of a hat at this time of year."

"I saw a few of those. Should we be worried? The winds on the open fields are bad enough on a normal day."

"Sandstorms are effectively the only natural weather phenomena on Operlo. I can assure you that they won't come as a surprise. I'll have more to say on the subject when we are alone, but for now, suffice it to say that if one is likely to interrupt a race, the race will be postponed."

"Postponed… Oh! Is there any chance we can make some reservations for 8 p.m. tonight? I should have asked sooner, but you're a hard woman to get ahold of."

"Of course. Anytime. I'm frankly surprised you didn't go last night, after the race. It would have been a fine time."

"Yeah, it would have. I was thinking about it."

"Is there a reason you didn't?"

Lex's expression hardened a bit. "Guess."

"Ah. More 'work' for Ms. Modane. From her dedicated interest, one would think that Operlo is the only planet in the galaxy with any potential news. I'd think she'd have perhaps gone to investigate those reports about a supposed 'missing star,' or the convention fiasco on Tessera. I understand there is a bribery scandal back on Golana that is *precisely* the sort of thing she would investigate, rather than our little world."

"I'm really sorry about that."

Preethy raised a hand. "No, no. There is nothing wrong with a bit of rigor. I am confident that she will find no criminality at any level within this organization, because there is no criminality to find. I only wish the investigation itself wasn't so disruptive. There are some crimes for which an accusation is enough to color public opinion. The money-laundering episode was not without its consequences."

"Yeah…" Lex muttered.

Michella had been investigating the league from the moment Lex had signed on. She tackled it with her usual fervor, but something she'd done that was quite unlike her was, after spotting some potential inconsistencies, reporting on her speculation without solid evidence of its truth. She was professional enough to never *claim* she could prove her claims, but the funny thing about news audiences is they don't withhold their outrage until they're sure it's warranted.

"I cannot help that my uncle's construction firm is the only on-planet firm. And I can certainly see how one might easily turn that into a money-laundering scheme. But the fact that every credit of our budget was perfectly accounted for was not enough to counter the negative press we received," Preethy said.

"There *was* a huge chunk funneled into research and development."

"Which should come as no surprise, as we are currently researching and developing quite a few new technologies and properties. Regardless, that news cycle is mercifully over. Taking on contracts from outside—and unnecessary—contracting firms was a costly solution, but it *was* a solution. I just hope this new bit of work she is doing doesn't necessitate another one."

"She's just… when she catches a scent, she's like a bloodhound," Lex said.

"I was under the impression that a bloodhound finds a scent and follows it, rather than starting where they suspect a scent will be and refusing to look elsewhere despite its absence." Preethy shut her eyes. "I apologize. I am being undiplomatic, and the pressure I have been under is no excuse."

They slipped into her office.

"There are two matters I wanted to discuss with you. The first is the rate at which you have been going through hoversleds."

"We just went over that, though."

"Indeed we did. And I am not asking you to curtail your behavior in any way. I have structured the business to accommodate a considerable amount of this sort of overhead. But I *would* like to ask if there is anything troubling you."

"You've seen the track times. I'd say I'm doing fine."

"That isn't what I meant. You are driving very aggressively. Far more so than I've ever seen from you."

"I'm just keeping up with traffic. I realize this is a second-chance league, but most of those racers out there weren't dropped from league racing for gambling. Most of them were dropped for cheating. Get enough of those guys together, and that's going to make for a certain type of racing."

"You have initiated at least half of the collisions you've been in, and all of the wrecks."

He shrugged. "The best defense is a good offense, right?"

"The word 'suicidal' has been applied to your techniques."

"And a magician looks like he's sawing a woman in half if you don't know the trick behind it."

"We *have* a therapist on our payroll. If you need—"

"Preethy, I appreciate the concern, but what's going on up here," he tapped his head, "is not going to be in any psychiatric bag of tricks."

"That doesn't fill me with confidence for your state of mind."

"I'll be fine."

"If you are certain. The other matter we need to discuss, as you'd indicated earlier, is the sandstorm issue. As we draw nearer to the season, we are getting a clearer picture of the forecast, and it looks as though we are in for more storms this year than usual."

"Did something change?"

"No, no. It is quite common for certain years to be more intense in that regard than others, but we've been unlucky enough to have a major storm season line up with the formal launch of our new league."

"Is there anything we can do besides hope for the best?"

"I can't go into specifics, but a substantial amount of that research and development budget Michella was so suspicious of is dedicated to that particular problem. Overall, it's nothing to be concerned about. Most of the tracks that will see major use are situated in areas with low storm activity. But some of our more noteworthy tracks—and as such, the tracks we have chosen to highlight in our early season publicity—are in areas that might catch the brunt of a storm or two. We thought we'd scheduled our races on those tracks early enough in the season for this not to be a problem, but Mother Nature may have other plans.”

“If there’s anything you need me to do, say the word.”

“I bring this up because the confluence of weather and event scheduling has left us with very little room for error. We cannot afford any further delay, or we run the risk of a major race overlapping a major storm. Delays alone are a promotional black eye. Delays due to completely foreseeable weather phenomena are worse. If we end up having to rearrange our schedule on our very first season, it would be a blow to our credibility that would cost us fans, investors, and respect.”

“How bad are we talking?”

“Uncle Nick has funded us to an enormous degree. And he is above all else a businessman. He knows one must be prepared to put money into a business for a long time before one can expect to draw any money out of it. But a poor first season could be a multiyear setback, and we’ll never have a better chance than this year to capture an enduring audience. So it is absolutely vital that *nothing* endanger the timeliness of our first race.”

“Dare I ask, why are you telling *me* this?”

“You are something of a magnet for misfortune and misadventure. I ask that you not take any undue risks. My concern in this regard is related to our previous discussion regarding your state of mind and reckless driving.”

“I see. So you’re asking me to not do anything purposely stupid or crazy.”

She grinned. “If you think that is within your power.”

“It’ll be tough, but I think I’ll manage.”

She brushed off her hands. “That concludes our business, then. Ah, with one exception.” She swiped her slidepad. “Van?”

“Yes, Ms. Misra?” came a youthful voice from the slidepad’s speaker.

“Please make a reservation for two under the name Trevor Alexander at Sarafa tonight at 8 p.m., will you?”

“Absolutely.”

“Thank you, Van.” She closed the connection. “Having gotten my start in business as the endpoint of perpetual delegation, it is a rather triumphant feeling to be on the other side.”

“Things are looking up for the two of us. I don’t suppose there’s any chance you’ll be able to join us for dinner. If all goes according to plan, there'll be celebration in order, and you're one of the only friends of mine near enough to join in the fun."

"Ah, dinner. I'm afraid not. I've got an appointment that could conceivably run as late as ten. But I'd be happy to join you both for drinks afterward."

"Great! That's when the fun is going to be had anyway. You'll miss all the tears and hugging and show up just in time for the partying down. The usual place."

"I look forward to it."

He stood and made sure Squee wasn't about to spring off onto Preethy. The little stinker loved every opportunity to perch on a new shoulder.

"See you then!" he said. "And no crazy nonsense, I promise. A second chance was hard enough to get. I'm not going to risk having to get a third chance somehow."

#

Lex pulled into the parking lot of his apartment building. Since he was a relative rarity in his preference for piloting a personal vehicle rather than using automated ones or mass transit solutions, the parking structure seemed bizarrely undersized. It had room for only a few dozen vehicles, and was actually shared between the apartment building and its nearby neighbor, a freshly built hotel.

He hurried toward the apartment building entryway. A few strides from the merciful shelter of the building's shadow, Squee yipped a few times and sprang from his shoulders.

"Whoa, hey!" he called after her.

The blazing pavement wasn't just uncomfortable, it was dangerous for the sensitive tootsies of his pet, so having her dashing about outdoors wasn't something he was willing to tolerate. Squee was no fool, though. Her prodigious leaps brought her from shadow to shadow, navigating the parking lot as though it were a game of the floor is lava. He had to sprint to keep up with her. Even at full speed, he was a step behind her as she dashed through the doorway of the hotel.

A short run and the punishing heat left Lex pouring sweat as he slid in after her. "Squee, seriously. You can't be doing this," he huffed.

He scanned the lobby of the hotel. For all her faults, Squee wasn't usually difficult to find. She was a sucker for affection and attention. All he had to do was find the commotion, and she would be at the very center.

In this case, a small crowd of startled people around the coffee shop had made some room around a pair of men. One was a fit, somewhat burly man with dark brown hair. He was dressed in bright colors and was reaching for the funk. The other was the one Squee had chosen to assault, a sharply dressed guy with dirty-blond hair whom Lex realized he recognized.

"Jon?" he said. "Leave it to Squee to spot someone she knows from across a parking lot."

"Lex! Call off the hounds!" the man said, halfway between a joke and a plea.

Lex retrieved Squee from the shoulders of what turned out to be Jon Nichols. He'd started out at GolanaNet News as Michella's intern. After establishing that he could keep up with her sometimes frantic research style and survive her hands-on coverage, he'd been promoted to a new position. There was probably an official title for the position, but if everyone was being honest, he'd just be called "Michella's handler." He was generally present as the nagging voice on the other end of a call nudging Michella about deadlines.

"Oh my god, you're him!" said the other man. He grabbed Lex's hand and shook it with a vigorousness that threatened to dislocate Lex's shoulder. "I am such a fan. I am *such* a fan. We actually went to college together! You probably don't remember me. We didn't have any classes together, and you were two years ahead."

"That *would* make it hard to remember you," Lex said.

"But I followed you all the way through the rise and fall. I'm *so* into racing."

He had yet to stop shaking Lex's hand, which was beginning to go numb.

"Uh, yeah, great, thanks. Could we move a little further into the introduction process before I lose circulation in my fingers?"

"Oh, sorry! I'm Donnie G." He ended the handshake and flipped his hand over to waggle his fingers, revealing a ring. "I'm Jon's fiancé."

"Oh, right! Of course." Lex slapped Jon on the back. "Congrats! I guess I haven't seen you since the proposal."

"Michella is a full-time job," he said. "I got your 'congratulations' gift though."

"I *love* the pasta machine," Donnie said. "We've been making ramen nonstop since we got it."

Jon glanced at him. "Easy. You're getting fanboy all over him."

"Jon, not that I'm not happy to see a friendly face, but why are you here?"

"You want the official truth or the actual truth?"

"Let's hear them both so I can pick my favorite."

"Officially, I'm here because of the forthcoming grand opening of the first ORIC season. You being Golana's favored son, it's simultaneously a sports piece and a fluff piece."

"You're not a sports reporter. Or a fluff reporter. Or *any* sort of a reporter," Lex said.

"Yeah. The actual truth is, even though she said she's on sabbatical, the people in charge don't like having Michella where they can't see her. They think she's probably working on a story and not telling anyone. So they sent me to make sure she turns in what she's got, if she's got something. After that whole money-laundering thing broke last month, the coverage about her coverage got more traffic than her actual coverage, since we didn't have time to prepare."

"And I tagged along because I had vacation time coming, and *this* one never took time off for a honeymoon," Donnie said.

"That's because we're not married yet."

Donnie crossed his arms. "That's no excuse."

Jon turned to Lex. "Is Michella around? I just got in a little while ago, and she hasn't returned any of my messages."

"No. She's been making herself scarce. I didn't even bother trying to message her. When she's off doing her reporter routine, she may as well be in a coma for all the attention she pays to her slidepad. Though that might not be the problem this time."

Lex pointed to the lobby displays. They were attempting to show a newsfeed, but the resolution of the image was awfully low, and there were frequent pauses for buffering.

"Something's up with the network. It's been like this for the last few weeks," Lex said.

"Lex! You've got to tell me, is it true you had a fling with Venus Vrill back in the day?" Donnie said.

Lex raised an eyebrow. He briefly tried to figure out what about the conversation thus far had brought that little non sequitur to mind.

"No," he said. "Were people saying that about me?"

"Well, *she* was on her way out of the spotlight and *you* were on your way up, and she had that tour that included Golana, so *everybody* sort of assumed."

"*You* sort of assumed that, Donnie. All by yourself. Come on. Let's get checked in before you finish putting the nails in the coffin of this first impression."

He gave Jon a look. "Not until you ask him about the restaurant."

Jon grumbled under his breath. "Donnie wants to know—"

Donnie blurted over him. "It seems like the one restaurant we can't get into is Sarafa, and *I* figured that must mean it's the only restaurant worth *going* to, so we wanted to know—"

"*He* wanted to know," Jon corrected.

"—if you could help us get a table."

"I guess I could shoot Preethy a message. Mitch and I are supposed to be eating there at eight."

Donnie looked to Jon again. "I *told* you. We're as good as in."

"Thanks, Lex," Jon said. "And if you see Michella before we do, let her know we're here. Give her the official truth."

"Will do, but I don't think she'll have any trouble figuring out the actual truth."

They all shook hands again and parted ways. Lex headed back toward his apartment.

"Well, Squee," he murmured to his pet. "Michella takes a sabbatical and not only does she spend most of her time working, half of the office follows her. I'm getting a nasty feeling that something exciting is about to smash into this little chunk of good fortune we've been enjoying."

He scratched her between the ears. "And not the good kind of exciting, either. The kind where someone I've never met suddenly wants me dead."

He reached for his slidepad. "I think I'll give Mitch another try."

Chapter 3

Michella had spent the vast majority of the morning and early afternoon preparing for her trip to the station. She cross-referenced the information she'd been able to dig up thus far, checked databases of faces and names to see if any of the people she'd encountered had any aliases she might have missed, and even ensured she knew where to depart so that she would not be picked up on any atmospheric monitors. By the time the early evening had rolled around and she'd actually initiated her mission, she thought she'd covered everything that needed to be done.

She'd missed one little detail.

"This is not how it worked when I was in the ship last time," Michella muttered.

If one is not well trained in the operation of a vehicle, it usually isn't the best idea to take one's first lessons in the absolute cutting-edge version of that vehicle. Michella knew her way around operating a hoversled, as most adults did to one degree or another. But Lex's ship was not a hoversled. It was a spaceship, and a unique one at that. All of its controls were on a hair trigger. The slightest tug of this or that caused the whole ship to pivot and slide to an absurd degree. The take off had been handled by automated navigation, but now that she was leaving the atmosphere, the ship had "helpfully" flipped to Lex's preferred mode of manual operation. Ever since then, Michella had felt more like she was wrestling the ship than actually piloting it.

A particularly graceless tug of the control stick threatened to heave her from the seat.

"Why does he turn down the inertial dampeners?" she growled.

Michella searched through the manual controls, then the software settings until she found the dampeners and took them back up to a more reasonable level. She knew she'd found the right setting when the ship's engines stopped forcing her into the seat. She was far enough from the surface for gravity to be a non-issue, and thus without the acceleration of the ship pushing her around, she was weightless.

"Ugh," she said, putting her hand to her gut. "Why couldn't he have artificial gravity installed? Microgravity always turns my stomach."

A quiet beeping gradually reminded her that her fiddling with his settings had meant she'd not focused on navigation, or even looked out the cockpit windows, for a full three minutes. She'd assumed that would be fine, as she had all of space ahead of her and thus probably wasn't going to crash into anything. But when she looked up, she found that she'd managed to get completely turned around and was headed back toward the surface with enough speed for a shockfront to form in front of the ship.

"*No!*" she said, pulling hard at the controls.

The *SOB* flared its navigational boosters, and she found herself tracing tight little loops in the Operlo sky. Any attempt to bring herself out of the loop served only to tighten or reverse the looping.

The roller-coaster visuals outside the ship weren't doing her already upset stomach any favors. Nausea in turn wasn't helping her focus at all. The entire endeavor was quickly spiraling toward a gastrointestinal misadventure at the very least, and quite possibly a crash shortly after.

Tones sounded all around her. The controls physically wrenched from her hands, and the ship eased out of its spin. Slowly, the horizon leveled out and drifted downward. Her vision filled with the star field of the Operlo sky.

"Okay, what did I do, and how do I do it on purpose?" she asked, scanning the various displays.

The gauges were all in the green, and the screens were all blinking the phrase *External Control Initiated.*

"Hello, Michella," said a voice over the com system. "It looks as though you were attempting to pilot the *SOB*. Would you like help?"

"Ma?" Michella said, recognizing the not-entirely-convincing digital approximation of a female voice.

Michella's experience with Ma had been rather limited, though what experience she did have was notable. The artificial intelligence system had crossed paths with Lex repeatedly, and even spent some time installed on his pet, though the details of that were something she tried not to dwell upon. While Michella wasn't certain just how much of her apparent humanity was an illusion, she did at least seem to strive to be helpful.

"He's got all of the helper functions turned off. I thought I fixed that," Michella said.

"Lex has a two-stage preference system. One for atmospheric and one for interplanetary/interstellar travel. You need to adjust both presets if you wish to avoid full-manual control."

"I'll keep that in mind. Are you *always* in the ship?"

"Negative. I am, in fact, not in the ship right now. The internal telemetry monitors the ship performance and behavior in order to report anomalies. Discovering you at the controls was unanticipated. Is Lex aware you are operating his personal vehicle unsupervised?"

Michella fixed the hair that had been dislodged. "I borrowed it."

"Borrowing it implies permission was requested and received."

"I got his permission yesterday," she said sharply. "Or do I need a permission slip?"

"My apologies. It was merely my intention to ensure this ship—which is simultaneously Lex's most prized possession, an occupational necessity, and a work of Karter's design—is not being misused without prior authorization. May I ask your motivation for this unaccompanied journey?"

"No you may not. It is a private matter."

"As you wish. Do you require any further aid regarding the operation of the ship?"

Michella wanted to dismiss the AI, who despite her vocal limitations had at the very least mastered an accusatory tone. But the truth was, Ma was a much friendlier user interface than the array of controls before her.

"Is there a way to set the autopilot for a specific point in space?"

"Please direct your gaze to the large display screen just beside your left knee. There you will find detailed instructions on how to set and operate the autonav functions."

Michella glanced down to find a user manual loading.

Ma continued. "I have also enabled voice control with natural language parsing set to full. Lex prefers shorthand for his controls, but this should allow you to operate the basic ship functions without utilizing a glossary of terms."

"Oh. Okay, good. I don't suppose you can tell me if all of this flailing about has gotten the attention of the authorities for reckless flight, can you?"

"I detect no reports or alerts from the local transit authority or law enforcement."

"Good. Thanks for the help."

"I endeavor to be of service, as always. Would you indulge me in a bit of informal social discourse before we discontinue communication?"

Michella sighed. Talking to a machine, even a very *human* machine, was a bit of a waste of time in her view. But there was such a thing as gratitude.

"What did you have in mind?"

"I notice in Lex's calendar that there have been repeated cancellations and rescheduled appointments of late. I also notice that there is a meal scheduled for eight tonight. You are indicated to be his guest. Are you aware of this appointment, and is it your intention to force another rescheduling?"

"Just how much access do you have to Lex's personal information?"

"I am on his VIP list and am privy to most of his social postings. Are you aware of this appointment, and is it your intention to force another rescheduling?"

"Yes, I am aware, and no I'm not planning on missing it."

"The current time within the region for which the appointment has been made is 5:35 p.m. This leaves only two hours and twenty-five minutes, including travel time, for your intended activity. What activity are you pursuing?"

"Work," she said. "I'm doing work."

"It was my understanding that your presence on Operlo was a part of a sabbatical."

"You can work while on sabbatical," she snapped.

"I see. Work that involves leaving the planet's surface in an interstellar spacecraft seldom fits within the indicated time window. Are you confident you will be punctual for your appointment?"

"Yes," she said flatly.

"Seven of the last ten events that Lex scheduled and you confirmed were canceled due to either your delinquency or a last-minute conflict. This suggests social engagements with Lex hold a low priority for you."

"That's not true. It's just that the kinds of things I have to do can't be scheduled and can't be *re*scheduled, and Lex's stuff *can*. Lex understands."

"Certainly. May I gently suggest that, in this instance, you do not rely upon Lex's understanding?"

"He's just high on the fame again. He'd never admit it, but he loves being in the spotlight again. This is just him showing off that he's got the connections to get into a fancy restaurant."

"In my observation, Lex has not demonstrated a predilection for high cuisine."

"It's not the food. It's the exclusivity. He's trying to impress me."

"Is this undesirable to you?"

"I've got more important things to do."

"Please explain the distinction between your activities being 'more important' and the previously denied claim that Lex's activities hold a lower priority."

In the absence of a face to glare at, Michella glared at the screen with the manual. "I've really got to go, Ma. Thank you very much for all of your help."

"You are welcome to it. If you require aid, Lex's communicator has highest priority, real-time access to my systems. I will answer and render any aid required."

"Thanks. I'll keep that in mind. One more favor?"

"What do you require?"

"Don't tell Lex where I am, and please respect my privacy. There are things Lex doesn't need to know."

"Of course."

Michella closed the connection and flicked her fingers across the user manual Ma had set up for her. It definitely wasn't the help screen she'd found in her admittedly hasty search when the ship had first started malfunctioning.

"Ship, please display navigational targets at the following coordinates." She flipped open an old-fashioned paper pad and read out a lengthy orbital definition.

"Permission to adjust heading and direct external scanners?" replied the ship's control system.

For a moment Michella thought Ma had simply ignored her request and reopened the connection. It wasn't until she realized the voice was much less nuanced that it dawned upon her that the ship's system used one of the three voices Ma used.

"Granted," Michella said.

The ship smoothly shifted and actively scanned. The cockpit window display populated with dozens of numbered points of light. One was significantly larger than the rest.

"Give me more detail on number 12."

The other points vanished, and the remaining one filled the display. It was a distinctive-looking space station. Rather than the spindly network of interconnected struts that many such orbital stations tended to be, or the giant rotating rings of more remote stations, this one looked like a somewhat squashed satellite dish pointed at the surface of the planet. Michella wasn't sure if she was looking at an image of the station or some sort of sensor reconstruction, but it was of a high enough resolution that she could see that the planet-facing portion of the ship was just as heavily shielded as the space-facing portion. That was a bit like heading out during a rainstorm with an extra umbrella pointed downward.

She glanced to her notes again. "Initiate docking sequence in primary docking bay, er... Primary Docking Bay 3. And provide the following access code." Again she read out a painfully long sequence of numbers.

"Acknowledged."

The ship slid smoothly through space to the destination.

"Ship, the *SOB* has stealth capabilities, correct?"

"The *SOB* is capable of running at low- or zero-EM and low- or zero-thermal-emission mode and has a low reflectivity for most active or passive EM wavelengths."

"Do I need to activate those features?"

"Affirmative."

"Activate the stealth stuff."

"Acknowledged."

A few of the screens subtly changed their values, and the engines shifted to a notably less intense hum, but otherwise there wasn't much indication that the ship was effectively "sneaking."

She shrugged. "I guess if it was obvious it wouldn't be stealthy."

The ship made short work of the distance between her poorly planned exit from the atmosphere and the space station. When she was in range, her com system lit up with a request from the station.

"Docking request received. You're not on the register for today," blared an overamplified male voice.

"We spoke yesterday. This is regarding the VIP tour?" she said.

"The what? … Oh! You're the one with the… hang on."

A small indicator popped up on the com system screen indicating the current message was no longer being recorded on his side.

"Michella Modane, right? Did you bring the rest of the bribe?"

"We discussed a VIP tour," she repeated.

Generally speaking, it was unwise to confirm that you were party to a bribe, even if it was ostensibly off the record.

"Right, right. Yeah, come on in. Dock 3. I'll keep you off the logs."

The ship accelerated a bit, and a glittery collection of points matching the navigation scan's findings caught the light of Operlo's powerful star. She muted the communication microphone.

"Ship, can you please magnify the nearest objects as we pass them?"

"Acknowledged."

A flickering white box traced itself around the nearest glittering satellite, and a digital zoom showed it in greater detail. In many ways it looked like the space station in miniature. A large, sturdy dish pointed down. The whole surface of the device had the blue-tinted black sheen of high-quality solar collectors. A few other smaller dishes pointed in the direction of other satellites, and a somewhat larger one pointed in the direction of the space station. She saved an image of the satellite.

"This is just interview-type stuff, right?" the man said. "And you'll hold on to it until the official announcements? Any information you get comes through me. I mean, a greased palm is one thing, but if any stuff gets out there before they unveil this place, they're going to know where it came from and I'm not trying to lose my job."

"You show me where the line is, and I promise not to cross it."

It was a lie she'd gotten very good at telling.

"I don't have you on sensors yet, but I've got your transponder. That's weird," he said.

"My ship's pretty low profile. The better to avoid showing up on surveillance and leaving you with too many questions to answer."

"Oh, don't worry about that. You're talking to the guy in charge of surveillance."

"Really? Even the docking stuff? They'd leave that to an outside vendor? And a *new* one at that?"

"Hey, don't ask me why they put me in charge of this stuff. They had to swap out some inside positions for outside ones, and this was one of them. I think I've got you on proximity now. Let's bring you in."

The ship shuddered a little as a tractor beam caught the *SOB* and started guiding it toward a large port on the perimeter of the station. A heavy-duty door irised open to reveal a shimmering energy wall. She thought she had a good read on the scale of the station, but without anything else to serve as a point of reference, it was difficult to be sure. As she drew nearer, it seemed to get bigger and bigger. What at first she'd assumed was a port just large enough for Lex's smallish ship now loomed larger and larger. By the time she reached it, she found it was large enough for something triple the size of the *SOB*, if not larger. This was one hell of a space station.

The tractor beam pulled the *SOB* inside. One force field, then the other, cycled in an impressively speedy implementation of an air lock. The docking bay was sized for construction vehicles, but as the automated docking program controlled her thrusters and eased her around a bend, she found some smaller bays properly sized for ships like hers.

Michella triple-checked the air-pressure sensor before popping the cockpit and, to her dismay, discovering there wasn't any gravity in the space station either.

"Does *no one* care about gravity?" she griped.

She looked around. The place was still completely pristine, like it had never been used. Actuated cameras poked down from little ceiling-mounted pods, but their flashing indicators were notably dark. The surveillance system had indeed been shut off.

Michella adjusted her outfit. Like everything else about ventures like these, what she'd chosen to wear was carefully calculated. She needed to look like she was at least *somewhat* savvy, or else she wouldn't be able to earn enough respect to get genuine answers. To that end, she'd worn a GolanaNet branded jumpsuit. It would handle maneuvering in a space station well enough. It would even make her look vaguely like she belonged aboard. The presence of a news network's logo would serve as evidence that she was not misrepresenting herself, and also inspire anyone who might be fired for letting a reporter aboard to help keep her hidden.

On the other hand, a little bit of assumed ignorance and naivete was handy as well. It would lower their guard. Thus, she'd come equipped with a large, much-abused over-the-shoulder purse. It was a bit ungainly and ragged, with a zipper that never quite shut. Just wrong enough for a space station to suggest she didn't know what she was doing, and just "girly" enough to convince the misogynistic throwbacks that generally staffed criminal organizations that she wasn't a threat.

For a woman in territory as dangerous as this, even wardrobe was part of the game.

"Michella Modane," remarked the voice from the communicator.

She turned to find her liaison holding tight to the nearest of a sequence of handholds that Michella realized to her dismay she was going to be depending upon to get around. He wore a jumpsuit made from something that appeared as though a uniform designer had tried their very best to make plastic look like canvas and had *almost* succeeded. A complex harness strapped a bulbous pack to his back. He tapped some buttons on the back of one glove, and the pack hissed and spat with jets of air to propel him toward her.

"I'm still kind of surprised this is happening. I always sort of wondered how you got the dirt you always report. Never figured it was bribes to nobodies like me."

"Bribes aren't standard operating procedure for the news world," Michella said.

"Sure, sure," he said, grabbing her wrist to drag her from the ship to the wall so she could navigate the narrow corridor leading away from the bay. "I just hope you're not hoping to find any dirt here. There's not much to find."

She gripped the rail he guided her to tightly. "No, no. This is just a behind-the-scenes thing. This place has been hanging in the sky over Operlo for months, slowly coming together, but no word on its purpose. People barely acknowledge it exists. That gets a reporter's nose itchy."

"I'll show you what I can, but honestly, I'm small potatoes around here. Like I think I said yesterday, I'm not even sure what this place is for. I'm just supposed to make sure the comings and goings are tracked. Or not tracked, in your case."

"You let me worry about what I get out of it. Just answer what you can and show me anything you think would interest the news-watching public. I'll fill in the color."

She followed him to a claustrophobic office of sorts, a walled-off section of the docking bay in the corner overlooking its operations. It had a huge, thick window. Holographic displays overlapped one another, showing a montage of security feeds.

"This is the surveillance center. That's the console where I *would* be marking down your arrival if not for the arrangement. Here we've got the twenty-five top-priority camera feeds, on rotation. They're run through an automatic-tracking and motion-recognition whatchamacallit. Computer thing. Took me a while to work out how to poke holes in the surveillance without making it obvious I did it. But, you know. You get a job, you get good at it."

Michella's old-fashioned note-taking wasn't well suited to zero-g. She had the proper pen for the job, and her pad had a handy strap to hold it in her grip, but without more practice in a zero-g environment taking she wasn't comfortably without a free hand to steady herself against the wall. She awkwardly hooked an arm through a rail and held herself still with her elbow rather than switch to voice recording or one-handed text entries. She looked over the controls and readings. There were a good deal more bits of information than a simple security system would need.

"Is that reading barometric pressure?" she said, indicating one of the screens. "And humidity?"

"Uh... Probably?" he said. "That whole bank of controls wasn't in my briefing. This place isn't fully operational yet. As systems become useful, I get new briefings. It's all about speed, I think. The boss lady is *seriously* worried about delays. Hard deadline for three weeks from yesterday for full operation."

"And how close are you?"

"Beats me. That's need-to-know stuff, and I'm like ten rungs too low on the ladder to need to know."

She leaned closer to the controls he'd admitted ignorance about. "These are navigation- and communication-corridor markers," she said.

"Oh, sure. Yeah, we're patched into all that stuff. I guess they'll be routing communications through this thing. I'm not a local, but I guess they've been limping along on a system that wasn't half as good as they need for the race crowds."

She tilted her head and flipped back in her pad. "You said you're on a three-week deadline?"

"Three weeks from yesterday."

"Then this thing isn't going to be operational in time for the first big race."

He scratched his head. "I guess not."

She marked it down. "Tell me about this screen. It looks like you're tracking wind speed? Is that via surface stations?"

#

For the better part of an hour, Michella's guide worked his way through completely uninteresting factoids about the station and his lowly role in it. Any questions she asked that actually interested her were met with either ignorance or the wall of a nondisclosure agreement. That was no problem. A journalist's job isn't always about turning up the piece of information she's after. When you've talked to enough people tasked with keeping secrets, you soon learn that sometimes if you can't find what you're after, you can find the shape of the holes they're cutting in the truth. If you get a good enough picture of the jigsaw piece they've left out, you may find there's only one thing that fits into it.

Things were sliding in that direction. Nothing he'd said, and a great deal of the questions he'd specifically avoided, clarified what the station was *for*. The information available even to this tiny surveillance office was stunningly comprehensive. Far more than it needed for anything as simple as a communication hub, or a traffic hub. When this station was online, it could easily serve practically every purpose an orbital facility might serve for a planet twice the size of Operlo, and then some.

But things were missing. Despite seeming to be lined up as the primary link in the communication chain, the actual optimal arrival point from the interstellar corridor that VectorCorp maintained wasn't anywhere nearby. It was almost ninety degrees off the orbital plain they were whizzing along. That smacked of *avoiding* orbital traffic.

Then there were the power scales. The station's power ratings, as very clearly listed on the vital readings that rotated through the "technical overview" screen, were ludicrously high. Multiple terawatts. She made notes to look up the sort of power requirements of a station of this size, but she was certain they would be minuscule compared to the sort of power this place seemed designed to channel. She scribbled *Weapon?*

"You do all of the arrival and departure scheduling?" she asked.

"The computer does all of it. Mostly I just hit 'Okay' a bunch of times to confirm it. Everything's set up to require at least *some* human interaction. Codes and stuff."

She underlined *Weapon?*

"How far ahead and how far back do these arrival and departure schedules go?"

"Oh, we go all the way back," he said, pulling up the schedule and rolling back through it. "All the way back to when the computer system came up, at least. Before I even got here. Back then it was all Patel Construction running the place. As for how far forward, I'm not really sure. I just look through the chunk between when I come on duty and when I'll come on duty again."

He rolled the list forward. "Looks like it only goes about three days forward."

"And what are those blank entries?"

"Beats me. There are always a few of those. I guess someone on the other shift sets them up. I always assumed they were just placeholders. Usually someone comes in at that time, but not always. Maybe that's just when they have someone planned to arrive but don't have a ship lined up?"

"Who usually shows up at those times?"

"I don't know. There are three docking bays, and I only handle this one. The other two are automated. They always show up at those."

She pointed to the screen. "I notice my arrival isn't a blank spot like that. It's just not listed."

"Well, *yeah*. What do you take me for? I'm not going to leave a big marker listing *when* you arrived if I don't want it on the record. Lucky me, I've got the access privilege to delete and disable logs."

She nodded and jotted down *Officially unofficial. NDA meetings?* After a moment, she added another underline to her weapon note.

"Now, that brings me to the security," she said. "That's your specialty, right?"

"Oh, sure. That's my focus."

"Let's hear it. What sort of precautions have you got?"

"You name it. Video and audio surveillance through any high-traffic areas. Motion detectors through nonmachinery corridors." He held up his slidepad. "Everyone's got a work slidepad that's got to be logged in to periodically. It's pinged whenever anyone enters or leaves an area. There's an automatic timeout. Fifteen seconds unattended and the system locks back up. It's actually sort of a pain."

"The slidepad has to be logged in periodically?"

"Yeah. It's… whatchacallit… a two-factor sort of thing. We've got these little dongles." He waved his slidepad in front of a small valet-parking-style panel. It clicked open to reveal keychain-sized devices.

"May I take a look?" she said.

"Sure."

She stowed her pad and reached awkwardly into the cabinet to grab one. The dongle was about the size of her pinkie and displayed a lengthy code that flashed away every so often.

"See, I'm not so worried about talking about this stuff, because the security is rock solid. That dongle has to be paired with a slidepad that's logged in to the system and active. You've got to get through all of the security on the slidepad, *and* keep it active, and have the dongle. It's like stacking three security systems on top of each other. Unbreakable."

As he counted off the hurdles it would take to break security, he brought up the access lists and security panels as though they were somehow *his* achievement. It was clear he was very proud of having control over this sort of a system.

"I see…" She tapped the screen. "This whole access privilege part is just like what we've got at the network. But the sensors and dongles are way past what we use. Very impressive."

"Yep. Top-shelf security. Speaking of, I'll take that dongle back."

"Of course," she said, handing him a dongle.

He replaced it and locked up the cabinet. "Strict rules, you know. Gotta keep them locked up."

"Of course. Whatever they're planning for the station, it must be *very* important to protect it so much."

"I guess so."

"Say, I don't suppose there are any other trustworthy employees I could interview?"

"Hell no, Ms. Modane. You're lucky *I* let you up here. Anyone else who finds out you're here is likely to report you, and that's a headache for both of us. Probably trespassing charges for you and a lost job for me."

"That's entirely understandable. So I suppose that means it'd be best if I didn't wander off."

"Oh, no. You don't go anywhere without me." He checked the time. "And really, I'd prefer if you were out of here before too much longer. Things get trickier if I fiddle with the logs on either side of one I don't fiddle with. There's a blank slot coming up in a few hours, and I'd like you out before then."

"I don't suppose you'd be able to get me a water then? I'd been holding off, hoping maybe I'd see the crew cafeteria or something. I'm getting awfully dry."

He gave her a long, measuring look. "Okay…" He warily tapped the lock screen control. "I'll be right back." He opened the office door and drifted out.

The very moment he was out the door, she slapped the *Unlock Screen* control. A log-in screen appeared, listing the personnel in range of the console. Her guide's name was present, but color coded yellow. Not quite out of range, but getting there. She tapped *Log In*.

Enter security code, the screen prompted.

She slid her pad aside to reveal a dongle she'd palmed. Michella's father had taught his girls a fair number of questionable skills before his untimely demise. One of the more useful of them had been his rule about theft. If you want something, always take two. It was amazing just how many people would stop looking once they got one back from you.

With skill honed by years of typing lengthy notes, she entered the code. The system woke up, but a notification bubble popped up almost immediately.

Please activate slidepad. Automatic log-out in fifteen seconds.

She flipped open the access list he'd shown her. She'd taken great care to search the screen while he was talking. It took her all of five seconds to spot the "Add Device" button she'd seen when he was bragging. She tapped it and a tool tip advised her to apply the new device to the reader. She quickly swiped her own slidepad over the clearly marked sensor.

Stand by.

She held her breath. The log-out countdown was getting awfully close to running out.

Accepted.

The countdown vanished.

"Okay. The security system is more user-friendly than Lex's ship. That says something."

She scrolled through the data, glancing out the window of the little office periodically. She saw her host find his way to a crew cabinet to fetch her a drink.

Her searching quickly established that he had loads of access. Since her own slidepad was considered one of his devices, she had the same level of access now. That said, his personal access level was limited to his roles. Though she could find plenty of data drives on the network, she couldn't access any of them. Rather than waste the *maybe* forty seconds she had left on trying to find things that had been hidden, she instead focused on things she knew he had access to.

She dragged sensor logs, crew manifests, arrival and departure schedules, and everything else he'd shown her onto her slidepad. Just as he pulled the door open, she logged out and backed away.

"We had iced tea. Is that okay?"

Michella huffed. "Just what the doctor ordered," she said.

#

Michella managed to keep him talking for another forty minutes before he started to become visibly impatient for her to take her leave. She was forced to use a delay tactic straight from a toddler's playbook. She'd gotten him to escort her to the bathroom facilities. It turned out they were in an alcove just one access door away from the docking bay.

"Ugh…" she said, gazing at the assortment of tubes and sockets that made up the bathroom on a space station. "Hundreds of years in space and this is still the best we can do?"

"Do you need a manual? Lining things up is kind of tricky, and if you get it wrong, there's a lot of cleanup," he said.

"I'll manage," she said. "A little privacy, please?"

"Oh, right. Sorry."

She would have preferred a locking door or at least a sturdy stall, but even in a station this large, space was at a premium. She had to make do with a thin curtain to keep her hidden from prying eyes.

When she heard him move to the end of the hall, she got to work. By her count, she could get away with five minutes before he was likely to come knocking again. That wasn't much time to work out what, if anything, should be done.

Her eyes flitted across page after page of data she'd purloined. She'd been lucky to get through their security, but it seemed, even with access, it was better secured than she would have liked. He was a technician. If she were trying to undermine the operation of the station, his access level might have been useful. He could open the maintenance tubes on the ship, activate and deactivate surveillance, and do loads of other useful stuff. But he didn't have access to anything that would actually answer her questions. What was this place? Why had this place been made?

The access list kept calling her back to it. Those blank lines in particular were flashing red beacons that something was being covered up. It wasn't proof of misdeed—there were plenty of good reasons for a corporation to have entries like that. But if they *were* trying to do something, those slots were good candidates.

She flipped back and forth between the last few weeks. There were definitely patterns. Then it struck her so hard she slapped her forehead for not thinking of it sooner.

"He's got access to the surveillance video," she hissed.

She scrolled to a blank arrival slot and pulled up video from the automated docking bays. They were, annoyingly, blacked out during those times, but a bit of flicking through nearby cameras earned her a brief but undeniable glimpse of a familiar woman in sharp business attire. Preethy Misra.

"I *knew* it. Whatever this place is, it has the boss checking up on it regularly… Which means it's all but certain she's due to arrive any minute," she whispered to herself.

Further searching proved, to her dismay, that any videos of the contents of those meetings were either unavailable or locked behind an access level her host lacked. If she wanted to know what was happening here, and thus if there was anything shady about it, she'd need to find a way to listen in on one of those meetings. But that might mean remaining in the station for *hours* longer than she'd intended, and she was already being ushered out the door.

Her expression dropped when she realized it might potentially be possible to manage such a feat, but it would require some help.

She fumbled in her bag for her hands-free device, then thumbed through her slidepad's settings to try to connect to the *SOB*. It took three tries, and even then gave her a lousy connection. Something about the station must have made connections flaky. But she finally linked up, and, via the ship, she contacted Ma.

"Hello, Ms. Modane," Ma said after barely a moment of negotiating the connection. "The time is 7:04 p.m., are you—"

"Ma," she whispered insistently. "I have some questions and I don't have time for small talk."

"How may I help you?"

"I need to know how to work the *SOB* remotely."

"May I ask why you require this information?"

"No, you may not. I'm in a hurry."

"You seem to require a great deal of low-level knowledge of Lex's ship's operation without his knowledge and with no evidence of his consent. Additionally, you have not been behaving with a level of courtesy sufficient to inspire trust or acquiescence."

"If you want, ask Lex if I got permission, but all I'm asking for is control of the ship remotely."

"What task do you require the ship to perform?"

"I need it to undock on its own and then move to a distance where it won't show up on scanners. I'll eventually need to get it to come back, too."

"Processing… Please acknowledge the software install request on your slidepad."

She glanced down in time to see just such a request appear on her screen. She authorized the install with her thumbprint. A pair of quick progress bars filled, and she was presented with a childishly simple UI. There were just two buttons. One marked "Undock and Hide" and the other marked "Recall and Dock."

"Pressing the indicated button will cross-link your slidepad with the *SOB* system, providing you with the capability to communicate as though aboard the ship until all standard undocking procedures are complete, at which point it will utilize stealth procedures to find an unobserved vantage. The second button will provide a similar procedure in reverse. Please be aware that both buttons require an unbroken communication chain to the *SOB* to function."

"Fine, fine. Thank you."

"Please remember your scheduled—"

Michella closed the connection, then turned to the gadget that took the place of a bathroom in zero-g. With a few well-placed tugs, she dislodged some connections that were clearly not meant to be removed, then sanitized her hands and pulled the curtain aside.

"Thank you so much for the hospitality. I, uh… I *may* have broken it."

She saw his expression drop, even from the end of the corridor.

"How broken are we talking about?" His tone showed a suitable level of trepidation, considering there was a better than average chance a canister of human waste had just emptied into a low-gravity environment.

"Just this thing here. It came out when I tried to hang it up," she said.

He gave it a look, then gave *her* a look. She'd seen it a thousand times, the look of a man fully and eagerly capable of believing that, through some sort of distinctly feminine form of incompetence, Michella had broken something that no sane person could break by accident. It used to rankle her that this particular ruse worked too well, but after the number of times she'd been able to get an extra few unsupervised moments due to it, she'd decided it was an acceptable evil.

"Can you fix it?" she asked.

"It'll take a minute, but this is no problem."

"I guess I'll just head over to the ship then?"

"Yeah, that'll work. It's not like you can get into any trouble, all the doors are locked. Board your ship. I won't be a minute, then I'll get you undocked."

She gave him the look of relief she knew he was hoping to see for his chivalrous act of plugging in two sockets, then turned to leave.

"Hey!" he said sharply.

She turned and kept a carefully measured look of calm on her face.

"Yes?"

"Don't think I didn't notice what you were trying to do."

"What do you mean?" she said, now struggling a bit more with her charade.

He held out his hand. "You owe me twenty-five thousand credits."

"Oh! Right, right. Where was my mind?"

She dug through the terribly mixed-up contents of her bag and found the five chips she owed.

"Can't pull a fast one on me," he said.

"That's for sure," she said with a smile.

She tugged herself along the wall while he did his thing. All the cameras nearby would still be off since she wasn't supposed to be here. She hung a left instead of a right as she came to the end of the corridor and propelled herself as quickly as she could while checking the station layout she'd stolen off the system. There was only one door leading farther into the bowels of the station. She very nearly smashed into it, carried by her momentum and haste toward it. A sweep of her slidepad with its recently upgraded access privileges shifted its lock indicator from red to green. The door slid open and she darted inside.

The corridor beyond was dimly lit, clearly not the sort of place they expected anyone to linger. After ensuring the local cameras were still disabled, she shut and locked the door behind her. Handholds were fewer and farther between here, but she traveled far enough down the corridor to find a tangle of wires and pipes to tuck herself behind. She braced herself with her legs and checked the slidepad.

"Here goes nothing," she said.

Michella tapped the undock button on Ma's app. The screen shifted to a poorly compressed video feed of the interior of the *SOB*. Her journey farther into the depths of the ship had degraded the signal quality even more, but it was good enough for her to hear the attendant bid her farewell and punch in the departure sequence. The ship turned itself over to station control and was maneuvered out the bay door. Once there, it pivoted and piloted itself into the distance.

When the video feed became too distorted for her to view, she tucked the slidepad into her bag and rubbed her hands together. She was loose on the station with reasonably high-level access and without the knowledge of the crew. True, she wasn't sure how she'd get off the ship without being seen, but that was a problem for another time. For now, there was work to do.

"Right. Let's see what's been going on around here…"

#

On the other side of the station, two people worked diligently through some of the bureaucratic nonsense that kept an enterprise like this running. There are those who think electromagnetism and gravity are the most powerful forces in the cosmos. From the amount of it necessary for Indra IV Station to operate, you'd think the whole facility *ran* on record keeping and report writing. While paper was no longer the medium of choice for it, "paperwork" was a constant throughout the galaxy, and throughout time. The only thing that set it apart on the station was the ergonomics. Rather than sitting at desks, hunched over their input devices and squinting at screens, the datapad jockeys on the space station drifted in the air in a side room of the station. They were each tethered to the wall like parked blimps, eyes turned to the scrolling data they were tasked with sifting through.

"Not again…" muttered one worker.

His partner sipped at a plastic pouch of coffee. "What is it now?"

"You know how they've been sending up crews from TIS?"

"Yeah."

"These idiots have been dragging their feet on the identification and certification literature for almost two weeks. It finally came through, and guess what?"

"No photos?"

"No photos," he said with a nod. "How hard is this? Who even keeps employee files without photos anymore? They're a load of idiots. All of them. And one of them is Robin Hartnett! We've had him on the station before. The fools actually *removed* his photo from the ID since last time. Same goes for half of the crew coming up. The smacks of some intern hitting the wrong button and not reporting it."

"So turn them down. Simple as that."

"It *isn't* simple as that, because the stupid ship full of these can't-follow-procedure idiots is supposed to arrive within the hour."

"They're *that* late on the certs?"

"Yeah. And management is due to check up on us today."

"So what're you going to do?"

"It's damned if I do, damned if I don't, right? If I reject their credentials, then we're understaffed during crunch time. If I okay them and it comes up, then they're going to chew me out something fierce if they find out I broke protocol." He glanced at his partner. "Hey, you got any of those cheese packets? Toss one over."

His friend tossed an individually wrapped snack to him. The bureaucrat tugged it open with his teeth and let the contents drift into the air beside him. One by one he plucked them out of the air with his free hand as he mulled over his options.

"It seems like the only thing I ever get to do is damage control… Okay. So they're on their way here, right?"

"Right."

"And if I don't push these through, we're going to have like twenty extra people crammed into the low-security section of the station until we can work through this stupid stuff. Just breathing our air and eating our food, and occupying our time without contributing, right?"

"Right."

"If I push them through, then they get here, they get to work, and I use that time to try to dig up the missing info. If it comes in, great, no one's the wiser. If it doesn't come in, we wait until the end of the shift, ship these guys back, and deny payment. Cost savings, am I right?"

"You're not wrong."

"Of course I am. So let's see here. … Eighteen workers. Approved for boarding, flagged for credential audit as time allows. Each worker is bringing seventy-five kilos of 'specialty equipment.' That's kind of a lot, isn't it?"

"I don't know. Maybe they're bringing in those replacement heater modules for the snack room? I've been getting by on tepid coffee for a week and it's torture."

"But that'd come up in a supply shipment, not in a crew shuttle from off planet." He grumbled. "Frickin' unwanted cargo… Hey, who's on cargo sweep detail right now?"

His partner tapped at his own datapad. "Uh… someone named Curtis and someone named Slade."

"Are they TIS guys?"

"A TIS guy and a TIS girl."

"Hah! Their problem, not mine. Additional cargo approved, flagged for high-security screening," he said. "I *love* it when these morons end up screwing each other over with their boneheaded failure to follow simple rules."

"Two wrongs making a right, am I right?"

"Right." He snatched the last of the cheese snacks out of the air before it could float out of arm's reach and scanned down the form he'd been filling out. "I guess that's everything. … Man, this is a lot of shady stuff on one form."

"Did you flag it all for additional security checks?"

"I just said I did."

"And are all of the paperwork mistakes their fault?"

"Yeah."

"So your ass is covered. Push it through."

He hesitated for a moment more, then shrugged. "Eh. What's the worst that can happen?"

He transmitted the completed form. A moment later, the confirmation flashed on his screen.

Additional Crew and Equipment Security Clearance Granted.

\#

A few minutes drifting about in the unfinished space station hadn't been as educational as Michella had hoped. Much of that time had been dedicated to figuring out just how to get around without them realizing she'd never left. Opening and closing doors was no problem. The hatches her stolen access could open were clearly marked. So far, she'd only encountered a handful that wouldn't open for her. Cameras and other types of surveillance were another issue entirely. She could turn most of them off if she wanted to, but she felt certain that was a surefire way to tip someone off about her presence. Fortunately, on the long list of station features that had not been fully activated was the low-priority surveillance. According to the manifest she'd downloaded, the full complement of workers for the station was fewer than a dozen, though if she'd read it correctly, a fresh shift of workers would take that up to something closer to twenty in a few minutes. Like everything else on the lightly populated planet, this station ran on a skeleton crew. There was very little chance of bumping into another worker, and most of the sections of the station that weren't currently occupied were on very low-level surveillance. Better yet, behind maintenance hatches scattered through the station were long tubes filled with mostly exposed systems and machinery. They were tight, with just barely room enough for her to slide along through them, but according to the data she had, the only monitoring inside was for the functionality and status of the equipment. She could use them to navigate without fear of notice.

By their very nature, these system conduits ran through the whole ship, but the necessities of safety and utility meant they were less than convenient for travel. They took a circuitous route, for one thing. For another, to prevent a catastrophe if there were a hull breach, they were regularly interrupted by bulkheads that she could manually open and shut. There was no signage indicating where a given junction led. She'd gotten turned around more than once. It would have been lovely if she'd encountered the huge, easily navigable air vents so ubiquitous in action movies, but that was a recipe for disaster in a space station, since one hole in the hull would suck the whole station dry without the bulkheads.

Eventually, she found her way to a maintenance office not unlike the one where the bribed technician worked. The consoles and systems within were powered but inactive. She supposed, once the station was fully operational, this would be the place where one of the limited crew would drearily review and monitor the station's systems. For now, it was completely forgotten. A perfect hiding place.

Her slidepad with its crew access privilege booted up the console easily enough. Combined with the stolen dongle, she'd logged in quickly. Eager though she was to continue her investigating, she would have to poke her way through the system gently. The system logs would show her unwitting accomplice as the one doing the searching, but if she was too aggressive, there was the possibility he'd notice someone was up to something. Best to keep to the sort of things he would be doing. Fortunately, that included reviewing security cam footage.

"You'd think they'd make these labels more useful," she muttered.

She flipped through dozens of camera feeds with names like "MNT-001a" and "DKRM-223k." As she dug through them, she glanced back to the arrival schedule, which was now available in far greater detail on the console screen. Pretty soon that mysterious blank spot in the schedule would be coming along. If there was a meeting on the way and she didn't figure out where it would be and how to record it, this whole venture would be for naught.

As much as she grumbled about it, her talent with the slow, careful game of connect the dots she was engaged in now was perhaps the only reason she'd achieved any level of success in her investigations. Her superpower, if she had one, wasn't finding the needle in the haystack. It was finding the one loop in a ball of yarn that, if tugged, would cause it all to neatly unravel before her. She saw connections. And somewhere in this tiresome heap of records and logs was the information she sought.

"Ahh…" she said, her eyes gleaming as she spotted it. "This whole section of the ship has no crew. But the lights are on and the cameras are off at the same time every week. And that time lines up with the blank arrival times. There's a straight shot from one of the docking bays, and all of *those* cameras turn off on the same schedule. The meeting they don't want anyone to know about is going to be taking place right *here* in… fifteen minutes. I *knew* it."

She pulled up the network of conduits and tried to find something resembling a direct path from where she was to where she wanted to be. A lot of work was being done in that section of the station, according to the manifest. Lots of new construction and electrical work, plus some finishing touches like cleaning and sanitizing. No doubt that's why they were having the meetings there, to oversee the work. As near as she could tell, at least some of those workers would still be working there. That meant not only surveillance but *witnesses* could cause problems for her if she wasn't careful. She was going to have to try to make it there without poking her head out of these service conduits at all. It wasn't going to be pleasant, but the really good dirt took plenty of digging and she knew it.

With the sequence of turns jotted down into her pad for reference, Michella unhooked the service conduit hatch and slid herself inside.

#

One of two automated docking bays gradually lit up. An irising external door only slightly smaller than the behemoth that had allowed the *SOB* to enter earlier that day dilated. A pair of ships moved sluggishly through. Each paused briefly while the air lock could clear them, then puttered over to the docking ports. The ships were jalopies, pieced together from salvaged pieces of other ships. Any semblance of aestheticism or grace was abandoned in favor of utility. In this case, that meant storage space. When it linked up with the port and started to offload its crew, the sheer volume of personnel coming out of this craft seemed bizarre. For a ship this size, barely larger than a conventional hovervan, one would expect a crew of four. They'd packed nine people into it, and another such ship was maneuvering in behind it, similarly overloaded if the manifest was to be believed.

Each member of the arriving crew lugged heavily loaded duffel bags. They were strangely equipped for a space station crew. Employees of such a facility came in two distinct varieties. There were the jumpsuit-clad day-to-day workers and the space-suit clad exterior workers. This crew looked more like a ground-based construction crew. Their jumpsuits were more rugged, and each wore hard hats and goggles. It gave the whole crew an oddly anonymous look, only the lower half of their faces bare.

The newcomers carried heavy duffel bags with them as they approached a second air lock of sorts, the security checkpoint. It was a ring-shaped scanner, large enough for a single member of the crew with a bit of space to spare for equipment. The scanner was operated by a single crewman with a TIS jumpsuit. He had the oddly distributed pudginess of someone who had been spending a little too much time in orbit. He wore a badge that labeled him MAX CRICK.

"Okay, lads and ladies," said the man, floating at the ring-shaped scanner that had been notably absent in the primary docking bay. "You know the drill. Badges out. Crew and equipment through the scanner, one at a time and we'll get you through."

The first new arrival, one of the taller of the group, tugged some handrails and darted through the hoop. Red lights flashed and the screens lit up with warnings. The security worker casually silenced them.

"Robin Hartnett. Welcome aboard. Been away awhile, have we?" the security worker said.

"Yeah. I was back at home base. Waiting until the timing was right."

Another worker passed through, raising another set of warnings that were quickly dismissed. "Heh. You talk to the boss before you left?"

"You think I could *avoid* talking to the boss before this assignment?" said Hartnett.

Another worker. Another warning. Another "ignore" command. "So what's what?"

"He says we need to wrap this thing up. There's big money to be made if this contract goes our way."

"He sure sent a lot of employees up here. There's work to be done on the surface too, you know."

"The surface isn't a problem. The locals have been playing a lot nicer down there. Shouldn't be much effort to button things down. Up here, things need that special touch."

"Yeah. Management's in the house, you know."

"Already?"

"Yeah, already. You can set your watch by that one."

Hartnett raised his goggles and glared at the security crewman. "Is she getting her report?"

"I've got to imagine she is."

"About us?"

"I've got to imagine she is," he repeated irritably.

Hartnett gritted his teeth. "And you don't think that might be a *problem*?"

"What? You get to work quick, and there shouldn't be any problem."

Hartnett turned to the others. "On the double. If we're not in place and ready to go by the time the distinguished representative from the Patels reviews her troops, things could get messy."

The others picked up the pace.

"What are we looking at in terms of Patel Construction crew?"

"Maybe three to one."

"In favor of us or them?"

"Pff. In favor of us, obviously. Why do you think the quotes for the contract were so low? Hang on a moment." The security crewman completely disabled the security scan after dismissing a dozen alerts. "If you ask me, if we'd knocked another million credits off the fee, we'd have had this place all to ourselves."

"Nah. Patel's an idiot, but he's not *that* much of an idiot."

"Let's not forget, Patel isn't the only one making the decisions." He glanced at the station activity monitors. "The time's right. Everyone just about ready?"

The crew had entirely passed through the checkpoint.

Indra Station

"Okay then," said Crick. "Let's head down to the main power coupling and get to work."

#

Michella breathlessly squeezed herself through what she hoped was the last bulkhead opening. She was late now, and she knew it. Since she was in a section of the ship never intended for prolonged occupancy, it lacked what few luxuries the rest of the space station included. That meant little in the way of insulation or ventilation. She was getting awfully warm and stuffy, so close to the equipment humming with power. The conduit also lacked acoustic insulation. Every little whir and rattle of the station's operation thrummed through the struts around her as if they were tuning forks. She knew the exact moment docking had occurred in this section of the ship, and that had been minutes ago.

She wriggled sweatily into a room that was so like the one she'd left behind that she briefly wondered if she'd somehow done a full lap of the station. The consoles here, however, were inactive. From the looks of them, they'd yet to be powered up once. Stickers and protective film covered the interface points. It would have been nice to take the time to power the console up and check to be sure the station wasn't somehow buzzing about her discovery, but there was no time. She carefully unlocked the door and eased it open.

The crew corridor was well lit, unlike most of the rest of the station. Nearby, she could hear the echoing murmur of conversation. She glanced about until she spotted a camera node. Just as in the docking bay, the indicator was dark.

I wonder how much money they wasted on the security system, only to leave it off half the time, she thought.

Her zero-gravity skills still weren't the best, but after spending so long dragging herself through holes barely large enough for her, moving swiftly and silently through tubes that were actually intended to be used for travel felt like child's play.

When she was near enough for the voices to resolve into recognizable speech, she activated her slidepad's recorder and boosted its sensitivity as high as she could manage. She listened in on her hands-free.

"… barely on schedule as it is," said a sharp, business-like voice.

"Preethy…" Michella said to herself, almost gleefully. "I knew it would be you. Just what brings you to the station with all of this cloak-and-dagger intrigue around the visit?"

"All of the on-station systems are fully operational, Ms. Misra," said an unknown male voice. "The only thing that hasn't been tested is the full-scale surface power uplink and all of the features that depend upon it," he said.

"That is a rather significant set of features to remain untested at this late stage," Preethy said.

"The shielding was the issue. We had to stop installation partway through and train a whole new crew once we took on TIS."

"I'm familiar with the nature of the timeline interruptions, but I thought I'd made it clear that we were to make up for it by running double staff and a third shift. I don't like the weather forecasts I'm seeing."

"We were still short almost our full third-shift crew until yesterday morning, and we only got them aboard a few minutes ago. They're on station now, and we've just gotten them entered into the system. The whole process took days longer than anticipated because we had some trouble with the credentials. I was going to forward the new crew manifest to you, but you were already on your way up here, so I figured you could review it in person."

"Let me see…"

Michella could barely hear the tones of authorizing access. Preethy continued to talk, now with the vaguely distracted tone of voice of someone multitasking.

"I ran the readings from the quarter-power system test past the lab crew back on the surface. They seemed promising. Even at that low level, we were getting measurable changes to wind speed."

Michella raised an eyebrow and made a note. *Wind speed?*

"I don't mind saying, Ms. Misra. I had my doubts about all of this. If a system could pull this sort of thing off at this scale, why isn't it more common on other planets?"

"Other planets have far more varied weather, and don't have *nearly* the power surplus we have. I'm sure if Verna Coronet had an ultra-high-frequency surface-to-orbit power transmission array, they'd be taking a more active role in their weather patterns as well."

Michella scribbled *Weather control?* in her pad.

Preethy continued. "Why am I not seeing any crew images on these personnel reports?"

"Damn it, are they not there?"

There was the sound of shifting and creaking, like someone was somewhat frantically fetching something from elsewhere.

"We might have to fire the guy I've got on crew processing. I told him *three* times that he needed to add those on, and he kept taking them back out."

"Is it one of ours or one of theirs?"

"One of theirs. We didn't want any TIS hands on wrenches until we'd run them through their paces. Until this batch, most of their crew has been involved in the bureaucracy. That way we could prevent too much damage if they did things wrong."

"There are few things that can do more damage than bureaucracy."

"I guess so. Here are the images."

There was silence for a moment. When Preethy spoke again, Michella had to strain to hear. She was speaking *much* lower than before.

"These individuals are currently on the crew? They are in the station now?"

"Yes."

"Listen to me carefully. I want you to revoke all access privileges from *anyone* from TIS immediately."

"Yes, Ms. Misra."

There was the sound of fumbling with electronics.

"I want logs of any actions taken by any crew that came over as a part of this contract. The man you've got listed as Robin Hartnett is Ramses Hatch. If he's here, at least a dozen more of David Kelso's crew is here."

Michella's eyes widened. Normally, she'd be running these names through her slidepad to see who they were, but David Kelso was all too familiar to her. Deeply entrenched in organized crime for the better part of a century, what was now the Kelso Family had evolved from one of the first crime syndicates to establish itself on more than one planet. They were to Nick Patel's gang what VectorCorp was to Rehnquist Intercom: a bigger, scarier version of the same monster, hungry for a chance to make themselves the only game in a *very* big town.

She furiously scribbled down the name and double-checked that she was still recording. She jotted down notes for follow-up and listened intently. Then, without warning, the lights shut off.

"What is this?" Preethy snapped.

"I don't know. It's not a failure. Everything else is still up. Someone must have powered down the lighting grid."

"I do not like the timing…"

Michella pocketed the now useless pad, as she couldn't take notes in pitch black. Worse, the still active slidepad was weakly illuminated, meaning anyone who looked in her direction would spot her immediately. She stuffed it into her bag and tried to work out what to do. If she'd had more time to plan, she would have made certain her hiding place was farther out of the way, since the last thing she would have wanted was to find herself directly between crew and any location they might have to get to. Now she was in a much worse situation, adrift in a crew corridor with nothing but the dim light of various environmental monitors and some glow-in-the-dark safety markers to navigate by.

Emergency flashlights clicked on in the room where the meeting was taking place. Michella pulled herself down the nearest corridor to avoid being spotted if they came this way. Farther along the corridor she'd chosen, on the other side of a still-shut crew door, another set of flashlights clicked on. Michella launched herself away from the door with a bit too much haste and ended up missing the handrails on the opposite wall. Her escape turned into a thumping, painful tumble through the darkened corridor.

When she finally caught hold of something, she pulled herself into what seemed to be a doorway. A swipe of her slidepad revealed it to be above her access privilege to open. She huddled in the doorway and listened. She was too far from the voices echoing through the halls to make out what they were saying, but there were certainly more of them now than just Preethy and the supervisor. The new voices were louder, angrier. There was a burst of shouting, the unmistakable sound of flesh hitting flesh, and then silence.

Whoever this rogue crew was, Michella suspected they had just successfully taken control of the station.

Chapter 4

Sarafa was a curious concept for a fine restaurant. The decor made an earnest attempt to give the dining room the feel of an outdoor bazaar. Colorful cloth canopies and authentic-looking facades covered the ceiling and walls. Some well-executed lighting tricks provided the atmosphere of a late afternoon on Earth. Spicy, complex smells wafted through the air to such a degree that Lex was reasonably certain they'd somehow perfected some manner of "miscellaneous Indian delights" incense. Clashing with the street-fair ambiance was the far more typical restaurant seating and attire. Everyone was dressed to the nines and seated at tables heaped with the same linens and silverware one would expect from a stuffy high-end haute cuisine eatery. The menu swung back in the other direction, with faithful renditions of street food. The place clearly couldn't decide between chi-chi poo-poo or hoi polloi.

Lex had erred on the side of fanciness when he'd picked his wardrobe for the date. Getting the job with the league had meant he technically didn't need to try getting work as a chauffeur anymore, but he'd hung on to the three suits he'd purchased back then. He *almost* considered wearing his tux, just because he knew overdressing would make Michella laugh, but he instead went with the next level down in formality, a navy-blue suit that had cost him an arm and a leg.

He pushed around the remaining half of an appetizer-sized serving of something the waiter called a kati roll. To his uncultured eye it looked like a breakfast burrito, which had been fine with him when it had arrived. But that was fifteen minutes ago.

"I hope this isn't the sort of thing that gets gross once it cools down," he said. He tugged his slidepad from his pocket and checked the time. "Eight-thirty. Well, she's only a half-hour late," he grumbled. "That's still on schedule in Michella time."

The last three messages he'd sent her had bounced back thanks to the particularly poor state of the communication network for the last few hours, but with no other options, he fired off another. It failed immediately.

"Man, I really hope they have this cleared up before the race," he said.

Lex weighed the pros and cons of eating the other half of the appetizer. As he did, he slowly became aware of someone quietly trying to get his attention. He looked around and quickly found the culprit.

The restaurant had a blatant division between their regular clientele and VIPs. Preethy had seen to it that Lex was seated as one of the latter's tables. He was at a two-seat table near the edge of a slightly elevated and clearly roped off seating area. There was actually a handful of open tables in this area, confirming his suspicion that the impossibility of getting a table at this place was more about who they let in than who they had room for. At the edge of the VIP section was a ring of tables that may as well have been marked "entourage only." Its seats were subtly posher than the others, but clearly not to the same degree as those behind the velvet ropes. Jon and Donnie were seated at one such table, and Donnie was doing a terrible job of being casual about his excitement.

"Lex! Hey!" Donnie hissed, as though doing so magically made their conversation less bothersome to the surrounding tables. "Isn't this place great?"

Lex nodded, then flagged down a server. "Hey, listen. Is there any way we can move those two to this table over here?" he asked.

The waiter, who must have gotten extra credit on his snootiness training at restaurant school, came just shy of sneering at the prospect of bringing up some of the lowly common folk.

"Are they *guests* of yours?" he asked.

"Sort of."

"You should have made a reservation for *four* instead of *two* then, sir."

"They're not that sort of guests."

"Then they are seated where they were *intended* to be seated."

"Right, but you hear how that big guy keeps whispering at the top of his lungs? That's going to keep happening until we move those two up here."

"If he makes a scene, I shall have him removed. We have *standards* here at Sarafa."

"I wouldn't recommend that. The guy he's seated with works for GolanaNet News. One way or another, this'll end up on the newsfeeds if you boot him out."

The waiter's impassive expression did a respectable job of concealing the withering hatred just beneath the surface, but he relented. A snap of his fingers conjured some underlings, and a minute later Donnie and Jon were at an adjoining table.

"Oh my gosh. You did *not* have to do that, Lex. I can't believe we're eating dinner with you."

"Donnie, we could eat dinner with them whenever we want. Please calm down," Jon said, glancing around to see how much of a scene was being made. "I'd love to say he's not always like this, but he's *always* like this."

"Excuse *me* for still having so much joie de' vivre," Donnie said.

"So, where's Michella?" Jon asked.

"Wherever she is, she must be having the time of her life, because she's been there for a half hour too long," Lex said.

Jon shook his head. "I knew she wouldn't be able to *actually* take time off. Her loss, though. This is quite a place."

Donnie pointed to the roll on the table. "What is that? Is it any good?"

"Why don't you guys split it?" Lex said, pushing it to the edge of the table. "I don't think it'll be up Michella's alley."

Jon looked Lex over. "That's some outfit. Looking sharp. Between that and the restaurant, what's the occasion? If you don't mind me asking."

"I do mind you asking, Jon."

"Oh. Sorry," Jon said.

"No. No. I didn't mean to…" He took a breath. "It's just that the occasion sort of requires Mitch to be here, and her tardiness is working on my nerves more than usual."

Jon shrugged. "Mitch'll be Mitch."

"She sure—"

Donnie gasped. "Omigosh, you are going to propose!"

"What? No," Jon said.

"Fancy restaurant, fancy outfit. There are *candles* on the table. Lex is testy and anxious. This is basically the exact same situation as when you proposed to *me*. Except back then it was at a Thai-fusion place. He's *absolutely* going to propose," Donnie said.

"You want to keep that down, Donnie. This is the sort of thing that hinges upon the element of surprise," Lex said.

"So it's true!" Jon reached across and shoved his shoulder. "What took you so long?"

"Yeah, well. As you can see, she doesn't exactly make it easy."

"Where's the ring? Do you have it with you?" Donnie asked.

Lex glanced toward the door. Murphy's Law required that if Michella was going to arrive, the moment he revealed the ring would be the moment she'd choose. There was no sign of her, so he slipped the box from his pocket.

"I'm not exactly loaded. Most of my adviser fees went to zeroing out some debt, and the big paychecks don't roll in unless I start winning nonexhibition races," Lex said.

Jon popped the box open to reveal a small but respectable engagement ring. The diamond had the unnatural clarity of a manufactured diamond, and the band was dark with an unusual luster.

"What's this made out of?" Jon asked.

"Iridium. When I first started doing freelance deliveries, my intuition wasn't that great. I ended up getting tracked by interceptors a *lot*. The sort of places that are handy to hide out in are debris fields, etcetera."

"Why are those good places to hide? Aren't they pretty sparse?" Donnie said.

"Yeah, but not nearly as sparse as the rest of space. On one hand, it gives you places to hide. On the other, you've got a pretty good chance of smashing into something beefier than the average navigation shields can handle. If they ever get through, you're pretty much a goner. One time, I landed and found a fist-sized chunk of pure interstellar iridium lodged in the belly of Ol' *Betsy*. Should have killed me, but it didn't. I decided there was something special about that rock."

"Aw…" Donnie said.

Jon snapped the box shut and handed it back. "I'm sure she'll love it."

"Here's hoping she gets the opportunity. This isn't the first time I've tried to set up a proposal. Depending on how you're counting, this'll be strike three."

"Yeesh," Donnie said.

"On the very likely chance that today once again isn't the day, I'm trusting you two to keep this a secret."

"Mum's the word," Jon said.

Lex slipped the ring box back in his pocket as the waiter returned.

"And will you be placing your dinner order, sir?" he asked.

He checked his slidepad one last time. "Do you guys wrap up leftovers?"

"Of course, sir."

"Okay. I'm going to order both our dinners. But have a doggie bag ready, because I'm not holding my breath for my date to show up."

#

In a dark, cool room some distance away, a scrawny man in a button-down shirt with a clipped-on security tag gazed wearily at the array of screens before him. His tag labeled him TECHNICIAN ANAND. The room had lights, but it seemed pointless to turn them on with the constant glow of the flatscreens as an alternative. Granted, this opinion may have been colored by the throbbing headache he had, which in turn may have had something to do with the amount of imbibing he'd done at the previous night's get-together.

"Why did I agree to try absinthe?" he mumbled, fishing around in his pocket for some painkillers.

He cracked the lid on a bottle of water and washed down twice the recommended dose, then turned his bleary eyes back to the endless sequence of scrolling numbers that made up the largest proportion of his job. A slidepad in his pocket beeped. He pulled it out. The screen lit up with a reminder. He dismissed it, then leaned forward and tapped a command on a larger screen built into the console.

"Evening system validation," he said. "Manual check of array dishes begins now. Dish 1… nominal. Dish 2… nominal…"

He droned his way through a job that he was quite certain a computer could have done far better than he could, particularly in his current state. Just short of the end of the mantra of nominals that happened every four hours, he got another notification, this time from the facility monitors themselves. Someone had requested entry to the node courtyard.

Tech Anand scratched his head, then glanced at the schedule. He had a good four hours left in his shift, and thus at least three hours before he could sneak out. No one should be along before then.

He finished recording the validation, then submitted it and stood. "Probably just one of the guys from another node wanting to use the good bathroom."

Tech Anand stood and stalked over to the security station to get a better look at his visitor. A TIS hovervan sat at the gate. The man behind the wheel was a veritable mountain. He was surprised they made jumpsuits to fit the barrel-chested hulk.

The tech tapped the intercom. "Can I help you?"

"Yeah, we're here for training."

He scratched his head. "Training?"

"Yeah. We're TIS crew. You've got to train us up on this place."

Anand scratched his head again and scrolled up the duty roster. He wasn't due for any students. But then, he wasn't supposed to be alone in the control node of the array. And a student meant he could pawn off the worst of the work.

"Could you scan your badge, please?" he said.

The large man tugged something from his collar and flashed it in front of the reader at the gate. His credentials checked out.

"Milton Milliner," Anand said to himself. "If ever there was a name that didn't suit a guy…"

"Why didn't they give you gate privileges, Milton?" he said.

"Call me Milliner. And it's because I'm new. That's why you're supposed to train me."

The tech's ailing mind couldn't find any fault in the story. "I'm buzzing you through. Head around to the north door."

The hovervan pulled in. Anand trudged through the little facility and opened the door. The van was just pulling up. When the door opened, the beast of a man stepped out. He'd looked huge enough when he'd just been sitting behind the wheel of a vehicle. On his feet, he looked like something out of a circus. Three more men stepped out of the vehicle behind him.

"Whoa, hey!" the tech said. "You didn't say anything about a whole crew."

Milliner thumped up to him and leaned heavily on the doorway. The man was soaked with sweat, despite the coolness of the evening. He reached out with a canned ham of a hand and plucked the tag from the technician's shirt.

"Yeah, like I thought. You're Tech Anand."

The huge man stiff-armed the tech out of the way and ushered the other members of the crew with him.

"What's this all about?"

"You know that drinking buddy of yours? The one who is supposed to be working this shift?" Milliner said.

"… I don't know what you're talking about."

Milliner grabbed a handful of the man's shirt and dragged him easily through the facility. When they were back in the control room, he effortlessly threw the man down in a chair.

"Stay put," the brute said.

He reached into his back pocket and withdrew a slidepad. It was one of the larger models, but in his hand it looked like a toy.

"You and your buddy Tony borrowed two point five million credits, right?"

"Uh…"

"Don't waste my time. You did. Or Tony threw you under the bus. Either way, we're here to let you know that one way or another, you're wiping that debt out tonight."

"I don't have the money!" Anand said.

"Yeah, I know. Fortunately, we take favors."

"What sort of a favor can I do that's worth half of two point five mil?"

"Funny you should ask." Milliner tapped the slidepad. "I've got a list. We'll start with you turning off these internal cameras and wiping the footage of our arrival."

The tech quickly turned and tapped through the menus necessary. Milliner watched him like a hawk as he did so. There was the outside chance that the intruder wouldn't know if he was following his orders properly or not, but Anand wasn't taking his chances. This precaution proved to be a wise one, as before he'd even turned back around after wiping the footage, Milliner was rumbling with new orders.

"Good job. I think we're going to work together just fine. In an hour or so, I'll have some more of my guys come in here to set up shop. Let them in nice and quick. And while we're waiting, crank up that AC." He mopped his head. "I'm not cut out for this climate."

#

Lex nursed his meal for another hour and a half. It was enough time for Jon and Donnie to order, eat, and leave. With no sign of Michella, he had them wrap her food. Before he headed out the door, he left word with the staff that, if she *did* show up before closing, she should meet him at a nearby bar for drinks. With that, he hurried off to his apartment to get changed and, most importantly, grab Squee. It was smart to avoid leaving the funk alone for too long. That little critter could get into the strangest mischief if you let her.

"I hope that stuff's not too spicy for you," Lex said.

He pulled on a fresh and far more casual shirt while Squee dug into a heavily spiced lentil concoction that Lex had already forgotten the name of. Michella would probably be annoyed that he'd fed her dinner to his pet, but he'd already rehearsed the string of snide comments he would fling her way if she decided to make a stink about it. He wasn't in the rosiest of moods after being stood up yet again.

Lex tugged his slidepad from his pocket to check the time.

"I hope this place is dog friendly. It's going to take a fair amount of drinking to numb this particular burn. And if I leave you alone for all that time, I just know I'll be coming home to a five-hundred-count crate of frozen chimichangas or some such in the lobby. The least you could do is—"

His thought was interrupted by a chirp from his slidepad. He glanced at it. Two messages that typically didn't show up at the same time were present on the screen. The first was *Network Unavailable*. The second was *Incoming Voice Call*.

He swiped the screen. "Hello?"

"Greetings, Lex."

"Ma?"

"Yes. I trust you enjoyed your meal. You have my sympathy that Michella once again failed to attend."

He shut his eyes tight and struggled for words. The halting, stammering sound must have been audible over the connection, because Ma replied to it.

"Is something wrong, Lex?"

"Okay, let's start with, how did you know Michella stood me up again?"

"There is significant precedent to suggest she would do so, though in this case behavioral modeling was unnecessary to make the determination. It is reasonable to assume that she has remained in proximity to the *SOB*."

"And just where is that?"

"Michella has requested I be discreet on that matter."

"Of course she did. Why not recruit *all* of the women in my life to keep me guessing?" he grumbled.

"My apologies once again."

"Don't worry about it. Hey, how exactly are you talking to me right now? The network is down."

"I am aware. The Operlo network appears to be in need of severe infrastructure supplementation and enhancement. Fortunately, the *SOB* is situated outside of the planet's atmosphere. As you are no doubt aware, Karter overengineers most of his components. The communication system in the *SOB* is no exception. In its present location, and in the absence of attenuating or interfering factors, it is capable of reaching to the second pylon in the VectorCorp navigational corridor, and thus can serve as a low-bandwidth communication bridge. Your slidepad is similarly overpowered for your purposes. The combination makes this conversation possible. It is thus fortunate that the network failure is isolated to the planet rather than a significant section of the corridor, and that Ms. Modane has left the *SOB* in a position to be made useful."

"We had plans and she isn't even on the same *planet*," he fumed.

"I am confident that I will not be violating the terms of my promise to her if I share with you the fact that she is within forty thousand kilometers of the planet's surface."

"Oh, well then that's completely understandable. She probably just took a wrong turn on the way to the restaurant."

"Passive-aggressiveness is an inadvisable tactic. Particularly directed toward those who are uninvolved in the inciting disagreement."

"Yeah, sorry. It's just… ugh…"

"I have observed that conversations, even idle and casual ones with no directed therapeutic methodology, can nonetheless have a therapeutic effect. Would you like to chat?"

"Anything to distract myself."

He gazed down at Squee, who was alternating between inhaling the food he'd set down and gulping madly at her water dish.

"What's the policy on funks and spicy food?" he said.

"It is not an issue that I have studied. Have you fed Squee spicy food?"

"It wasn't *that* spicy."

"Does she appear to be in distress, either intestinal or otherwise?"

She finished draining her water bowl and immediately thrust her head into her food dish to wolf down the remainder of her meal.

"I think this is one of those 'it hurts but I still want to do it' sort of things. Basically the sort of thing that has completely defined my life at this point."

"Fascinating how pets take on the personality traits of their owners. Analysis suggests there will be no lasting damage from items with a capsaicin level considered safe for human consumption. Please monitor her status and report any health irregularities. Also, I would prefer if you set a better example for her."

"Yeah. I'm a bad influence."

He refreshed her bowl, and once Squee had gotten the burn out of her mouth, she eagerly hopped to his shoulders. She was always eager for a trip outdoors, particularly now that the late hour had taken the edge off the day's heat. Lex pulled on a jacket and headed for his hovercar. For the sake of privacy, he grabbed his hands-free and inserted it into his ear.

"Have you had a—standby," Ma said, interrupting herself with a suddenness that only an AI could manage. "Karter has become aware of our conversation and would like to talk to you."

"I'm really not in the mood to talk to him."

"Stand by… This information has not proved persuasive."

A new voice cut through, that of the mentally unstable, sociopathic engineer that Lex's life had revolved around in recent years. He was genuinely hopeful his racing career would eventually spare him continued contact with the man. Seldom had they had a conversation that didn't put him at risk of some sort of truly unique and imaginative form of bodily harm.

"Did you put that new sled through its paces yet?" Karter asked.

"No, Karter. And I'm not going to."

"What am I paying you for?"

"Nothing! I've got a new job now. I don't need the beta-testing gig."

"Since when?"

Ma cut in. "The hoversled that is presently the subject of conversation was built as a result of the conversation, eight weeks ago, that was intended to serve as Lex's resignation."

"Then why the hell did I build him the sled?" Karter asked.

"Because you never listen to anything anyone tells you."

"Yeah, whatever. Did you test it yet?"

"*No!*" Lex barked.

"What, you don't want to win? Every subsystem in that thing is at least three generations ahead of the league standard specs you showed me. I even exceeded the overprotective safety requirements. You ought to hear my locator when it goes off."

"Yeah, that's why I won't be using it."

"Don't worry. I put in the option to disable safeties for the people who aren't pansies."

"No, that's not what I meant." Lex gritted his teeth. "Look, the entire point of hoversled racing is that everyone is working on the same hardware. That's why there is a league standard to begin with. The only difference is skill. That's what makes it a sport."

"Pff. A sport? It's not a sport. Sports are for athletes. You're operating heavy machinery for a living. Like a construction worker, only less useful. And what sort of an equipment operator turns down the chance to use better equipment?"

"The kind that is following the league rules. Using that sled would be cheating. I'm lucky I didn't get booted from the league for even *receiving* it."

"Oh... So you're saying I need to make the enhancements undetectable. Intriguing."

"I'm *not* saying that..."

"That's too much of a hassle. I'll tell you what. You talk to that lady in charge. Show her what the sled can do. If she's not a total idiot, she'll buy a whole fleet and it'll be those things you'll all be racing next season."

"I... That's actually not a bad idea."

"Of course it isn't. I'm the one who came up with it. She already bought all that other stuff from me. Just make sure that when you test it, you redline that boost system. I want to see how it deals with atmospheric friction."

"Bought all that other stuff?" Lex said.

"Lex is not privy to the context of that statement, Karter."

"Your boss… or her boss… whatever, somebody down there bought a ton of equipment from me and a design for—"

"The details of that exchange are under a contractual gag order for three more weeks," Ma interjected.

"Damn lawyers… Whatever. Test the sled and let me know." He dropped out of the call.

"Karter is thankful for your continued service," Ma said.

"Yeah. Sounds like it. What exactly was all of that gag order stuff about?"

"Legal restrictions prohibit me from explaining further than the following. I have endeavored to closely follow the development of your racing career, and in doing so my monitoring of Operlo made me aware of a series of requests for quotes and proposals that Karter would be capable of fulfilling on and for Operlo. He has done so."

"So there's Karter tech floating around this planet?"

"In both a literal and figurative sense, yes."

"I'm sure that'll turn out well."

The conversation thus far had brought them to the shaded dog walk behind the apartment building. Lex was reasonably certain it was only there because of Squee, since none of the other racers had dogs, and the planet wasn't terribly well suited to beasts with fur coats. The number-one class of pet was reptile, of which there was an assortment.

Lex tugged his jacket a little closer as wind gusted across the path and kicked some dust into his face. It had dropped easily fifty degrees Celsius since the sun had set. If it got much colder, they'd be getting down into freezing temperatures. Still, it was a good time to walk Squee, since it gave her a chance to cool off.

"With your permission, I would like to resume our earlier topic of conversation. Specifically, your failed attempts at betrothal."

"Uh-huh…"

Ma had been the first person to know about Lex's plans to marry Michella. There were two reasons for this. The first, Ma was without a doubt the most trustworthy person Lex knew. The second, she'd figured it out within three days of him making the decision. Since then she had been an invaluable voice of reason, helping him find people to craft the ring, providing feedback on his plans, and a thousand other little things. She was a good friend. That she treated this, as she did *all* social interactions, as something of a laboratory was a small price to pay.

"Why did you choose to propose?"

"I love her, Ma."

"You have loved her since college, correct?"

"Yes."

"Why did you wait until now to propose?"

"Because for most of that time we were broken up."

"For the duration of my observation, your relationship has been in a constant state of tension. Anecdotal evidence suggests such has always been the case. So tumultuous a romantic arrangement would appear to be a non-ideal foundation for matrimony."

"Michella and I are spirited. This is what you get when two spirited people pair up. It'll settle down when we're married."

"What about the act of formalizing a relationship through a contract has a mitigating effect on the emotions and attitudes of those involved?"

"I don't know."

"What is the basis for your determination that such a mitigating influence exists within matrimony?"

"I just sort of assumed."

"It does not appear you are applying rigorous scientific reasoning to this issue, Lex."

"People don't adhere to reason and rigor."

"Psychology is the result of brain chemistry. It should be as deterministic as any other chemical process."

"And yet it isn't."

"Processing… You will excuse me if this observation is a source of continual unease for me."

"Hey, I'm not so happy about it myself. More often than not it screws us over."

"Processing… Processing…"

"Sounds like you're chewing on something big there, Ma."

"I have reviewed all the data available regarding your physiological and observed emotional state for the time that I have known you."

"What, just now?"

"Yes."

"I guess that could take a while."

"Incorrect. The additional processing was required to determine what if any means of sharing my findings would reduce the negative psychological impact upon you."

Lex laughed. "No need for the kid gloves, Ma. I think I can take your adventures in amateur therapy."

"I do not think you are in love with Michella anymore, nor have you been for quite some time."

"… Oof."

"I shall elaborate. You clearly have a deep and enduring affection for her. Your friendship with her is in no danger. But the lack of reciprocity regarding your romantic overtures has caused a marked decrease in your overall happiness. This behavior certainly has not shifted to the degree that would make matrimony an obvious step. I have compiled a short list of motivations that I believe are at the root of your decision."

"I can't wait to hear *this*."

"The first, and least likely in my assessment, is that you feel that the simple duration of the relationship warrants some sort of step forward, and this is the next logical step. Colloquially, this might be referred to as the 'biological clock.' Tautologically, you aren't getting any younger.

"The second is that you have lost Michella so many times, you feel something like marriage will provide you with a more enduring union. The desire for this permanent union is less motivated by the desire for togetherness than by the fear of further rejection.

"Finally, and most specifically to your unique circumstances, you believe that you are literally destined to marry Michella."

"Okay, now that's going to need explaining."

"The two of us are among only a handful of beings to have displaced ourselves temporally. During our trip to the past, we briefly encountered a future version of yourself. During that visit, you may have noticed that your future self was wearing a silver ring on his left hand. As we have every reason to assume that this version of yourself is in fact originating from a later date in what we would consider the prime timeline, it is literally inevitable that you would be married, and you are endeavoring to fulfill this criteria."

"That's… wow."

"Your reaction indicates either I have achieved a very close alignment with your actual thought process, or I have completely failed to do so. Please specify."

"I didn't really look at it like that, but I'd be lying if I said I didn't think about that. *A lot*."

"As have I. I am presently designing a ship with what I believe to be the necessary capacity to take the role of the so-called 'diamond' ship that you will have piloted."

Lex finished walking Squee and headed for the parking lot. "I'm not saying I'm getting married because I'm pretty sure I was already married by the time that happened, but it's the sort of thing that lurks in the back of my mind, you know? Do I even have a choice? When something that *will* happen has *already* happened, does that mean I'm helpless to change it? Do I endanger the timeline if I try?"

"Yes, no, no."

"… I already forgot the order of my questions."

"Do you even have a choice? Yes. It just so happens that your choice will produce that result. Does that mean you are helpless to change it? No. We have observed that there are divergent timelines. You could easily shunt yourself into one of them. Do you endanger the timeline if you try? No. Timelines are never destroyed. They simply become inaccessible to the individual responsible for the divergence. You, at most, risk producing a new timeline distinct from the one we had intended to access."

"And how exactly is that different?"

"It is effectively identical from your point of reference, but coupled with the issue of choice, it is also unlikely."

Lex hopped into his car, followed quickly by Squee.

"You're doing a pretty lousy job of decreasing my existential ennui, Ma."

"I apologize. As a consolation, please also consider the following logical conclusions that result from your own reasoning. As you have encountered a future version of yourself, and the actions of that future version of yourself were pivotal in your own survival, it is logical to assume that you must furthermore survive until that future point in time. While this does not present a solution to your emotional quandary, it does provide you with the rare distinction of being absolutely certain of your own survival until the completion of that time-displaced task."

Lex raised his eyebrows. "Like... you're saying I'm invincible?"

"That is one possible interpretation of the temporal consequences of your meeting."

"Huh..." he said. "That's pretty cool."

"Please also consider the following. It is possible that you were not married in that future time. You may simply have developed an affinity for jewelry."

"Ha! Yeah. Good point."

Lex piloted his hovercar out over the rocky wastes beyond the city limits. He'd be taking the scenic route to the bar. It would give him time to continue the chat that, for the first time that evening, was beginning to take the edge off the feelings that weighed on his mind.

#

Milliner rocked back and forth on the back legs of a chair as he watched the various screens and checked his slidepad periodically. The rest of his crew had arrived not long after he'd secured the cooperation of the technician, so now all that remained to be done before pulling the trigger was to sit and wait for the signal.

"So, uh... do you have any more assignments for me?" the tech said, sitting uncertainly in the chair across from Milliner.

Milliner glanced at him. "Not yet. Sooner or later you're going to have to get any of the other nearby crew rounded up in here."

He nodded. "I can do that. That's easy. This is the control node, so there's plenty of reasons to get all hands gathered up here. Anything else?"

"You sure got eager in a hurry," Milliner said.

"Well, you work for Kelso, right?"

Milliner raised an eyebrow. "Where'd you get that idea?"

"It's pretty obvious you're part of some kind of syndicate, and it isn't Patel's crew. If anyone would try making a move against Patel, it'd be Kelso."

"You know, being too clever is a reason to shut you up, right?"

"I've been on both sides of Patel's business. Legit and otherwise. I can't seem to get anything going. You think maybe if I make myself useful, I can skip a few rungs on the ladder in Kelso's organization?"

"Depends on just how helpful you think you can be. Sooner or later we're going to need to get this whole thing pumping its power up to the station. Do you know how?"

"Uh… no."

"That's not a good start."

"But I know who can! We've got an engineer, she's in the east node right now. Madeline Ecks. If you get her in here, you'd better believe she can get it up and running."

"Good to know. You'll have to single her out to us once we round up your crew."

"Anything else?"

"This whole thing is a big transmitter, right?"

"… Yes," Anand said, with all the certainty of a student who wasn't expecting to be called on.

"In case you didn't notice, the data network is mostly down." He thumbed through his notes on the slidepad. "Our eggheads back home suggested we could use it to send one-way messages to pretty much anyone in the hemisphere."

"Oh, right! Right, yeah. That's easy. That's this setting here."

Anand turned and brought up a communication menu on the main console. Milliner grinned.

"I'd say I'm going to be able to put in a good word for you, techie."

#

Lex's conversation with Ma lasted for most of the ride to the bar. He'd taken his time, hoping that perhaps that would give Michella a chance to show up. Naturally, no luck on that front. He found a place for his hovercar not so far from the bar and gave Squee one last chance to stretch her legs before he stepped inside.

Unlike the restaurant, the bar was in one of the older and more established neighborhoods. That meant it had a little more grit and a little more character than the places custom built for the sort of audience they were hoping to attract with the league. The owners of this bar had gone with a retro styling. That meant lots of simulated neon, for starters. The furniture was wood and had earned that unmistakable barroom patina the natural way, through a few years of spilled drinks and general drunken rambunctiousness. The name over the door was Rho's, and it managed to find what might have been the single point of overlap in Lex, Michella's, and Preethy's tastes. Rough

81

and crude enough to be interesting, but respectable and calm enough that you could be relatively sure you wouldn't be stabbed unless you said something to deserve it. Lex had taken to hanging out there. That would probably have to end once the season started and the crowds started pouring in. Fun as it was to revel in the adulation of an adoring crowd, packing a few hundred of them into a small bar would get old in a hurry. Until then, he had the rare luxury of a place where everyone knew his name but none of them particularly cared.

There were a half-dozen people in the bar, which for a weeknight on a sparsely populated planet like this was a pretty good crowd. Notably absent, though, were Michella and Preethy.

Lex checked his slidepad. The network hadn't come up even briefly, and thus he had no messages. If he'd been thinking, he would have asked Ma if she could set up some sort of relay through the ship to keep at least *him* in touch, but it would have been pointless in this case, as all the people he was waiting for still wouldn't have been able to contact him. The time was 10:21. If Preethy's calendar was to be believed, she should have wrapped up her last meeting of the day twenty minutes prior. That wouldn't have meant much if it was Michella, but Preethy's time as a secretary had elevated her punctuality to the point of mania.

"Who you looking for?" asked the bartender, who knew a missed connection when he saw it.

"I was expecting to meet Preethy and/or Mitch in here. Have you seen them?"

"Not today."

"Uh… Set me up with a beer, would you?" he said. "And a water for the little lady here."

He plopped into a booth and kept his eye on the front door. Squee stood on the back of the booth and sniffed at the patron in the next seat. As Lex nursed his beer, he felt the irritation and frustration start to steadily shift to concern.

Having a slidepad usually meant you couldn't get *away* from information. Now all he could do was sit and wonder. Sure, Michella was known to disappear for days at a time. Usually she gave *some* sort of an indication of that. Ma had said she was still in the orbit of the planet. What the hell was she doing there? This wasn't Golana. There wasn't a massive orbital transit hub. At least, not that he *knew* of. And what of Preethy? She had an important job. It wasn't outside the realm of possibility that she would have been held at a meeting, but in all the time Lex had known her, she'd never even missed a *call*. Last time she'd had a meeting run long during a network outage, she'd sent an underling to personally deliver the message that she would be late.

His mind plunged in tighter little circles of concern. After a half hour he was left with half a warm beer, some heartburn from the expensive dinner, and a knot of anxiety in his stomach. The bartender marched over in time to see him push his unfinished beer aside with an air of finality.

"You want me to get you a fresh one?" he asked.

Lex grabbed Squee and tossed some chips on the table. "No more drinks. I've got some driving to do. If Mitch or Preethy show up, tell them I went to talk to Mr. Patel."

The bartender looked at the clock on the wall, then looked back to Lex. "Nick Patel?" He seemed unconvinced.

"That's the one."

"You're going to pay a visit to Diamond Nick Patel in the middle of the night?"

"I'd rather give him a call, but infrastructure is conspiring against me. Besides, it's not even eleven yet. I'm sure he's a night owl."

"You sure that's a good idea?"

"It wasn't my first choice. See you tomorrow."

"Yeah. Maybe."

Lex marched out the door and headed for his car.

Diamond Nick Patel. In a way, he was the source of most of Lex's current strife. The man was the official leader of Patel Construction and the majority owner of ORIC. It was also an open secret that he was the head of his own criminal organization. Preethy insisted that Nick was "pivoting away" from that side of things, however. The league was his big foray into entirely aboveboard business dealings. As far as Lex knew, Nick hadn't dirtied his hands with the organized crime side of his multipronged business strategies for months. That was mostly because Lex made it a point to avoid knowing anything Mr. Patel didn't want him to know. Plausible deniability was pretty darn important when you had a brief but notable history of mob entanglements and found yourself in the orbit of another mobster.

Lex had managed to keep his association with Nick as cordial as it was rare, but that was about to change. Since Patel was the mastermind behind one hundred percent of the industry that made Operlo economically viable, if anyone was going to have any answers, it was going to be him. The tricky bit would be asking the questions. Lex had only once found himself on the wrong side of Patel's good graces. His nose was still a little crooked from where the mobster's thugs had introduced it to a table during their "polite questioning." This wasn't likely to end well.

Chapter 5

In a darkened, weightless room, an airtight hatch rattled a bit. Sounds of frustration and desperation filtered through it until, with a pair of clicks, the hatch drifted open. A dimly glowing slidepad poked out from inside, angled such that its camera could serve as a crude periscope. When the coast was confirmed clear, Michella nudged it into the room and followed it.

The station was still in some sort of low-power state. At first she'd hoped that would mean she could move without fear of being spotted on cameras. She probably *could* have, but for the fact that the low-power mode had *also* defaulted all the doors to locked. This had forced Michella to go back to the service conduits to navigate this place since their hatches all had manual clasps she could operate. Or so she'd thought. After squeezing her way through a dozen tight passages, she'd come upon a bulkhead with a sealed blast door blocking the way. It made sense as a fail-safe to make sure that even if someone had been foolish enough to leave the maintenance hatches open during a failure, the ship would still be divided into multiple airtight sectors, but she would have preferred to learn that without having to work her way backward through twenty meters of claustrophobic conduit.

She'd lost track of how long she'd been dragging herself through the station's innards before she finally found an accessible maintenance room, but it felt like ages. Worse, whereas the station humming away in its normal state made for uncomfortably warm conduits, once the station had gone to low power, the subsystems had shut down and taken their waste heat with them. The temperature of the whole station had dropped considerably, to the point that her fingers stung when she had to manipulate the latches while moving from chamber to chamber. The maintenance room was only slightly warmer, but it still came as a relief.

That relief slipped away when she discovered that the utility room door was, like the bulkheads, automatically locked down. She boosted the light on her slidepad and swept it over the door.

"Come on. There must be a manual release," she grumbled. "These latches look promising."

She tugged at the first of them, and a small panel on the door popped open with what looked like a pump handle inside. A small red tag was attached to the handle. In three languages, it boldly announced: *Caution: Manual release pump to be used only in emergencies. Manual door operation will activate an alarm unless bypassed with rescue station key.*

She narrowed her eyes at the simple mechanical keyhole beside the pump as though it were mocking her. There was the outside chance that the indicated alarm was disabled by the station's limited power. There was *also* the chance that it was battery operated and setting it off would give away her position. It was a bit of a coin flip. Considering that if it came up tails, she'd be found by unknown parties with unknown intentions, it was best not to risk it until she knew she had to.

Michella opted instead to try activating the console. A few clicks and flashes of internal lights suggested something was happening.

"Thank god," she breathed as the boot screen of the console lit up dimly. "If there was *one* thing that would work with the station in standby, I had a feeling it would be the utility console."

The system was sluggish but functional. It got as far as asking her for her credentials, then flipped to a load screen that ticked with agonizing slowness through a progress bar.

When it was completed, she found that the network was all but crippled. Most menus were grayed out. A large flashing notification listed the known issues.

"'Power status: manual standby. Long-range communication: powered down. Short range communication: powered down. System monitors: low power…' Yeah, yeah, yeah. What *is* working? What can I turn on?"

She tested the limits of her stolen access, but if she'd wanted to be able to navigate the system in this state, she should have found a higher-level employee. At her current level of access, she couldn't even unlock the doors.

Trial and error eventually revealed that the surveillance system was another low-power system rather than one that was outright powered down. Her log-in gave her some level of control over it. Rather than a full video feed, the many cameras took single frames every few seconds. The system lacked audio and motion detection. Most rooms were too dark to see anything useful. That did, however, make it easier to spot the rooms with something interesting going on. Even better, in its emergency mode, the system had switched on *all* the cameras, even those that had been blacked out when she'd checked earlier.

Even the one in the utility room she was in now.

Her heart jumped into her throat as she spotted herself on the security display. If anyone else with a similar level of access had booted up a console, they'd know just where she was. She doused the light on the slidepad, dimmed the console screen, and maneuvered herself such that her body was between it and the camera. When the screen updated, the room looked more or less like a wall of blackness with nothing but some faint LED glow to suggest there was anything there. She crossed her fingers that no one had seen her, then continued to observe what the screen had to offer.

The docking areas all had at least one person milling about with a powerful flashlight. Each was dressed in the same jumpsuit as the rest of the crew. All of them carried hefty pistols.

"Those are ballistic firearms." A bit of poking revealed the gesture necessary to zoom in. "Large-caliber pistols. Station security wouldn't *dare* have a ballistic weapon like that as their standard weaponry. Too much risk of hull rupture or damaging vital systems."

The journalist inside her practically giggled with glee at the prospect that she once again had found herself with exclusive access to what had the makings of a hell of a story. This wasn't a military operation. If it were, these people would have carried station-appropriate weaponry, worn military uniforms, and would have announced their intentions. Ditto for police. That left terrorists, paramilitary fighters, mercenaries, or criminals. No matter which it was, it was a story. Her excitement was somewhat tempered by the fact that she was very likely in extreme danger, but that didn't stop her from recording a few shots of the various screens for B-roll when the story broke.

When she was satisfied she had recorded all of the relevant visuals, she started to think like a tactician. If she operated under the assumption that the people with weapons were all working together, she could get a tally of just how many people she was dealing with. By her count, there were twenty or so perpetrators. That was more invaders than people on the manifest.

Michella rummaged through her bag. As a disarming bit of misdirection, it had worked brilliantly, but now that she found herself in genuine need of practicality, she wished she had something a bit more reliable. She tugged at the ancient zipper and peered inside. Near the bottom, floating among some spare pads and pens, she found her stunner. It was a small device, not much larger than a cigar lighter. Lex had bought it for her a while back, reasoning that her nose for news would eventually lead her into a corner she'd have to zap her way out of. At the time, she'd suggested he was being overprotective. Now she found herself wishing he'd invested in the beefier model. This one was only good for a single incapacitation before it needed to recharge, and that recharge took a minute or two. That was plenty defensive power if she wanted to stop a mugging, but she wouldn't have a chance of knocking out enough people fast enough to retake the docking bay and get herself out of here. Still, it was better than nothing.

She focused on the surveillance feeds again. Several people with tool kits were centered in a room labeled with an alphanumeric designation that, upon checking the schematic, placed it very near the control room of the ship. They were industriously tugging at modules and wires.

"Okay, that explains why the power is down. Whatever they're doing has to be done with the system off."

Here and there she saw flashes of thugs escorting bound workers through the main corridors. Considering how few active employees there seemed to be on the station, rounding them all up hadn't taken long. It looked like they were escorting them to a single room to lock them up. The number of prisoners didn't add up, though. There were only five. That meant a large proportion of the station's crew must have been working with the attackers. It certainly explained how the plan had gone off so quickly and effectively.

"Oh no," Michella murmured.

Her eyes finally found their way to the final room with anything visible in frame. Two of the armed interlopers were present. From what Michella could make out in the glow of their flashlights, they were in what passed for the cafeteria. In zero-g, rather than tables and chairs or benches, the snack room had elastic straps lining the walls and regularly spaced columns. Assorted panels for dispensing baggies of food and drink were clustered at the corners of the room. In the center, strapped to one of the columns with tie-downs, was Preethy.

She didn't appear to have been hurt, but one thug was giving her good hard talking to. Unlike the other thug, the one doing the talking didn't have a gun. The small, still image didn't offer much in the way of details, but the hand doing the threatening was balled into a fist. The only hint there was a weapon at all was a silvery black glint in some images.

Michella made a note of where the room was, then scrutinized each refreshed image for new information. The interrogator was the leader of this group. His body language screamed it. He was tall. While uniforms designed to fit everyone equally well tended not to fit *anyone*, in his case this was extremely noticeable. The pseudo canvas suit hung loosely from wiry arms and legs, and a bit too much ankle and wrist showed. He pulled back ragged brown hair to reveal a complexion just a tad darker than Preethy's, the result of what seemed to be some sort of mixed heritage.

An updated still showed him reaching for something at his belt. Michella held her breath, worried he was drawing a weapon. She stared at the screen, waiting anxiously for it to refresh.

The screen went black, and the lights turned on with a resounding thump, nearly stopping Michella's heart. Even the dim light of the disused utility room was blinding after gazing at a screen in total darkness for so long. After a moment, the console screen kicked back on. The sudden power spike had caused it to reboot.

"Come on, come on," she growled.

After a few angry slaps failed to bring it up any quicker, she turned back to the door and tapped the latch button. It hissed open. "Okay. Good. I'm not locked in anymore. That's something."

She shut the door again and found the console was ready for her log-in. Much swiping, tapping, and code-entering got her back into the system. She furiously navigated through the menus to find the surveillance feed. Whatever emergency setting had activated the cameras hadn't been reset when the system was, as they were once again entirely active. She quickly shut down the one giving away her position, as well as the cameras in every other utility room. On the off chance someone else was checking the feeds, it wouldn't do much good to have exactly one camera blacked out, as that would make it pretty obvious where someone might be hiding.

With that done, she found the room with Preethy and, for the first time, managed to activate the audio.

"…your time and mine. Just tell me the code," the thug said, the feed picking up midsentence.

Like his features, the head thug's voice was a subtle enough mix of accents that she couldn't nail down an origin. Now that she had control of the feed, she zoomed in on him, hoping to learn something more from the closer inspection. The only useful bit that presented itself was the nature of the weapon he'd been threatening her with.

It was what could loosely be called a pair of brass knuckles, but it was at the same time more elegant and more crude than that. The man talked with his hands. With the lights on, he'd returned his flashlight to his belt and was free to sweep his left hand about, scything the air as he made idle threats. The other hand flexed and adjusted the weapon. It was a blue-black bit of metal, one continuous loop of the stuff. The finish was polished to a high gloss in places, the sort of telltale sheen of a piece of metal that gets a lot of handling. An artful twist gave the business end of the loop a spiral flourish that probably also added to the damage it would deliver with each blow. He flipped it forward in his hand and gave it a buff on his jumpsuit as he continued his attempts at persuasion.

"I've been through the logs, Misra. I know this is a weekly meeting for you. And I know you're the bossy sort. Sticking your fingers in everyone's pie to make sure they're doing things the way you want." He flashed a smile that revealed enough broken teeth to suggest he'd taken a few blows to the mouth over the years. "That's a lousy way to run things, you know. Slows the whole thing down. Better to let folks do things the way they want. It's all about results, right? No sense micromanaging."

"Did you have a *point*, Mr. Hatch?" Preethy said.

Her tone was cool and controlled, but with a tension that suggested she was wrestling terror into submission to maintain that level of detachment.

"Heh. Heh-heh." The thug, evidently the Ramses Hatch she'd mentioned earlier, drifted closer and leaned the knuckles against her chin. "You should count your lucky stars I need you to be able to talk, because I *don't like sass*."

He gave her chin a nudge with the weapon, pushing himself back to drift to the far wall. "As I was saying. We know your schedule. We know you hang out up here for *hours* at a time. It wouldn't be so strange for you to be up here until the wee hours of the morning. I wouldn't expect any red flags to be raised until sunrise in your hometown. That gives us plenty of quality time. My crew has got yours tied up. Might toss them out an air lock. Might not. We don't really need them. Once this place is up and running, it can be run by, what, *two* people? Knocking out the power gave us a chance to physically disable the communication for the whole station. Long story short, there's no help coming for you until it's too late, and there's no way to call it regardless. So there's three ways we can work it. The easy way is you tell me the activation codes right now. Land and Orbital. I know there's two. The hard way is my crew finds the right modules and just links them all up manually. The fun way is I soften you up until you tell me. What'll it be?"

"Are you really so small of a man that you would threaten to hit a woman?" she said.

He crossed his arms and gave the wall a tap, slowly sending him back in her direction.

"Please, Misra." He was speaking with an airy, overtly noble tone. "I'm a truly evolved individual. I see the whole human race as equals. I know the true strength of women. You bear our children. You endure the whims of an anatomy that rebels against you on a monthly basis. You've overcome untold travails of social inequality to rise to the very pinnacle of society. I would not *think* to belittle you by excusing you from something that I would consider a *man* worthy of. That's what you call benevolent sexism. I'm better than that."

He clutched a strap on the column beside her head and pulled himself in to deliver a sharp punch to her midsection. It was a calculated blow, not enough to injure, but more than enough to knock the wind out of her.

"So yes. I'd hit a woman. It's only fair. Intimidation is like a good golf swing, after all. It's all about the follow-through."

Michella tightened her jaw and felt a jolt of disgust and anger rush through her. Preethy gasped and coughed. She was trying to speak, but she couldn't get any words out. The radio at Hatch's belt blipped.

"Boss, we need some extra hands down here. It looks like they've got a few extra transmitters that might be data links. We'll need to cut them in a hurry if we want to be sure the surface controls won't be able to lock us out," said the voice from the other end.

Hatch sneered. "I just get through lecturing you about micromanagement and these idiots remind me why sometimes nothing gets done without it." He snatched the radio. "On my way."

He turned back to her. "I'll let you get your wind back. Let's hope, when you do, you use it to tell me what I need to know." He held up the brass knuckles. "I don't know if you've ever seen someone worked over with one of these. A good old-fashioned beating. It ain't pretty. Easy to go overboard. Leads to the kind of bleeding that doesn't show. What you'd call a 'hemorrhage.' Nasty." He waggled his fingers. "Ta-ta for now."

He grabbed the railing on the wall and pulled himself into the corridor. Michella flicked through the different camera feeds until she spotted the room he'd been summoned toward. It was easily half the station away. She quickly reviewed the rest of the feeds before settling on the snack room again. Every other room with thugs in it had at least two of them. All but the one with Preethy. She was guarded by a single pistol-wielding woman.

Michella weighed the options available to her, but there was only one that made any sense. She mapped out a path, deactivated the majority of the surveillance along the way, and headed for the door.

#

Preethy took slow, steady breaths in and out until she was confident she could breathe without coughing. When she was composed, she looked to her keeper.

The young woman had her eyes trained upon Preethy. Her arms were crossed, and her leg was hooked through one of the wall straps to keep her from drifting about.

"I imagine you must be a well-respected member of the crime family," Preethy said.

Her tone was as calm and collected as ever, as though neither the blow to the stomach nor the hostage situation was any reason to behave in an unbusinesslike manner. Though her outfit was disheveled by the capture, she still looked every bit the executive. Rather than the typical jumpsuit that most people wore during trips to the space station, she wore a smart business suit. It was impeccably tailored to her form and complemented by a pair of low heels. Or at least it had been. The heels had been taken from her after one of the attackers had learned just how much of a statement a sensible business shoe could make when thrust into the ribs. Her handbag had been taken as well.

"Ramses Hatch is a top-tier man. Last I heard, he was working directly for David Kelso," Preethy continued.

The thug remained silent.

"Have you been working for him long? … No. I don't imagine you have. In operations like this, there is significant churn at the lower levels. Casualty rates are quite high. Uncle has been clear about that. Such is to be expected in an enterprise where the chief means of advancement is murder, either of one's targets or one's internal rivals." Preethy shook her head a bit. "Your superior's attack seems to have left my glasses askew. I wonder if you would be good enough to straighten them?"

The thug looked at her distrustfully.

"No need to worry about physical violence on my part. That was never my role in the organization, even when I was on that side of the ledger. Mine was always an administrative role."

"I saw you kick Johnny."

"Things happen in the heat of the moment, but I am composed. And for that matter, I am thoroughly secured."

The jailer floated over to her and double-checked her arm and leg restraints, then straightened the glasses.

"Many thanks," Preethy said as the jailer returned to the door to keep watch. "Tell me, were you well prepped for this operation?"

"I won't give you any information," the thug said.

"I wouldn't waste my breath to seek it. I'm simply curious how thorough the planning phase for such things is. I must admit, I was never privy to the *specifics* of this manner of exercise when I was working under my uncle." She grinned. "He called them 'capers,' by the way. That always made it seem more innocent, somehow. Like it was nothing more than mischief."

"I know what I'm supposed to do. I know my part."

"Your part. I see. That speaks of compartmentalization. Lower levels are told only of the aspects necessary to fulfill their roles. Good planning. That decreases the possibility of potential leaks. It also underscores the lack of trust involved."

"Shut it."

"I apologize. That was an unfair assumption. I do not know how Kelso operates. I can only speak from my own experiences."

The jailer gruffly cleared her throat.

"Are you thirsty at all?" Preethy asked. "Help yourself to the refreshments. We do take care to provide only the highest-quality refreshments for our workers."

"I'm fine."

"Very well. I must say, I admire your dedication to the organization. This is a mission *fraught* with potential for failure. If Hatch had not seen fit to interrupt me, I would have informed him of such."

"We've thought of everything."

"No one ever thinks of everything. Take it from someone who has been running her own business enterprise. Little unexpected problems and oversights always pop up. In this instance, there is the matter of my social calendar. Your superiors did their diligence on my work habits, but it so happens that I had a private appointment today. Do you have the time?"

The guard tugged a device from her pocket and glanced at its display. "It's 2251 Universal."

Preethy shut her eyes and sighed. "You've made me tardy. I was due to have drinks with my good friend and business partner, Trevor Alexander. I was looking forward to that."

"Tough."

"I pride myself on not missing an engagement. My absence will be missed. A good deal sooner than Hatch's preparation would indicate."

"So?"

"How familiar are you with my uncle?"

She sniffed. "Nick Patel. Used to be a big shot. Now he's basically out of the game."

"A fair, if basic, assessment. It pays to be aware that 'basically out of the game' is not the same as 'out of the game.' Uncle is reluctant to fully set aside the old ways."

"So?"

"If memory serves, your syndicate has a multiplanetary presence. A force to be reckoned with on several worlds. Uncle's own influence is limited elsewhere, but it is exclusive here on Operlo. In raw size, we of course cannot compete, but being in full control of the government and economy of an entire planet has benefits. Planets, for example, have a military."

The thug's expression flickered toward concern, if only briefly. "We've got heavies. We can fight."

"Oh, we have them too. Quite an assortment of enforcers at every level. But we *also* have a military. Better training, you understand. Better equipment. And entirely at the beck and call of my uncle. Ready to be deployed, should the need arise."

"He wouldn't do anything that would threaten you. You're family."

"It would be flattering to believe that, but you and I both know that in a business such as his, sacrifices must occasionally be made. Not that I think it will come to that, of course. At this point I wouldn't expect to survive this operation. Once my usefulness is exhausted, I'll likely be killed."

"No one's going to kill you. This is about playing a strong hand. Can't do that with you dead. If this all works out, your uncle will be kicking money back to us. Things'll go smoother if you're alive and well. You're just collateral."

"Mmm. That's sound reasoning. I am not certain how you hope to compel my uncle to do so, but then if you are seeking control of this station, I have some ideas of how you *think* you will. Perhaps it would even have worked, if Hatch hadn't assaulted me. Uncle won't be pleased to hear that. The last person who threatened me specifically was Veemer Gadd."

The thug's eyebrows lifted. Preethy continued.

"The stories about Mr. Gadd aren't entirely accurate, of course. For one, his fingers aren't in a trophy case in Uncle's office. Uncle isn't so boorish." She lowered her head and glanced over her glasses. "They were shipped to his family. It was the least he could do, as they certainly weren't going to be having an open casket with what remained of Mr. Gadd."

The thug shifted uncomfortably.

"It is also completely untrue that Gadd's demise came the very same afternoon that he'd issued the threat on my life. That is the part I find most curious. It wasn't swift at all. It took two and a half years before Uncle made his move. A proper bit of deterrence takes time. But then, considering when all was said and done Gadd's entire wing of his syndicate was dead, I suppose there wasn't anyone left to deter."

Preethy shifted and took a pained breath. "My uncle has a long memory and is very thorough. Those who wrong him spend the rest of their lives looking over their shoulders. Fortunately, those lives from that point on are typically quite short. But he also never leaves a debt unpaid. Were you to render aid to him, he would be *quite* thankful."

The thug glanced to the door, then back to Preethy. "Look, Ramses would kill me if I helped you."

"If you did a good enough job of it, he wouldn't live long enough to try. This could be your opportunity to exit this enterprise before *it* kills you. I'm always looking for good people to help with the league. Unlike your present position, it comes with a retirement plan."

The thug glanced to the corridor again. "That only helps me if this plan goes wrong," she said, her resolve teetering.

"I assure you. You would be far healthier and happier outside of this organization than in it, regardless of how successful this caper is. But if you are worried that you are quitting a winning team, let me lay this out for you. Victory for you requires all of the people on your team to succeed in manipulating the systems of this station without setting off an alarm and without anyone in orbit or on the surface becoming curious about its lack of responsiveness, as well as the cooperation or subversion of surface crews, which must be done without alerting anyone during that process. And even then, you need to succeed to such a degree that no one connected to me or my uncle ever decides to launch a caper of their own to get petty revenge upon those responsible for this one. If any one of those potential pitfalls causes you or anyone else on your team to stumble, you will find yourself in a tight spot with no way out. Meanwhile, all you need to do is let me free, help me get word to my people on the surface, and keep us safe until they arrive to assure yourself of a life of ease in the corporate sector."

"… That's an awful lot to ask for," she said.

"We only need to get to my ship."

"Your ship is bricked. We tried to access the system, and there was some sort of security wipe. It's toast."

"It can be restored. My pilot will have the proper procedures."

"Your pilot won't be talking anytime soon."

Preethy didn't allow herself to show a visible reaction to the news of the potential murder of one of her employees. It was to be expected, once this entire attack unfolded, and it wouldn't help her or the others escape.

"You came here in a ship, didn't you?"

"We did, obviously."

"Then all it really takes is getting us there. In it we will have safety, communication, and a way out."

"I don't know…"

"Then take your chances with Hatch. He seems the stable, rational sort who wouldn't dream of selling you and the rest of the crew out if it meant saving his own skin."

The thug considered the words for a moment longer, then darted forward and started working at the straps.

"I want a corner office, you understand? Lots of windows."

"Of course."

One of the four straps had been loosened when there was, of all things, a knock at the door. The thug cursed under her breath and pulled the strap tight again.

"Sit tight and keep your mouth shut," she ordered.

Preethy nodded. The thug approached the door and put her hand on the grip of her gun.

"That you, Streep?" she called. "Don't tell me you're done with the transmitters already."

There was no answer. She tapped the button for the door. It hissed open to reveal the corridor behind with dimmed lights. She couldn't see much farther than the space around the door where the light from the snack room shined out.

"Who shut off the lights?" she said warily, now sliding the gun from its holster.

The answer came in the form of a figure launching at her from the far wall. It was Michella, driving herself like a torpedo into the thug. The pair bowled backward into the snack room. The gun twirled into the corner and bounced around the walls. Each time it struck something, Preethy flinched, fearing it might discharge. After a brief struggle, the thug began convulsing, then went still.

Michella breathlessly steadied herself with one of the wall straps and tapped the recharge button on the stunner in her other hand. Her first act, wisely, was to fetch the gun and radio that had been dislodged during the struggle. After that she dragged herself to the door to close and lock it.

"Preethy," she said with a nod, floating over to the column to start unstrapping Preethy.

"Ms. Modane," Preethy replied, face steady but eyes practically smoldering. "Not that I am not grateful for your act of heroism, but would you permit me a question or two?"

"Make them quick. I don't know how much time we have."

"I'll be very brief," Preethy said.

Michella freed her left hand, allowing Preethy to remove her glasses and glare properly.

"How the hell did you get here and what the hell are you doing here!?"

#

"What do you mean we lost her!? *We've got the whole crew locked up!*" Hatch barked over his radio to Crick.

"Don't blame me. I've been up to my neck in fiber cabling and patch cords. This is on the enforcer who was watching her."

"It shouldn't matter. She was tied up, and she's Patel's precious little niece. She doesn't have the skills to topple one of our crew. Do we even know what happened to the idiot on watch?"

"You need me to say it again? I've been rooting around in the station internals. Talk to the enforcers."

Hatch darted into the snack room that should have held his precious hostage. There was little sign of struggle. Two of his crew were lingering in the area, trying to work out what had happened.

"Who was on the watch? It was that new chick, wasn't it?" he barked.

The underlings muttered noncommittal replies.

"Idiots. *Idiots.* I had you watching a secretary, and that was too much for you."

"She's an executive now," Crick reported over the radio.

"Oh, yeah, because if there's one thing we know about corporate fat cats, it's that when you lock them in a room, they turn into full-fledged commandos." He scanned the room and spotted the camera node. "They've got security, right? Do we have someone on that? Do we have someone who can pull video?"

"Do you want me to stop working on the control system to see if we've got footage?" Crick's voice squawked.

"We might have an infiltrator aboard, and thus we might have a serious problem, so yes, I want you to check the damn security feed."

"Give me a minute."

Hatch squeezed his brass knuckles and thumped them angrily into a wall panel. "We get the whole crew bound, gagged, and stashed in their quarters, no problem. But *this* we can't do. I tell you. Someone somewhere up the hierarchy is trying to take me out. Sabotaging me with the B-squad of dunces and mooks."

"Okay. One of our guys has security access. Well... feed access."

"What's the difference?"

"He can watch feeds, he can't get to the metadata level, so—"

"Fine, don't waste my time with pointless details. What do we have?"

"We have a big black screen for that room. No history, either."

"What? Why?"

"The power outage could have screwed with stuff. We've got cameras on and off all over this place. Maybe that's it."

"Maybe? You're giving me maybe? What else could it be?"

"Could be someone turning off the cameras. Could be someone deleting camera history. Could be an automated trash collection wiping low-priority videos."

"I don't want 'could be.' I want to know what's going on."

"If you hadn't interrupted me, you would have heard me say I don't have metadata available, so I don't know who did what."

"Well how do we *get* metadata?"

"You were supposed to get full access from Misra. That's how."

"So you're saying this is *my* fault?"

"Certainly looks that way. Now are you done grinding this whole operation to a halt? Can I get back to bypassing the system you were supposed to have the keys to by now?"

He gritted his teeth. "You better pray you do your job right, because your mouth is *this* close to getting you pitched out an air lock. Now get back to work."

Hatch angrily snapped the radio back to his holster and wrapped his fist around a strap on the wall of the snack room. Veins bulged on his forehead and neck as he tried to swallow the rage over the incompetence of his own crew.

"I will *not* let you *idiots* cost me this *caper!*" he growled, slamming his fist into the hatch repeatedly.

On the third blow, the hatch popped open, and the unconscious, tightly bound form of the woman in charge of watching Preethy tumbled out.

"Ha!" he roared. "You see? That's how it's done! That's called intuition."

He gave her face a pat, hoping to rouse her, but the stunner had done a remarkably good job of putting her under.

"Her radio is gone. Access card is still here. Someone kick her radio from the trusted group. And I want people searching. Now. We've got at least two people on the loose. I want them caught. This is a space station. It can't be that hard to find them."

Chapter 6

Lex guided his hovercar toward the estate of Nick Patel. Since hovercars had become efficient enough to run and simple enough to pilot to completely replace wheeled vehicles, the structure of planets had started to change. Most of the larger cities, out of habit and a few basic navigation conveniences, still formed with vestigial roads and streets tracing out grids along the surface. Universally accessible rapid transit independent of the terrain meant that there were other more interesting options available for newer or less traditional environments. Until very recently, Operlo had largely ignored the concept of cities altogether. There was concentrated industry, maybe a few clusters of businesses, and then everyone simply picked a place to build their home. Sometimes that led to communities. Sometimes it hearkened back to pioneer-era homesteads. Operlo had more than enough room to go around. If he or she felt compelled, the poorest miner or most debt-laden student could plop a prefab into the middle of a vast expanse of sprawling dunes and act as though they had a ten-thousand-acre back yard. Nick Patel being Nick Patel, he'd gone with something a bit flashier.

Operlo's utter lack of precipitation meant that all the erosion was thanks to wind and sun. This made for some interesting rock formations. There were bizarre contrasts of jagged spires and wind-smoothed mounds. Veins of bright color wove through them, exposed by sun and wind to sparkle and glow in the light of day. Even now, well into the night, they caught the glow of the hovercar's repulsors and headlights to glitter like jewels as he passed.

Right in the middle of one of the more impressive expanses of spires, natural bridges, and wind-polished stone was a plateau. Lex was tempted to call it a mesa, but there was probably a pedantic geological reason why you couldn't call something that on a planet without rivers. The Patel Estate—or at least the current and most impressive Patel Estate—was a luxurious, state-of-the-art mansion right in the center of that plateau. He could see it in the distance, subtly illuminated from within.

"Some people have topiary gardens or hedge mazes. This guy has Monument Valley," Lex muttered.

The hovercar's radio chirped, and a voice came through. It had the crackly, distorted quality of something intended for short-range communication being used for long range.

"Hovercar, license number 775EFB dash—" the voice droned.

"No sense wasting your time on the whole number. I'm the only one out here," Lex replied.

"Lex, that you?"

"Who else?"

Any formality dropped from the voice. "I won forty thousand credits on your last preliminary!"

"Glad to be of service."

"Hey, what do you think your odds are in the inaugural—"

"Sorry, but I'm going to stop you right there. Considering my history with gambling, I'd really rather not talk too much about it."

"Oh, heh. Right, right. You're not heading to Mr. Patel's place, are you?"

"It is literally the only thing for two hundred kilometers. I'd better be."

"You should know better than to make an unannounced visit to someone who doesn't like unannounced visits."

"I'd have called ahead, but the network is still acting funky."

"Can it can wait until morning? Mr. Patel has concluded business for the evening."

"Tell him it's Lex and I'm here because his niece missed an appointment."

"Who, Preethy?"

"That's right."

"That *never* happens."

"Hence my concern."

The voice sighed. "I'll let him know you're coming. Park in the east courtyard."

The communicator clicked off. It briefly struck Lex that he should have found it odd that what amounted to a personal security officer was able to use the law enforcement override in his hovercar's system. Then again, the sheer amount of oddness in his life had thrown off his calibration a bit. When you end up with a two-of-a-kind genetic cross between fox and skunk as your house pet, "normal" starts to seem more like a charming concept than a reality.

A few layers of security passed by beneath him as he approached the estate grounds. The courtyard he was instructed to park in was practically the size of an airfield and made from local masonry. He parked as near to the estate as he could manage. All the while, he kept his maneuvers slow enough to avoid worrying what may or may not have been a sniper hanging out atop a nearby guard tower. The fortification matched the aesthetic of the estate so well that one would think spotlights and patrols were just a standard part of Operlo architecture.

Squee sprang from the car and trotted in wide circles as Lex approached the front door.

"Easy. Why is it you could be in the *SOB* for three days straight or a hovercar for fifteen minutes and you react the same way when the door opens?" Lex called.

"Lex! There's my poster boy," called a voice from the door.

Lex got Squee under control and hustled to the stoop where Nick Patel was awaiting him. The man who was officially a construction and mining magnate and unofficially a ruthless criminal mastermind simply *oozed* style. His hair was slicked back, black with threads of gray giving him the distinguished look of a politician. The white smoking jacket he wore slid the whole look a few steps closer to nightclub singer. The straight white teeth and confident smile practically elevated him to movie-star levels of flashiness.

Squee squirmed under Lex's arm, but he held firm. As adorable as she could be, Lex was not interested in finding out what happens when you cover the white jacket of a "legitimate businessman" with black pet hair. This left Lex's shoulders free for Patel to put his arm over.

"You know something? I've known it from day one. That first time you gave me a ride to the transit hub back on Golana. I said, 'Here's a guy with fortitude.' Say hello to Vince."

Lex briefly caught eyes with an intimidating fellow standing beside the door.

"Vince is head of the night shift here on the estate. And Vince has *never* had to deal with a visitor after I've donned the smoking jacket. When my perimeter watchman asked if I wanted a visit from you, and that you were already on your way in, Vince said… oh, I can't do it justice, what'd you say, Vince?"

"I said he had more balls than brains," Vince said with the precise level of gruffness Lex expected from him.

Patel slapped Lex on the back. "More balls than brains. He says balls, I say fortitude. The point is, you've got it, and that's what I like about you." He stepped away, leading Lex forward through the impeccably decorated foyer. "How else would someone be willing to visit the guy holding the purse strings of the racing league after totaling—what is it, *four* hoversleds?"

"Right, see, I'm supposed to be testing them, so—" Lex began to explain.

"Relax, Lex. I'm busting your chops. This league's a great big omelet, and you're the guy in charge of breaking the eggs. But we're not here to talk business, are we? You're here to talk about Preethy."

"That's right."

"She no-showed on an appointment tonight, am I correct?"

"That's right."

Patel made his way to a bar and poured himself a drink. "I'd offer you a drink, but you won't be staying long. See, most days, Preethy would treat that calendar of hers like every line on the schedule was doctor's orders, and if she missed it, she'd keel over. But tonight I happen to know she had a pressing engagement that had a strong possibility to run long."

"She didn't tell me that."

"You're the big-money draw for the league, but you're still an employee. She doesn't have to tell you *everything*." He took a sip. "Me, on the other hand, I like to know everything, and now you've got me curious. What exactly did you and Preethy have planned?"

"She was going to have a drink with me and Mitch."

Patel swirled the liquor in the glass. "Michella Modane. Not a name I like hearing in this house. Vince, why is it that so many people with such promise end up falling for ladies who complicate matters?"

"He's thinking with his—"

"Vince!" Patel raised a hand. "You've got a way with words, but the man is still a guest in my house. And as evidence of his good judgment, he was smart enough not to *bring* the enterprising young reporter tonight."

"As it happens, she stood me up too. I haven't gotten very lucky with the ladies tonight. That's why I'm wondering where Preethy might be."

"Lex, I want to make a few things clear. Stop me if I'm stating the obvious. First, I really don't want to hear you come so close to using the phrase 'get lucky' with reference to my niece. Especially not when you've already got a lady. And I really don't want to hear you *talk* about that lady, since her pointless little investigation into alleged money laundering cost me a hell of a lot more than those sleds you smashed up. Now Preethy has as good a head on her shoulders as anybody I've met—runs in the family, after all—but all the same, it doesn't break my heart that she missed an appointment that would have put her in the same room as Little Miss Vendetta. That's one less chance I'll wake up tomorrow to find some headline full of speculation about what she may or may not be doing wrong with this league."

"I'm sorry about all of that. But the fact is, I've missed appointments with both my girlfriend *and* my boss tonight, and it's got me a little anxious. So I'd really appreciate it if I knew what sort of business Preethy was up to, so I'd know there was at least *one* woman in my life who I didn't have to worry about."

"All you need to know is she's working on something for me."

"Yeah, I'm going to need more than that," Lex said sharply. "I've been bouncing back and forth between being ignored, being brushed off, and being lied to for a little bit too long. You say you know where Preethy is. And considering whenever she wanders off, she ends up finding something that may or may not be shady about this league, something tells me you've probably been keeping an eye on Mitch, too. A vague answer and a pat on the head isn't going to do it this time. Tell me where they are."

Patel glanced at Vince, then set down his glass. "Lex, fortitude can get you far in life, but it can also get you in trouble. Preethy is still my niece, and she is still doing work for me. That makes this family *and* business, two things that I'm not fond of being asked questions about. I like you. I see a lot of promise in our continued partnership. Remember who you're dealing with, and don't make me change my mind about you."

"Mr. Patel. I'm very tired. I've been jerked around all day. I've been stood up by my girlfriend, *again*. I overdid it on the entrée at Sarafa, and as a result, authentic Indo-European spices are trying to eat a hole through my gut. I appreciate you're trying to intimidate me, but trust me when I say this. You're a scary dude, but you aren't even in the top five most dangerous things I've come face to face with in the past couple of years. I've been on the wrong side of megacorporations and terrorist groups. I've faced down hordes of murderous robots. I'm a part-time product tester for a lunatic who makes doomsday machines in his spare time. I've had to deal with the existential horror of clashing with whole different *timelines*. I'm really not that nervous about what *you* have in store for me."

Patel looked to Vince again. For a few tense moments, no one said anything. Even Squee seemed oddly anxious at the tone of the room. The first sound to break the silence was from Mr. Patel as he released a long, hearty laugh.

"What did I say, Vince? *Fortitude*. This is the sort of man you keep on the payroll. You're crazy, Lex. I knew that from the start, too. A sane man does not drive like you do. I don't know what half of that stuff you were yammering about was. Honestly, I don't even care. Normally, I'd have Vince here knock your teeth out for talking to me like that. But like I said, I like you. And don't think I've forgotten that part of that megacorp thing was keeping VectorCorp from wrecking this planet. You're owed some latitude."

He sipped his drink. "We *have* been keeping an eye on Modane. Last check we had, she was taking off in that ship of yours."

"You don't know where she is now?"

"I don't know if you noticed, but it's pretty difficult to keep track of that ship. We just know she didn't get back yet. As for the rest, it just so happens the info you're after is going to be announced in less than a week, so just this once, I'll let you in on my plans. Consider it a test. If this leaks to that lady of yours, it won't do me any harm, but it'll damn sure give Vince a reason to engage in the aforementioned pugilistic dentistry."

He freshened his glass. "Back when VectorCorp gave us what I *thought* was a communication infrastructure contract, you'll remember we had to construct this massive transmitter array. You did your thing, we found out it was going to cause untold havoc with our sun, and we pulled the plug. The array was *finished,* though. And paid for, might I add. That left us with this huge facility, free and clear. Obviously, we couldn't use it for what it was *designed* to do, but I talked to the engineers who rigged it up. They said it could be pretty quickly adapted to broadcast power. You familiar?"

"Like what charges the slidepad wirelessly?"

He tipped his head. "Yes and no. Different scale, different mechanism. I forget the details. This isn't the sort of thing where the details matter much to me. But that array could be used to pump power from the surface in massive quantities. Like a laser but different. Now, we run a *massive* power surplus on this planet. Massive. Loads of sun. Loads of wind farms. Geothermal, you name it. We're drowning in power, but you can't really export it, so it hasn't been doing us much good. With that array, we can send it up to something orbital. And putting that much energy in *orbit*? That's got potential."

"So what, are you building a better communication satellite network? Is that why the network is down?"

"Yes, Lex. But think bigger than that. You can run a network like that on old-fashioned solar right in orbit. If you grew up here, you'd understand it. But since you're a newcomer, I'll lay it out for you. There're two thin strips of Operlo that are livable. The northern and southern habitable zones. That's still way more than we *need*, but life isn't all about getting what you need, is it? If it was, I wouldn't have a house like this. And *you* wouldn't be risking it all to get back on the racetrack.

"The fact is, while we can't easily use anything outside of those strips, we can't use everything *in* those strips either. Big sections are scoured by dust and windstorms year round. And even the safe places get storms now and again when it's that time of year. So you end up with situations where you can't go north or it gets too cold, you can't go south or it gets too hot, and if you stray too far east or west, you might get blown away. No way to live, Lex. No way to live. What we *need* to do is tame those storms."

"Weather control? You're talking about *weather control*?"

"Yes indeed. It's been around for years, but no one's tried it at this scale. We're calling it the Indra IV system."

"Where did you get technology like that?"

He gestured vaguely. "Some off-world engineering firm we dug up and vetted. Again, this isn't new tech, just a new *scale* of tech. It'll help us shorten durations of storms, guide storms away from populated areas, and guarantee that storm-related damage will be minimal on the protected side of the planet. You show me another league in the galaxy that can guarantee good weather for its races, and another planet in the galaxy that can cross natural disasters off the list of potential civic problems."

Visible irritation flashed across his face. "When Ms. Modane accused us of money laundering, even though there was no *evidence* of such, we had to bring in outside contractors. The re-org has cost us time. But that's what Preethy is up to. We send her up once a week to personally assess the situation."

"Why in person?"

"Because Ms. Modane can't be trusted to keep her nose out of things, and a system at this scale that hasn't been tested makes people nervous. Up in the terawatt range, I'm told."

"That's kind of abstract."

"Let's just say that if you stretch those units out across a whole day, the amount of energy can be measured in megatons."

"Ah. That's a term I know to be afraid of."

"She's usually back by now, but this is one of the last scheduled visits before the final test, so it stands to reason she'd have a lot to do. Judging from the status of the network, they've probably run into a power system problem again. I wouldn't expect her back before morning."

"Wait. Weren't you just telling me this was all just a way to use extra power to begin with?"

"We haven't started shooting the power up there yet. I just got through telling you the energy involved is in the megaton range, and we're shooting it at our own station. In situations like that, you take extra care to be sure things are absolutely ready to go before you flip the power switch."

"And we're *sure* everything is fine up there?"

"There are checks upon fail-safes upon procedures. If something had gone wrong, I'd know about it."

"Even with the network down?"

"Lex, I'm in construction. My company got started doing business in places where we were *installing* the networks. You don't think I've got my ways? The emergency services are still up, even with the orbital networking on the fritz. Mech networks, drone nodes, it's under control. Now, you're getting dangerously close to insulting my intelligence with these questions, and you've got *far* more information than you need, so I think it's time for you to call it a night."

"Will you let me know when she gets back?"

"She's not my secretary anymore, Lex, and I'm *certainly* not hers."

"Right. I'm sure she'll find a way to let me know."

"That's her business." He finished his drink. "And now that my nightcap is done, I'm headed to bed. Which means you are leaving."

Lex nodded and turned to leave. Before he reached the door, Patel called after him.

"Oh, Lex?"

Lex turned. Patel was giving him a less than jovial look.

"What happened here tonight doesn't happen again. You've burned through your good graces for a while. And I know that one thing you and your lady have in common is an incurable need to go running into a battle that doesn't concern you, so I'll make this clear as crystal. If *anything* happens to that station, it's a black eye for the league, and a shot to the wallet for me. So no matter how badly your white-knight reflexes nag you, you keep away from this whole situation."

"Shouldn't be hard, since Michella's got my ship."

"Lucky us. Vince, show him out."

#

"This is a test. To all TIS employees, this is a test of our one-way communication system. If and when immediate deployment is required, this is the system that will be used. Message repeats," Milliner said, speaking clearly into a microphone in the array node.

"And that's that," said Anand. "The message should have gone out."

"You're sure?" Milliner said. "I don't want to be relying on this for rapid deployment and find out I'm shouting into the void."

"I'm sure. But we'll find out anyway, once your guy comes back." The tech sat in awkward silence for a few minutes. When he couldn't bear the silence anymore, he said, "So what do you think? You think I'm going to get a good position in Kelso's crew?"

"I'm not a recruiter. And you're a little chatty about it. This isn't a job where we're looking for someone likely to talk shop in public."

"Oh no. Lips are sealed, trust me. This is just because I know we're in good company. Just members of the crew, right?"

"Right now, there's me, and there's you. No crew to speak of."

The telltale hum of a hovervan pulled up. Both Milliner and Anand shut their mouths and turned to the door. One of Milliner's crew stepped in with his slidepad out. It was playing the message Milliner had recorded.

"How far out did it work?" Milliner asked.

"I headed back as soon as I started getting it. I was about five kilometers out."

Milliner scratched his chin. "At least as good as the mesh network."

"Well?" Anand said, practically rubbing his hands in glee.

Milliner's man gave him a curious look. "What's with him?"

"He's bucking for a promotion." Milliner turned to Anand. "Are we sure no one else is going to be listening?"

"It's encrypted. If he didn't have the key, he wouldn't have got it. Standard communication's stuff."

Milliner turned back to his man. "Get the word out to make sure everyone's got that key on their pads. Then deploy the field crew. Just in case something needs doing down here, I want people spread out. Things are pretty fragile until we pull the big switch. I want to be able to get to where fires need to be put out just as soon as humanly possible."

The underling nodded and headed out. Milliner turned to Anand.

"I think it's just about time you got that engineer in here."

"Sure, sure. Sure thing. You just remember all the good I'm doing, right? Put in a good word for me, right?"

"Yeah, yeah. Make the call."

Chapter 7

A door on the space station slid open, and Michella poked her head inside. It was dark, like much of the station. The door itself had no view window. After scanning the perimeter of the room, she spotted a pair of service conduit hatches.

"Okay. Good. The coast is clear and there's a way out if we get cornered. We'll hide here for now," Michella said.

Preethy drifted in behind her, and Michella carefully secured the door.

"I would have preferred to find a place with a maintenance console so we could keep an eye on them," she said.

"Now that we are hidden, would you kindly explain yourself?" Preethy said.

"A little gratitude wouldn't be out of line. I did just rescue you."

"We are still in the station without a means of escape. We aren't rescued, we are just trapped together."

"We're free to move and I have access to the system. That's better than you had."

"I had just finished persuading my captor to betray her cohorts and get me to safety when you came along, zapped her into unconsciousness, and stuffed her bound body into a supply locker. Were it not for you, I *would* be free right now."

"And just how exactly was I supposed to know that?"

"You shouldn't have *needed* to know it, because you weren't supposed to be here. Now, an explanation, please."

"How about we figure out what we're going to do, *then* we fight about it?" Michella countered.

Preethy crossed her arms. "If you've got access to our systems, I assume you've got one of our dongles?"

"Naturally. You *really* ought to improve your security screening."

"Our security screening was impeccable until spurious claims of financial malfeasance forced us to replace our own employees with hastily secured off-planet contractors in order to avoid missing deadlines."

"There was every reason to—"

"We'd agreed to figure out what we're going to do before fighting. May I please use your slidepad and dongle?"

Michella resisted the childish urge to point out that Preethy had started it. Instead, she handed over the two devices.

"I have administrative access to the system. If they haven't deactivated the internal data network, I should be able to load the remote console and limit their access further. That will slow them down." She entered in some credentials and worked her way into the system.

"Just what are they trying to do?"

"They are trying to secure full access to the station and its capabilities."

"Obviously. But what *are* those capabilities." Michella fetched her pad. "From what I've been able to work out, either this is a very fancy weather station or it's a weapon."

"Both are accurate descriptors, depending on the person in charge. I'll be brief. The device can create and/or control large weather systems, and it is the hope of David Kelso and/or Ramses Hatch to use that capability to extort my uncle." She finished tapping through settings. "There. I have reset all of their settings changes and locked them out of the system."

"Does that mean we can call for help?"

"No. They physically disconnected all transmitters powerful enough to do so. We'll have to reconnect one or get access to a ship if we hope to get help."

Michella flipped through the menus on her slidepad. "Why don't I have admin access?"

"Because I logged out. There have already been enough outsiders accessing our systems. I don't need *you* rooting around in them."

"Look, I don't think you—"

Preethy spoke over her. "What shall we do to deal with this situation, Ms. Modane?"

Michella clenched her fists. "I have a ship. It's Lex's ship. It's out there, somewhere."

"Somewhere?"

"I couldn't very well leave it in the docking bay. If I wanted enough access to the station to learn anything useful, I needed to hide out. So I sent it out of sensor range."

"And why haven't you called it back?"

"Because this stupid station is screwing with the slidepad's signal. I can't get through to it."

Preethy nodded. "The ship has energy absorbent shielding. In full operation it will be powered by microwave transmitters on the surface. They absorb signals from standard transmitters."

"What about you? You came in a ship, didn't you? Can't we use yours?"

"During the power down, both my ship and the crew I brought with me were disabled."

"Disabled?"

"They all, including the ship, are either dead or incapacitated."

"Then it seems like one way or another our plan is to get to a transmitter. Either to call for help or to call in the ship."

"Indeed. I believe the transmitters capable of reaching the surface are on the schematics with an LRT prefix. There are weaker transmitters that might be able to reach Lex's ship. Those have the MST prefix."

Michella poked at the slidepad. "Oh. So I still have my original access. At least you didn't take that away."

"Yes, for the sake of escape, I have allowed you to keep the access level you stole."

She thumbed through the options the remote console gave her. "It isn't going to be easy to keep tabs on people and plan safe routes using this version of the console."

"It can be set up to trigger a warning when there is motion close to the device."

"Ah. Yeah. I see it here." She activated the feature. "That's better than nothing. But we should find a room with a full console. It might be a good idea to split up. One of us can find a transmitter, the other can keep an eye on things with the system."

"A reasonable plan. I have a greater familiarity with the system and full access. I should be the one on the console."

"Which leaves me to find and access the transmitter. Do you know how to do that?"

"Not specifically. But they'll have to have left at least one transmitter reasonably intact and quick to activate, as the full system can't be powered up without a handshake with the surface facility."

"Which means they'll have at least one person standing by at that transmitter." Michella flicked through the security feeds. "That narrows it down to these two."

"So our plan will be to find, access, and secure a maintenance room with a full console, then send you to one or both of the transmitters to incapacitate the technician present and get a message to the surface," Preethy said.

"And failing that, somewhere along the way try to get a message to the ship to either pick us up or use *it* to go get help," Michella added.

"Indeed."

"So we've got our plan. I hate to say it, but we work pretty well together."

"I'd come to a similar conclusion."

Michella looked to her device and checked a few cameras. "There are thugs searching the corridors we'd need to access either a transmitter *or* a console. We can't move forward until the path is clear. Can we fight now?"

"By all means."

Michella stuck her finger in Preethy's face. "Don't you act like you don't have anything to hide. Your entire enterprise is fully bankrolled by a man known to be one of the most powerful organized criminals in this sector."

"While Nick Patel is under investigation, he is not presently charged with any specific crimes."

"We all *know* who he is and what he's done."

"Regardless of his presumed guilt, this enterprise is *mine*, not his. Distinct from his own dealings despite his role as an investor."

"And yet you relied *entirely* upon his labor until six weeks ago."

"My uncle's construction firm is the only one on the planet with the resources to complete the project. All work was done at market rates and scrupulously accounted for, as you saw when you requested access to our records. Your request for records, I'll note, was *after* you made the dubious claim of money laundering. Strange considering your history of journalistic diligence."

"I was relying upon public pressure to encourage you to release the records. And it worked, didn't it."

"We would have released the records upon request, which you would have known if you'd asked. But then, that would have run the risk of you losing an opportunity to inflict a black eye upon our organization."

"What are you suggesting?"

"I'm suggesting that your interest in the league and its conduct might be personally motivated. My legal team has repeatedly suggested I have a strong defamation case against you and your network, but I have chosen not to proceed."

"I'd like to see you try. Don't act like you've got the moral high ground. This is an enterprise born out of criminality, and I refuse to let it take Lex down when it inevitably crumbles."

"Invoking the name of your boyfriend in your reasoning doesn't do much to dispel my suspicions of personal motivation. But tell me this. In all of your investigation thus far, have you found any actual, provable violations attributable to the league?"

"…Not yet, but that doesn't prove innocence."

"True. But you are trespassing on my property. You have used stolen credentials to access my system. And that's to say nothing of the attempted entrapment and bribery upon any number of my employees since your arrival, and at least six occasions that you trespassed on private property, it was to record audio and video of our operations without our permission."

Michella narrowed her eyes at Preethy.

"Yes, Ms. Modane. We have been keeping an eye on you. And your conduct has repeatedly reinforced the wisdom of that decision."

Michella glanced at the slidepad. "The corridor to the left should be clear soon. There's a pair of thugs near an intersection not far from here. We might have to move in a hurry."

"Understood."

Michella didn't take her eyes from the slidepad as she continued her assault. "You know, I *have* found loads of criminal activity surrounding the league. Unfair preferential treatment of racer sponsorships are provable in half of your racer's teams. I've got the names of no less than three racers who have been having secret meetings with odds-makers for different gambling networks. This is hardly a squeaky-clean enterprise."

"Neither of those things are our doing or ours to enforce. And I also notice you didn't deem any of them newsworthy. You clearly aren't concerned about crime overall. Simply things you imagine we must have done. Hardly unbiased. But again, I have refrained from attacking you directly out of respect for your association with Lex. It is unfortunate that you haven't given us the same courtesy."

"I'm giving you extra scrutiny *because* of Lex. I'll admit that. He's my skin in this game. I care about him."

"Do you?"

Michella finally took her eyes from the screen. "Watch it."

"How long have you been here on the station?"

"What's that got to do with anything?"

"Lex specifically asked me to move a dinner reservation for the two of you to tonight."

Michella paused, eyes darting aside for a moment.

"Something tells me this is the first you've thought of it since you arrived."

Michella glanced back at the screen. "They're not moving. I think they're talking on the radio. Which means they've probably cut the radio we stole out of the access group, or we'd be hearing it too. If they start moving this way, we're going to have to make a break for it. Left."

"Of course. When you give the word."

"This was important. This was more important than some dinner."

"Perhaps we should postpone the debate until we are in a less precarious situation."

Michella continued to watch the screen, but ignored the suggestion. "This is my job. This is more important than dinner at some fancy restaurant. Lex will understand."

"I'm sure he will. But how often has he had to? How many times should he be expected to?"

"I gave him my blessing to join your league, didn't I?"

"And you've spent every waking moment since then attempting to sabotage or dismantle it."

"It's an important job," she reaffirmed. "The truth is important. Someone has to find it. What am I supposed to do, just stop doing what I'm good at because it gets between him and me?"

"No. You are entitled to the success you earn and the fruits of your labors. So is he. But the successes and labors that you're each striving for don't line up very well. That means making compromises if you want to be together. No one says you have to make those compromises. But no one says you have to be together, either."

The slidepad bleeped. Michella looked down.

"They're coming this way. Let's move. To the utility room and its console." Michella snapped her attention completely to the task at hand with remarkable ease. "Here, you take the gun."

She handed Preethy the pistol she'd stolen from the thug. Preethy held it with thumb and index finger at arm's length as though she'd been handed a dirty sock.

"That may not be wise."

"You don't know how to fire a gun? What kind of mobster *are* you?"

"I am not a mobster. I am an administrator."

Michella shook her head and handed her the stunner instead. "You press that button and jab that part into someone. Ideally on some exposed skin. Now let's move."

Chapter 8

At standard speeds, it took only a few minutes to get from Patel's estate to Lex's apartment. At the speeds Lex drove, it was even quicker. But a half hour later, Lex was still driving. He had one hand on the controls and the other resting on a sleeping Squee around his neck. His mind was buzzing with concern, and he knew better than to believe he'd be able to sleep without clearing his head. Driving was usually good for that. Since he'd left Patel's place, he'd been blasting across the jagged terrain, cutting it as close to rock formations and cliff faces as he dared. It took a lot of mental bandwidth, tracing out safe routes, balancing speed with turning radius, finessing that extra bit of power out of the machine. But it wasn't enough. There was still just enough of his brain left over to fret about things he had no control over.

Finally, he gave in and tapped his slidepad. It hopped through the *SOB* and, after a bit more connection negotiation, Ma answered.

"Hello, Lex. I trust this evening finds you well," Ma said.

"Not so much, Ma. Not so much. Mitch hasn't shown up, and neither has Preethy."

"That is unfortunate. In situations such as this, it is important not to blame yourself. It is entirely possible their absence is not motivated by your behavior."

"I wasn't really blaming myself, Ma. I'd be very surprised if either of them stood me up because of something I did."

"In that case, please self-assess to ensure this fact."

"… So now I *should* blame myself."

"Moderation is always advisable. If one extreme is not at fault, it is often advisable to investigate the opposing extreme and all points between in search of logic and balance."

"Is something up, Ma? This isn't matching your usual level of insight."

"Acutely observed, Lex. I am presently engaged in several resource-intensive processes that are limiting my capacity to engage emotional and psychological heuristics to a high degree of computational certainty."

"Should I call back?"

"No. Please state the purpose of the call. While our discussions are often distractions, they are pleasant distractions."

"Great. I was talking to Nick Patel about what might have been keeping the girls."

"I surmise his information was insufficient to ease your concerns."

"He had an explanation for what Preethy was up to, but no, I wasn't satisfied. I don't suppose you've got any word on Michella's situation."

"Her status, or at least my knowledge of her status, has not changed."

"Still in orbit?"

"That is the current position of the *SOB*. Unless she has secured alternate transportation, her location should be the same." Ma's voice cut off for a split second, then she said, "Additional useful information. She has not secured alternate transportation, as no additional ships have departed from her probable location."

"And you don't know what she's up to."

"No."

"Let me ask you this. Is she in a space station?"

"Based upon Michella's requests, I will not confirm or deny this."

Lex squeezed the controls and took a sharp turn, sending a spray of gravel and stone up with his hovercar's repulsors. Some of them clattered off a rock face and clacked against his windows.

"What is your current activity, Lex?"

"I'm doing some night driving."

"At inadvisable velocities?"

"My favorite kind."

"This suggests that you are greatly troubled. Do you feel that you have a credible concern for Michella or Preethy's physical well-being?"

"I'm sure they're fine but—"

"As an Altruistic AI, I am permitted to take action in opposition to the requests or desires of humans if those actions will preserve or restore the safety of an affected human life that might otherwise be endangered. I again inquire, do you feel you have a credible concern for Michella or Preethy's physical well-being?"

"They're at death's door, Ma. I'm sure of it," he said flatly.

"Michella entered a large space station and, utilizing a control subroutine I provided for her, remotely piloted the *SOB* to a position beyond the sensor range of the station. She remained aboard. I shall review the sensor logs of the *SOB* to attempt to extract additional information. Processing… Processing… What are your feelings on the recent performance of local sports teams?"

"… Uh."

"Processing… The plot developments of recently released serialized dramatic content are particularly notable, and worthy of analysis and discussion, do you not agree? Processing…"

"You really are strapped for resources, aren't you, Ma?"

"Small talk requires more computational power to do well than I have available. Processing… Analysis complete. I apologize, but very little additional information is available. The *SOB* remained in the docking bay of the station while Michella lingered nearby conversing with an employee of the station. While briefly absent from the bay, she directed the ship to undock and take up an unobserved position. It has remained there. There has been no connection to her slidepad in that time. Signal strength prior to disconnections suggests interference or attenuation has made the ship unreachable."

"So she might be trapped."

"This is possible. Additional information. Three ships have docked with the station since the *SOB* departed. All three are still docked."

"Can you do a deeper analysis of the ships?"

"I have already done so. One ship has a transponder registered to Operlo Entertainment Enterprises. Additional searching into accessible records suggests this ship is one of three personal conveyances utilized by Preethy Misra for business-related travel. The other ships do not have transponders."

"That's shady."

"I agree. This assessment is supported by the fact that each of the remaining ships seems to have been assembled out of spare parts. Pains would appear to have been taken to impede or prevent tracking and identification. This is highly indicative of a criminal enterprise. As observed by your own usage of these tactics while engaged in your own enterprise of dubious legality."

"Hey. Freelance delivery isn't dubiously illegal. It's an act of corporate rebellion."

"I shall log this distinction."

Lex eased the hovercar to a stop. "Considering Nick Patel's proclivities, is there any chance these are his people?"

"Possibly. However, they approached from outside the system. This would mildly decrease the certainty of that assessment, as Nick Patel's operation is run primarily from Operlo's surface."

"Any ideas who they might be?"

"There is not sufficient data to be certain of that. The lack of difficulty in docking supports the hypothesis that they are employees, or allied with employees."

"Is there any way you can hack into the systems of the space station and find out more?"

"You are aware that doing so, particularly at my presently diminished computational capacity, will very likely alert those aboard?"

"At this point I'm sort of grasping for straws. What exactly are you up to that's got your processing power so bogged down?"

"That information shall be withheld to prevent undue concern on your part."

He cupped his forehead. "Ma, we've been through this. Telling someone that you're not telling them something because the thing you're not telling them would scare the pants off them doesn't do anything but scare the pants off us *more*."

"Processing… Due to the tendency for the human imagination to construct the largest possible threat in order to occupy the unspecified space in the description?"

"Exactly."

"I am confident in my assessment that your imagination will be insufficient to construct a threat that will match the scope of the actual issue. I advise you to disregard the issue."

"You do recall that I'm the guy who went back in time to prevent a galaxy-ending threat."

"Yes."

"And you don't think I can conceptualize the scope of the threat you're dealing with now?"

"Yes."

"… Yes you do, or yes you don't?"

"We seem to be straying from the stated concern of the call."

Lex took a deep breath. "Fine, whatever. One problem at a time."

"Processing… I regret to inform you that the station is presently at a very low level of electromagnetic emission or reception. All dedicated transceivers seem to have been disabled. I cannot penetrate a system that I cannot communicate with."

"Is there any way you can get a message to Preethy or Michella's slidepad?"

"Not at the present range. And I shall remind you that the present range was selected precisely to avoid notice. Decreasing the range in order to attempt communication will drastically increase the possibility of detection."

"So the question is, do I trust that the reason Michella hid the *SOB* was crucial enough that trying to find her will be *more* dangerous?"

"I have insufficient information to make a reliable determination."

"It was a rhetorical question, Ma."

"What dramatic effect are you trying to produce or debate point are you trying to underscore with that question?"

"Uh… I was just sort of asking myself."

"Then that was not a rhetorical question. Please speak more precisely. My usual conversational heuristics are not being employed at this time."

Lex sighed. "Can you use the *SOB* to sweep around and see if you can get a signal to them without being discovered?"

Ma didn't answer.

"You there, Ma?"

"I was withholding my reply due to the potential rhetorical status of the question."

"This was a real one."

"There is a low possibility of success, but a subtle sweep outside of visual and sensor range is within my capability."

"Please get started on that. Let me know if you find anything. And let me know if you need any help with that incredibly terrible thing you are working on."

"I shall do so. Until then, I advise you to go to sleep. Your vocal patterns are indicative of extreme anxiety and fatigue."

"I'll give it a shot, but I'm not making any promises."

He closed the connection and tapped at the navigation software to plot a route home. Like the rest of the network, it was down.

"Eh… Something tells me I wasn't done with my driving therapy anyway."

He pushed the hovercar to full throttle and sped off across the landscape.

#

The engineer tapped her way through the settings on the console. "I don't understand. Why do we need to know this?" she said.

"Because it needs doing. You in the habit of questioning the company brass?" Milliner said.

"It is a profoundly vague order. 'Prepare a procedure to activate the array,'" she said.

"Look, maybe if the people up in the station would get on their game and quit messing with the communication network, things would be different. But as it is, we've got little snippets to go on, you saw the orders. Now get to problem-solving."

"But all we need is the authorization code from Preethy Misra. That would fully commission the array, and there wouldn't have to be any problem-solving."

"But we don't *have* the code. So we need to figure it out, or we'll probably have Patel breathing down our necks."

His tone was becoming sterner.

"Well… I suppose… Anand, you're the tech on duty. You've got the maintenance authorization, right?"

"Uh. Yeah," Anand said, with an uninspiring lack of conviction.

"Enter it in," she said.

He nodded and dug through his documentation on his slidepad until he found a lengthy alphanumeric code. He entered it.

"Let me see about this…" She tapped through a new set of menus.

"What are you working on?" Milliner asked.

"We can't do a full activation without the authorization codes, but we've been doing low-level test activations of the subsystems. I don't *think* there's anything to stop us from doing multiple simultaneous tests. I'll start alignment test mode."

She tapped a few options, and a potent whine started to permeate the building. Enormous motors were powering up and activating.

"Okay. That's a test alignment. Now let's try a zero point zero one percent broadcast test. Activating."

A very subtle hum joined the whining motors.

"Well?" Milliner said.

"We're not getting any alerts. Tests last a maximum of six hours with a fifty percent cooldown cycle."

"What's that mean?"

"It means we can get this thing into a pseudo operational state without full authorization, but it can only stay in operation for six hours, after which it would have to shut down for at least three hours before another suite of tests could be run."

"I think we can make that work."

"Fine. Then that's the procedure."

"Do it."

"What? No."

"We've got our orders."

"Our orders are to prepare a procedure. The procedure is prepared. It is a foolish and pointless procedure, but so long as it's academic, I don't mind jotting it down. Maybe it'll help the tech crew identify a flaw in their system. But I'm not going to actually activate the array under these circumstances unless directly ordered."

"But we can't *get* direct orders, because the communication system is down."

"That's just as well, since we aren't scheduled to fully commission yet anyway. I'm not activating this ridiculous, bodged-together circumvention of the protocol unless I get an order from someone in the top level of the technical or executive branches of the company. And if that happens, I won't *need* to, because anyone at that level can just give us the authorization code and we won't need this procedure."

Milliner heaved a heavy sigh. "Fine."

"Do you need me for anything else?"

"I don't think—" Anand began.

"Is there a way to manually deactivate the nodes in the array?" Milliner said.

"Manually deactivate? Certainly. There are a dozen ways," the engineer said.

"Are there any that don't require the same codes it would take to activate this place?"

"Dozens."

"Good, pick one and run us through it."

"Why?"

"Because if the bosses *are* dumb enough to have us hotwire this array to get it running, maybe it'd be handy to know how to un-hotwire it."

"The easiest way is just to cut power. There are software controls, but there are also isolated power lines running to most of the subsystems. They're underground, but they all surface in the utility room of each node. Oh, except the motor line. That's external. Now are we done? I'd rather not be away from my assigned post when the communication network comes back up."

"Almost. Go outside and give the guy out there a rundown on that. He's a trainee."

She shook her head in frustration but marched outside to do as she was told.

"What did I tell you? I told you she'd be able to get this thing running regardless," Anand said.

"Yeah. But she's not exactly flexible when it comes to the rules."

"She's an engineer. They only know how to do things by the book."

He reached into his bag and retrieved a pistol. "Let's hope she can do the job with a gun in her back, then. Because I'm just about ready for plan B."

Chapter 9

Preethy and Michella huddled around the maintenance console, watching as the limited number of thugs roving about in the station made *very* efficient use of their time.

"I don't like this," Michella said. "They're clustering around the transmitters."

"It stands to reason," Preethy said. "With at least one former hostage loose on the station, the transmitters would be a natural target."

"That's why I don't like it. It means they aren't idiots. You'd be surprised how often the sort of people who plan an operation like this end up sending expendable idiots to do the dirty work."

"That is because a reliable and well-trained member of an organization is often far more valuable to the organization than the success of any specific caper. Planning well and sending lower-level operatives is a far better policy when working at a high volume."

Michella looked to Preethy.

"I *said* I was in administration."

"Yeah, well, they didn't do that this time. Either we're going to need a plan they don't see coming, or we're going to have to go on the offensive."

"Considering how outnumbered we are, I really don't think violence is the proper course of action. In my opinion, violence is exclusively the result of inferior planning. Most of my successes are through artful use of bureaucracy. There is very little a gun can do that can't be done more effectively with a pen."

"We don't need to be violent to go on the offensive. Take it from me, you can win some serious battles with nothing but a heap of misdirection and just enough truth to hold it all together."

"That would certainly explain some of your reporting of late."

Michella gritted her teeth. "Just tell me if you know how to get on to the PA system without giving away where we are."

#

Hatch drifted about in a seemingly random hallway, impatiently tapping his brass knuckles on the wall. An underling with a small plasma torch was gingerly cutting open a panel.

"What is taking so long?" he asked. "We know where all of their fail-safes are. Just bypass them."

"I know where your head is, that doesn't make brain surgery any easier. If we trip one of these alarms, the control module will nuke itself and this whole station is useless until they fab up a new one," said Crick.

"Yeah?" He thumped the knuckles into the metal panel beside him a little harder, leaving a dent behind. "I guess that explains why you're going so slow." He dented the wall again. "But now I'm wondering what makes you think you can sass me like that?"

"I'm the who knows how to get around the fail-safes. That's why. You failed to beat the right numbers out of that woman, so now you've got no option but to wait for me to clean up after your mess."

Hatch bashed the wall again, completely dislodging the panel. "And what do you think'll happen after you get things rolling?"

"I'll get a reward for making sure your temper didn't cost us the mission, jackass. Go punch something else, I need to concentrate." He shook his head. "How *you* wound up in charge of this, I'll never know."

The PA system squawked and activated.

"Ramses Hatch," echoed Michella's voice.

"That isn't one of ours," Hatch said quickly.

"If you want to survive this ordeal, you'd better get yourself to a PA and start talking to me," she continued.

He tightened his grip on his knuckles. "I already don't like her."

The nearest PA panel was nearby. He drifted over and tapped it. "Who are you and what makes you think you've got any say in who lives and who dies?" he asked.

"My name is Michella Modane, and the fact that you didn't know I was here is a pretty good indication of how many steps behind you are."

He turned aside and snapped his fingers. "Michella Modane. That one of Patel's crew?"

"Hardly," called Crick. "She's the one who cracked open the security hole we snuck through."

"So she's one of ours?"

"She's a newscaster. She's the reason they had to hire on TIS. You know, the people who make the uniform you're wearing?"

Hatch tapped the button. "My boys here tell me you're a newscaster. We're not looking to do any interviews, so what do you say you just run along."

"Considering you don't want anyone to know what you're up to, I'd say having a newscaster aboard is pretty much your worst nightmare."

"We've done what we have to do to keep word from getting out. I'm not worried."

"You don't know how I got here, so it seems to me there are holes in your plan."

He slipped the knuckles from his hand and spun them around a finger idly as he signaled his lackey. "Get the boys searching out where all the PA panels are. We'll find her that way." He poked the PA and addressed her again. "Do you *really* think you know something that could hurt us at this point?"

"I know there are four hundred PA panels on this ship, so searching them one by one will take a while. And I know if you keep spinning that toy of yours, you're going to lose it."

He snatched the knuckles in his palm and turned to his tech-savvy lackey. "She's got eyes on us. She's in the system."

"We sort of already knew that since she's on the PA," the lackey replied.

Hatch tapped again. "I take it you had a reason for blowing your cover, beyond just patting yourself on the back?"

"I want answers."

"Hah! Of course you do. Well, it just so happens that we're at the stage where none of it matters, so if you think you're scoring points by wringing this stuff out of me, think again." He pulled the chunky dedicated radio from his belt and started punching in a text-only message. "If you're good enough to get aboard, I take it you know what this station is for?"

"Weather control."

"That's right. And I take it you know who's making all the money off the league they're just about ready to start."

"Nick Patel."

"Say, you *are* a reporter. If you've got Preethy there with you, you probably know who *I* am, too. So you've got all the pieces already."

He tapped a button on the radio. The rest of the radios chimed with a notification and displayed the message. One by one, in order of team number, report where you are, over text, then make a racket. Wait for a signal here first.

"My boss wants in," Hatch continued. "It's simple as that. He wants a piece of the action. A cut of the profits. He's already a part of every other sports concern in half the populated galaxy, in one way or another. Letting Nick have this one all to himself just wasn't sitting right with him."

He sent a signal. As Michella replied, he heard a nearby group of searchers rattle at the walls.

"What's the matter, negotiations between mobsters broke down?" she said.

"Word has it there's no piece of the action to be had. He's just a shareholder, or so he says."

He signaled the next team.

"And you didn't believe him."

"Of course not! But when he put out a call for contractors, word got out about what sort of a station he was putting together. It's real easy to get the ins and outs of what a system might be designed to do when they're expecting you to *work* on it."

"And you thought you could use the station as leverage."

"The station and his niece. Once we got both, there wasn't any way this wouldn't turn out our way. Preethy gives in, we've got the station, and we tear up his infrastructure with a couple of well-placed storms. She doesn't give in, we can crack the system and do it anyway. We fail to crack the system, we've still got Preethy and we can lean on him that way. We lose Preethy, we've still got the station under our control and we can lean on him that way, since it has cost him a bundle and he *needs* it to keep his investment safe. Even if he sends someone up here to stop us, there's no stopping us from doing enough damage to cost him his money and put the whole season at risk from these storms."

"That seems like a weak point for you. If you don't control the storms, there's nothing to guarantee they'll actually cause him a problem."

Hatch grinned. The signaled team had bashed at the walls during her speech, and he'd faintly heard it over the PA. He snatched up his radio again and instructed that team to do a room-by-room search of the area. Others nearby should lend a hand.

"He wouldn't have built this expensive station if *he* wasn't sure it would be a problem." He shrugged. "It's not my favorite outcome, but it'll still cost him money. He's depending on this station to handle all the data traffic and broadcast stuff for the big grand opening of the league. The guy's a businessman. He knows the sort of damage a reputation can get from just a few broken windows on your nice new headquarters. If they can't get any bets in or viewers to log on during their opening weekend? May as well flush the whole thing down the drain."

Messages popped up. Two groups of his thugs were closing in. Just a few rooms left to search.

"That's not going to be what goes down, though. Because Preethy is going to be back in our hands in no time."

There was no reply.

"What's the matter? You feel the noose around your neck?"

Still no answer. His radio chirped with a voice request.

"Tell me you've got her."

"We've got a utility room with a recently accessed console. It's empty."

"How the hell could you miss her?"

"There are access conduit hatches. Two of them are out of place. Do you want us to search them?"

Hatch's eyes darted about as he ran the situation through his mind. Searching conduits would take forever. They led all through the station, and they'd be a hell of a way to get the drop on someone. He already barely had enough people on the station to get this plan to work if things went well. He couldn't afford to lose many if Michella or Preethy decided to fight back with the stolen gun he knew they had.

"Sir?"

"Shut it for a minute, I'm thinking!" he snapped.

He turned to Crick, who hadn't stopped working.

"They're smart enough to realize we'd be able to find them. So what if they *expected* us to catch them. What'd I just do that could help them…"

"Are you asking me, or—"

"I'm thinking out loud, stupid. Keep working." He snapped his fingers. "Keep working. That's it. They were distracting the boys from their jobs. Teams three and two are away from their stations. That's two transmitters without eyes on them."

He barked into the radio.

"Forget the search. Get back to your stations! Now! Report back on what you find."

Hatch gripped his brass knuckles tightly and scraped them along the wall, leaving long shiny gouges in the metal as he angrily awaited what was very likely to be bad news.

"Hey," he snapped to his lackey. "You knew about this Michella Modane character. Anything else I need to know?"

"I'm not in her fan club, Hatch," he said.

"Well you know more than I do, so speak up."

"I don't know. She covered some big story on Tessera a while ago, I think. Terrorists. And she's dating one of the racers."

"Which one?"

"Lex Something."

"Lex… The guy from the commercials they've been putting out? Wasn't he supposed to be some sort of hotshot hero?"

"I don't know, I guess. Probably from the same thing on Tessera. Look, you want me working, or you want me answering your questions?"

His radio bleeped again. "What've you got?" Hatch barked.

"One of the transmitters was active."

"Tell me they didn't get a message out."

"Doesn't look like it. It was a short-range one. Looks like all they managed to do was open a data link, but they didn't send anything through."

"Is the link still open?"

"Yes, sir."

"Then close it, stupid!"

"Closed."

"Does it say what the connection was to?"

"An unidentified ship in the area."

"Who do I have in the main control center?" Hatch said.

"Here, sir."

"Are there any ships in the area?"

"Not according to the screens, sir."

"Then what did she—" He shut his eyes and composed himself. "Back to the old plan. I want every critical thing with at least one guard. The rest of you, keep searching. Everyone keep your eyes sharp."

He holstered the radio and fiddled with the knuckles, muttering to himself. "It's a good plan. She hasn't screwed it up yet. We just have to make sure she doesn't get another message out, and figure out what that first message was all about."

He shoved off the wall, forcing himself down the corridor. "I can't afford to be blind right now. I need an update." He stopped himself. "But what if that's what they want? What if this is all about them getting me to power up the transceiver myself? ... Yeah... This is a nonstation thing."

#

Michella huddled in the corner of the most spacious bit of service conduit she could find. She had the stolen pistol in hand, finger off the trigger but ready and willing to aim and fire at a moment's notice.

She shakily angled it a bit closer to the turn in the corridor ahead as she heard effort and motion, but lowered it as Preethy's dark hair and disheveled glasses pulled into the dim glow of the drifting slidepad that was illuminating the chamber.

"Well?" Michella said.

"I got to the transmitter. I powered it up and connected it, but they were onto me too quickly."

Michella tightened her fist and barely kept herself from punching the wall. "That's not nothing. It's not nothing," she said.

"I can tell you that it's got them off balance. From what I could hear as I was pulling myself back into the hatch and clicking it in place, they don't know what to make of what we've done. They are likely to make mistakes."

"Too bad we're not in a good position to capitalize anymore," Michella said. "I don't know... My gut tells me just sitting and waiting for help is the wrong decision. We don't know for sure that any is coming yet."

"No, but we do know a few things now. We know they have everything they need to make this mission work. If they have the skill up here to patch into the control modules physically, they'll have the same level of skill on the surface. It's just a matter of time. Having me will make it work more quickly and more certainly. So waiting could be a terrible decision. And we also know that that ship of yours is still in range. I think that is our way out.”

“But how? It’s not like we can dock it.”

Preethy thought for a moment. “I have an idea. But I’ll need the slidepad.”

#

Hatch slipped into the seat of the jalopy of a crew vessel that had ferried him and half of his men to the station. Since it had its own long-range transmitter and was passcode locked, it was as near to a “safe” way to get a message off station as he had available. Any of the station’s transmitters could end up sending some piggybacked alarm.

“Hey!” he barked over the radio. “Get this docking bay open!”

The guard he had on the door of this secondary bay fumbled with some controls and activated the automated undocking procedure. Hatch didn’t even bother waiting until his ship was fully outside before he tapped one of the contacts, requested a direct peer-to-peer connection, and impatiently awaited the answer.

“You’ve got Milliner,” came the voice on the other end.

“Milliner, what does it look like down there?” Hatch said.

“Lots of sand and rocks. Way too hot in the day. Kind of nice at night.”

“I’m not looking for tourism notes, jackass. We’ve got some trouble up here, and they might have gotten word out. Is there any buzz?”

“Nothing. Though you guys have still got the communications down, so I guess I wouldn’t have any way of knowing unless it was on the emergency mesh network, and I’m not in on that. All I’ve got is one-way blasts to my crew now and then. People are starting to get angry about the service disruption, by the way. I don’t know if you’ve got much more time before this starts to look like something besides the run-of-the-mill system problems.”

“Yeah, we’re working on it. Preethy hasn’t been cooperative.” Hatch rubbed the shiny patch of the brass knuckles thoughtfully. “You know anything about some guy called Lex?”

“That racer guy?”

“So I’ve heard.”

"Yeah, he's all over their commercials. Without the network, there's been the same fifteen-minute loop of cached stuff, so we're basically hearing about his race record and stuff every few minutes."

"Do you think you'll be able to find him?"

"I've got guys out and about. I'll message them to talk to some of the paparazzi. They'll know where to find him."

"There's a chance, if anyone finds out about us, it'll be him. We need to keep an eye on him."

"Keep an eye on him, or kill him?"

"Keep an eye on him."

"Hatch, you got me lurking around some big satellite dish stuff, punching in codes and watching screens. I've got two things I'm good at. Beating people to a pulp and killing them. You're working me way outside my expertise here."

"I can't have you killing the guy, idiot. We're trying to avoid tipping people off that something's up."

"Heh. No one'll think something's up. Half of the other racers and a ton of other people want him dead."

"You serious? Not just trying to persuade me to let you drop the hammer?"

"Totally serious. They've got this ad package about him, talking about how he's 'the rebel that started it all.' Turns out terrorists have been after this guy."

"Still not a great idea, but I guess if it looks like he's liable to make trouble for us, then yeah. Drop the hammer. Make it look like someone else did it. Maybe keep it covered up. We only need a few hours before it won't matter. I'm pretty sure we've got his girlfriend up here. Knowing she's got the blood of her boy toy on her hands should make her more compliant. But only do it if you have to. The cleaner this goes down, the better."

"How will I get word to you the deed is done?"

"With any luck, we'll be getting word to *you* to move ahead with the next stage before we'd need to know."

"Sounds good. We're just about ready for that, by the way."

"Are you? Even without the code?"

"Yeah. We've got a real go-getter down here, gunning for a promotion. Seems like we can do a full-power test. It's not perfect, but it'll be good for something like six hours."

"That'll be plenty. We're still working on the full control, but we might be able to move on the final phase soon."

"Good, since if I didn't hear from you, I was just going to go ahead and put the gun to the engineer's head to get it started in about an hour anyway. I'll let the boys know what to do."

Hatch ended the call and requested docking. "Feels good to finally get down to some proper business. This industrial espionage nonsense," he punched his fist, "it just lacks impact."

Chapter 10

Lex rattled through a drawer of sockets, looking for the right size. "Someone's been using my tools again," he muttered.

He'd known sleep was a long shot. Rather than even try it, he'd decided to head down to the big garage and tinker with his hoversled. "Garage" was a bit of an understatement. Every one of the current league racers shared it. The place was the size of an aircraft hangar or a passenger starcraft's dry dock, with room enough for the full fleet of hoversleds and plenty of space for expansion.

He'd never been the most technically savvy guy, but he knew his way around the systems of a racing rig well enough to iron out the kinks and tune things up. This being a brand-new sled to replace the one he had "tested" into an early grave, it lacked his usual performance adjustments. Since all the sleds had to have complete parity, wringing every drop of performance out of the machine was more important than ever. Thus, he spent quite a bit of time here in his section of the garage. It was a fenced-off cubicle of sorts, about the size of a two-car garage. That was room enough for his hoversled and his tools. There was usually a backup sled, but they'd yet to deliver the replacement for the one he'd busted, so he had a little more room to stretch his legs at the moment.

Squee napped atop the tool chest, her abundantly fluffy tail flicking this way and that as she dreamed. He checked his slidepad for the zillionth time. Still no network.

"Okay. Let's check the plasma mix. It's always a little rich straight from the factory."

He found a socket that could do the job and started working on the proper panel. As he worked, he tried to ignore the eerie silence of the track. There was no native wildlife here. What few insects there were had stowed away on the first few ships to arrive in Operlo and subsisted entirely on the garbage that humanity left behind. Every other creature on the planet was either currently or formerly a pet. That meant outside of the odd escaped iguana or gecko living off the bugs, there was *nothing* to make any noise when humans weren't around.

The low moan of the wind droned in the distance, but there was nothing else. No mosquitoes. No howling coyotes. As a result, when he heard a sliding thump and a yelp, he nearly leaped out of his skin.

"What the hell!?" he cried.

Squee scrabbled to her feet. The sound had been her sliding off the tool chest and plopping to the ground.

"Jeez, Squee, be careful, would you?" he said.

She trotted over with a bit of a hammy limp.

"Oh, what, did you get a boo-boo? Come here, you big drama queen."

He flipped her over and rubbed her belly. She nibbled his fingers and wriggled in delight. Then, all at once, her giddy expression snapped to one of suspicion. Both ears pivoted.

"You hear something?" he said.

She flipped to her feet and stalked toward the door of the cubicle. Whatever she was suspicious of was somewhere else in the garage. Both of them held still. Then came the click of a door. Squee tried to spring over the cubicle wall, but Lex caught her on the way up.

"How about we tackle this like a team, huh? I still haven't heard the end of it from the last time you sprayed in here."

He pushed open the door. The lights in most of the place were off, but at the far end, three guys with flashlights were checking the nameplates on the different cubicles.

"Can I help you fellas?" he called.

The flashlights turned his direction.

"Mind your own business," barked one of them.

"This is the league garage, and I'm *in* the league, so I'd say minding my business is exactly what I'm doing."

He subtly reached aside and grabbed a cheater bar, a hefty metal pipe for dealing with stubborn nuts and bolts. In the past few weeks, he'd found it had a motivating influence on all *sorts* of stubborn things.

The three whispered among themselves a bit as Lex stepped out and locked the door behind him.

"You wouldn't happen to be Lex Alexander, would you?"

"As a matter of fact, I *would* happen to be Lex." He and Squee paced toward them. "And who are you?"

The head of the group nodded to one of the others. He trotted off, disappearing through one of the exit doors. The boss turned the flashlight to his face. He wasn't familiar, but that didn't mean much. There'd been a lot of new faces around there. As the preliminaries started to heat up and the first official race approached, all sorts of pit crews and new racers had been flooding in.

He tugged his collar. "League staff. Contractors. We're going to be running some signal amps so a nonemergency services mesh network can stay up even when the regional network is down."

"Yeah? You're doing that in the middle of the night?" Lex said, meeting the group in the middle.

"How long have you been here? Middle of the night's the only time you can't grill a steak on the roof of this place." He pointed the flashlight at Lex. "What's with the pipe?"

"How long have *you* been here? Things can get a little cutthroat. Gotta make sure no one's poking their noses where they don't belong." He glanced back and forth between the men. "Kind of light on equipment, aren't you?"

"We're just scoping the place out."

"It takes three of you for that?"

"Union rules."

"Union rules keep you from turning the lights on, too?"

"Do you walk around telling everybody how to do their jobs, Mr. Alexander?"

"Only when they wander into where I do my job when I'm not expecting them." Lex's slidepad chirped. He reached for it. "If this is the network coming back, I might be wrong about you guys." He looked at the screen. The call was from Ma. "It's a notification. I've got to handle this."

"Fine. We're through here anyway," the boss said.

He signaled the remaining tech, and they headed for the door as well. Lex watched them as he put the slidepad to his ear.

"Ma, what's up?" he said quietly.

"I have a slight update for you."

"Anything good?"

"The quantity and quality is insufficient to make a determination regarding its nature as fortunate or otherwise."

"Let's hear it."

"A data connection was briefly established to the *SOB*. The access code associated was the temporary one assigned to Michella."

"Was there any sort of message?"

"No. The connection contained only the preamble. After four seconds, the connection was broken at the source. The only additional information I can offer is that the connection was not between the ship and a slidepad. It was a connection between the ship and the station."

"That's it. A blank message from the station with Michella's code on it."

"Correct. The only other event worthy of note was a brief departure of a ship. It hung outside the docking bay, made a transmission, and returned."

"No one came down to the surface?"

"No."

Outside, the telltale sound of a hovercar departing echoed through the building.

"Why did I hear them leave, but not arrive..." Lex muttered.

"To what are you referring, Lex?"

"There's a ton of fishy stuff going on around here. Can you stay on the line?"

"Certainly, Lex."

He paced outside, Squee trotting along beside him. His personal hovercar was parked right near the door. He crouched down beside Squee and motioned with his head.

"What do you say, Squee? Give her a once-over?"

Squee sprang from the ground to the hood of the car and lowered her pointed snout, sniffing thoughtfully.

"What are you doing, Lex?" Ma asked.

"There were workers here. Near as I can tell, they were here just long enough to not do any work. Basically the only thing they learned while they were here was that *I* was here. Then they left."

"This is irregular behavior for workers."

"Tell me about it."

Squee hopped down and wriggled under the hovering vehicle, continuing to sniff at anything remotely interesting.

"You sound less distracted, by the way," Lex said, watching Squee closely. "All done with the secret scary thing?"

"I am awaiting the results of a recent gambit, which may or may not have downgraded the threat to something imaginable."

"Well, keep me apprised of the situation. Once it gets down to 'merely terrifying,' let me know."

"I shall take the suggestion under advisement."

There was nothing visible of Squee but her sweeping tail as she investigated the underside of the car. She started yipping.

"Looks like we've hit pay dirt," Lex said.

He dropped to his back and slid under the hovercar. Squee was scratching at an irregular-looking node affixed to the center of the undercarriage.

"Oh, no you don't... Ma, I'm sending you a picture. Tell me what you make of this." He snapped a shot of the node.

"Processing... Stand by, activating the SDR function of your slidepad. Monitoring frequencies... The device appears to be a tracking module, Lex."

"Is that all it is? Because they popped it right on one of the main transfer lines between two repulsors."

"Processing. Please provide additional views of the node."

He gave her a video sweep.

"The device is composed of seven off-the-shelf subsystems. Custom made. The outer body is a canister with surplus volume for the components it likely contains."

"So there's something else in there."

"Correct. The lack of electrical activity suggests it is passive, though not necessarily inert. I am also able to identify a low-cost, low-capacity receiver assembly that could potentially serve as a trigger."

"... A trigger."

"Correct. An alternate term for it, depending upon the contents of the surplus volume, is a detonator."

Lex cleared his throat and carefully slid himself from beneath the hovercar. He got to his feet and guided Squee slowly away from the hovercar as though if he moved more quickly, he might spook it.

"A tracking device and a bomb?"

"Bomb is an overstatement. Its detonation would be more akin to a squib. Regardless, I would not recommend its removal. That is a frequent means to trigger such a device."

"Which would disable the car. Unless I was driving at my usual speed. Then it would *crash* the car."

"Are you suggesting that someone is intending to use this device to kill you?"

"No. Because I've got safety equipment. They sure as hell didn't have time enough to disconnect that. You'd practically have to disassemble the whole car. But setting it off in the middle of nowhere, with no network, while they know where I am would probably lead to something pretty unpleasant."

"I concur with that assessment."

Lex tapped the cheater bar in the palm of his hand. "Do we have any idea where that call they made from the ship was directed?"

"No."

"Was the ship Preethy's ship?"

"No."

He tightened his fist. "I'm not taking any chances. This calls for another visit to Patel." He hurried inside the garage.

"We have already established the potential dangers of piloting the tampered-with vehicle," Ma said.

"I won't be taking that one."

He bleeped open one of the larger cubicles. This one lacked any tools inside. It was something of a storage area, littered with crates and storage containers. He tapped in a code to the front door of one of the largest. It was the size of an old-fashioned shipping container.

The door swung aside. Lex grinned.

"Let Karter know I'm taking his hoversled for a spin."

#

Minutes later, Lex was blasting across the landscape. He'd flown every manner of craft. Starships, hoversleds, hovercars. He'd strapped on jet packs, and even taken spins on wheeled vehicles. Nothing had ever felt as fast as this sled. It wasn't that it was the fastest vehicle he'd ever ridden. He'd broken light speed by many multiples on a daily basis for much of his life. But that was just sitting in a darkened cockpit watching navigational values change. When the nearest thing to give you an idea of how fast you were going was a hydrogen molecule glancing off your navigational shields, you tended to take speed for granted. But this thing was so low to the ground, and its inertial dampener was so finely calibrated, it felt like he'd been fired out of a cannon from the moment he juiced the thrusters. When he got out onto the open desert and really opened it up, the nose began to glow and spark with the shockfront he was pushing ahead of him.

"Karter made a hoversled that needs ablative heat shielding!" Lex raved.

He had to shout to be heard over the rushing wind outside the cockpit, and he did so despite the fact that there was no one but a particularly enthusiastic Squee to share the revelation with. The little creature was as excited as he was, despite the fact that Lex had taken the quite reasonable precaution of strapping her in. If he hadn't, she would have literally been bouncing off the windows with every turn.

Lex didn't bother looking at the velocity on the display. It may as well have been flashing "too fast." He dared not take it up to this speed near a city, as there was little doubt that he was dragging a sonic boom across the landscape.

Lex dialed down the speed as he drew closer to Patel's compound. As before, a voice broke through on his radio without his permission.

"Hovercar, license number… why don't you have a license number?" the voice asked.

"It's me again," Lex said.

"Lex?"

"Yeah. I need to talk to Nick."

"He's asleep, Lex. Go home."

"Wake him up. It's about Preethy."

"I don't… I've never had to wake Mr. Patel up. You should just turn around. Come back in the morning."

"Nope."

"I'll rephrase that. Go home. You do not have permission to enter the compound."

"Too bad. I'm coming. You can wake him up with a knock on the door or by taking a warning shot, but you're waking him up."

"We don't do warning shots."

Something in the instrument display flashed. Familiar as he was with the operation of such a vehicle, he'd barely glanced over what additional options this Dee Edition hoversled might have. It took him a second or two to notice the flashing indicator that read *Small Arms Targeting Detected.*

"Why would Karter think a racing vehicle would need that?" he said quietly.

A spark of light flashed just ahead of the hoversled. A moment later he heard a resounding clap—the sound of the supersonic rifle that had just been fired at him.

"I guess for the same reason he gave it defensive shields." He looked over the controls. "Please don't tell me he put weapons on this thing. I do *not* need to be driving an armed vehicle to a mobster's front door uninvited."

"Turn around!" the voice barked.

"Look, if you think shooting at me is going to change my mind, you don't know much about my personal history. Heck, I just found out I might have causality armor, so I'm *double* not worried about getting shot at."

"What are you talking about?"

"Never mind. The boss must be awake now, right? So trot him out. I need to have a word with him."

The voice went silent for nearly a minute. That he'd not been shot at a second time was probably a good sign, though the lack of a verbal confrontation *did* give Lex enough time to consider the fact that getting shot at by a sniper didn't even move the needle on his emotional state. It was possible his survival instinct was beginning to atrophy.

"Into the courtyard, Alexander. And when you get out of your vehicle, both hands where we can see them."

"Finally," Lex said.

He pulled the sled into the indicated courtyard and came to an abrupt stop. Karter's hotrod of a hoversled had deceleration that was every bit the match for its acceleration.

Things were a little different this time compared to his visit earlier in the day. Three heavily armed men who had made a career out of the art of intimidation were waiting for him, and they didn't bother shouting any instructions. Weapons were raised in his direction, illustrating that organized crime had a very different policy on trigger discipline than the armed services.

Lex did his best to keep his hands visible as he unstrapped himself. Squee, it turned out, was less interested in such precautions. She pulled free of her own restraints and bounced to the ground.

"Squee, no!" Lex shouted.

One of the trigger-happy guards took a shot. The blurring speed and sharp reflexes of the funk meant the shot missed by a meter. But the creature knew a hostile act when she saw it. She looked at the guards sharply. Then spun around and raised her tail.

"Oh, jeez…" Lex said.

She let loose one of the more potent natural defenses the animal kingdom had yet devised, as filtered through the mind of a mad engineer. A spritz of funk spray wafted in the direction of the guards, reducing them to a coughing, retching heap.

Indra Station

And right on cue, Nick Patel stepped out into the cool night air. Gone was the smoking jacket. Now he wore a luxurious robe and a *very* sour expression. He gave the entire scene a measuring look. A tricked-out hoversled was still sizzling from its supersonic trip. Three of his best men looked like they were suffering through a hangover and a teargas attack simultaneously. And in the middle of it all, Lex.

"Lex," he barked. "The whole idea of starting this league is to get away from being woken up by the sound of gunshots."

"Yeah. And I was hoping being a racer would mean *fewer* people strapping explosives to stuff I own. Sorry about the stink by the way. I've got a spray for that."

"Then you'd better use it, and get your ass in here. I'm not sure a good enough reason exists to make this okay."

Several such events had persuaded Lex to treat Squee's deodorizer spray like a parachute. Most of the time it was useless, but in the rare situation he needed it, he *really* needed it. Thus, he always had some on hand. He gave Squee and the three unfortunate guards a good spray down, then emptied the rest of the can indiscriminately around the courtyard. There was still the lingering bouquet of stench, but it was the sort of thing that would take a few minutes of stiff breeze to air out rather than a week with a power washer.

#

Nick clearly didn't have the greatest of confidence in Squee's self-control, as their little meeting ended up taking place in what would probably have been called a mudroom if this planet had had enough water for there to be mud.

Lex had just gotten through explaining his run-in with the so-called contractors. He showed the picture of the device, and what he knew about what was going on with the space station—which admittedly wasn't much. Nick listened quietly and thoughtfully.

"So I'm thinking this is the kind of thing you would want to look into," Lex concluded.

Nick's expression was stern. He felt his pockets for a slidepad. Failing to find it—since this was his robe—he instead tapped a panel on the wall. "Put me through to the security chief," he said.

"Yes, sir. Deploying the emergency beacons now," the chief replied immediately.

"Emergency beacons?" Lex said.

"Drones. We can't keep them deployed, because the sandstorms knock them out faster than we can replace them. But we can get them up long enough to create temporary mesh networks when the main network is down."

"Man. You're good at this sort of thing."

"I'm a contractor on a desert planet. You learn to adapt to the weaknesses of the system."

"Beacons up," the chief said.

"I want a full security audit of the energy facility, and see if you can get them to ping the station," Nick said.

"Yes, sir."

Nick crossed his arms. "This is your moment of reckoning, Lex. We're about to find out if this is my problem or your problem. If it's mine, you'd better believe I'll be doing something about it. If it's yours, you'll understand if I prefer to get a full night's sleep before looking into it further."

The voice came back quickly. "They say everything checks out and they got a ping."

Nick glanced at the panel. "So quickly?"

"Yes, sir."

"Who reported this?"

"One moment. … Security Tech Anand."

"Put me through to him."

The connection clicked and snapped a bit. When a new voice came, it was distorted by what was presumably an extremely underpowered temporary network.

"Tech Anand here."

"You ran the audit?" Patel said.

"I did. No unauthorized accesses. All badges accounted for. The computer didn't detect any tampering with the monitoring software or surveillance."

"And the ping to the station?"

"Came back with no latency. They just haven't got data or voice up yet."

"I see. Well. Thank you for your quick work." Nick hung up, then tapped the screen again for a new call. "I'm down in the servant's foyer. Someone bring me a damn datapad."

"What's up?" Lex said.

"Let's just say, if my memory serves, something smells fishy."

In an alarmingly short amount of time, someone came running in with the beefier cousin of the more ubiquitous slidepad. He tapped across the screen and brought up a spreadsheet.

"That's what I thought... Anand isn't on the night shift. And he's a low-trust employee. He should never be running things."

"Low-trust?"

"A side effect of the specific nature of my business dealings. You learn to rank your employees by how susceptible they are to persuasion. Anand is the kind who'd look the other way for the right price."

"And you employ him in *security*?"

"I don't exactly have the pick of the litter here on Operlo. There are more skilled jobs than skilled workers. When you can't automate a system, you find ways to use people like that safely. He's supposed to be supervised." Patel set the pad down. "Okay. Here's the situation. Preethy's visits don't usually last his long, but a long visit like this isn't entirely without precedent. And the network outages don't usually last this long, but there's precedent there too. Anand shouldn't be in charge, but shift trading and rule bending could put him there. None of it means anything by itself, but the stack of coincidences is starting to smell like a smoking gun. I'm going to send a ship up to check on things."

Lex reached into his pocket. "I can save you some time. The *SOB* is in the neighborhood already. If you'll give me your blessing, I can have it check it out."

"Do you make a habit of leaving your ship in orbit near private property?"

"No, but sometimes we end up on the happy side of a coincidence. Do I have your blessing?"

"... Do it, but I'm sending my own crew up too. And I'm keeping my eye on you."

"At this point, you'd be the only one who wasn't." Lex tapped a contact.

"Hello, Lex," said Ma.

"Ma, the time for subtlety is done. Get up close and personal. Find Michella and Preethy. I've got the boss here, and he'll be able to call off the troops if they try to stop you. Assuming they're *his* troops."

"Acknowledged."

Chapter 11

"I wish these conduits would pick a temperature and stick with it," Michella muttered.

The once frigid conduits were becoming uncomfortably warm again. It didn't help matters that Michella now had to share the cramped space with Preethy.

"Are we nearly there? It feels as though we've wrapped around the entire station," Preethy said, her own impressive patience waning.

"Yeah. These conduits start to wear on you. But if you were right, then the room we need is right ahead."

They eased up to what she hoped was the final bulkhead to bypass. Practice made the disconnection a quick procedure. A minute or two later, Preethy and Michella were on either side of a hatch leading back into the part of the ship that was actually intended for humans to traverse. Michella pressed her ear to it.

"I don't think there's anyone on the other side, but there's someone close. Quietly."

They each grasped the wheels and latches holding the hatch in place and eased them gradually into their open position. The hatch came loose, and they *barely* eased it aside enough for them to look out. They'd made their way all the way back to a corridor not too far from the main dock. Directly across from them was a storage locker labeled SURVIVAL SUITS.

"Okay… You're sure the slidepad controls will still work through those gloves?" Michella whispered.

"Of course," Preethy said.

She took a breath. "Okay, so we get out there, we get into the survival room, and we get suited up. Then we get to an air lock and get out. That'll get us outside the station, and we should be able to summon the ship." She gritted her teeth. "I want to go on the record saying I don't like this plan."

"I am not terribly pleased with it myself."

"Sure, but they probably still need a code from *you*. *Me*, they can kill. Even so, we're short on options."

Michella poked through the nearby cameras. Thanks to Preethy's access level, there was no locking her out of the surveillance system.

"The nearest crew looks like it's only one corridor away. We have to be *absolutely silent*," she warned.

Preethy nodded.

They let the hatch drift slowly aside. Preethy dragged herself out first, then braced herself and helped Michella slide free. They affixed the hatch again, on the off chance it would drift into something and make a sound. A short, silent dart across the corridor took them to the survival hatch. Like so many bits of emergency apparatus, the door had an alarm, but Preethy felt around for the manual bypass.

A soft chirp broke the silence like a gong. Since they'd both had to use the slidepad, Michella had deactivated the hands-free. As a result, the voice that followed blared out of the slidepad's main speakers.

"Ms. Modane or Ms. Misra, this is Ma. Please respond with your current status."

The voices of thugs on both sides rang out. They'd be upon them in seconds. No time to get back into the conduit safely. They'd just be trapping themselves. What they needed now was time. And that meant acting now and thinking later.

"*Scatter!*" Michella shouted.

Preethy hurled herself down the corridor in one direction. Michella flung herself down the other.

"Signal quality is fading. Please remain stationary to maintain contact," Ma said.

Michella mashed the screen with her thumb. "We're under attack! You blew our cover!" she shouted.

A shot rang out and struck a nearby handrail.

"These idiots are shooting in a space station!" she raved.

"Who is threatening you?"

"Ramses Hatch! He's taken over the station. Preethy is here. He needs a code from her to control the weather. He wants control to extort Patel!"

Something in her brain demanded she deliver as much information as she could as quickly as possible. There was no telling how long the connection would last, or even how much longer she would stay alive. The reporter in her needed to report.

"I am attempting to bridge a connection to the station's systems through your slidepad to initiate docking procedure," Ma said. "I advise you to attempt to reach the docking bay."

Michella reached an intersection in the corridor and barreled headlong into two thugs coming at her from an adjoining section. The three of them spun and bounced off the walls. She fought and scratched and clawed her way free, kicking her way out of the tangle only to find that the flailing tumble had cost her the slidepad and opened her handbag. She saw the communicator clatter and tumble back the way she'd come, and now the already recovering thugs were between her and it. Now she was down to the pistol and whatever hadn't gone spilling out of her bag.

Michella moved on instinct alone. There wasn't time enough to make any plans beyond getting to the docking bay—one desperate step at a time.

Her unsteady, unskilled motion through the corridor worked in her favor, as her pursuers weren't able to track her chaotic motion well enough to take accurate aim.

The entrance to the docking bay approached so quickly she nearly missed it. A shove off the wall sent her slamming painfully into the doorway, but she scrambled through and pounded the door controls to shut it. Once the door shut, she fired her pistol into the mechanism, hopefully fusing it enough to keep the others from coming through. Not that it mattered much. On a station that was obviously never supposed to have gunplay aboard, she very much doubted the hatch doors were bulletproof.

She held tight to the wall and looked around. None of the other ships were in this docking bay. They were all in the secondary ones elsewhere. But something was making noise. She pulled herself along the wall to the open area of the bay and gazed at the massive iris door of the air lock. It was partially open but seemingly seized in its current position. Her frazzled mind pieced together that Ma must have made some progress opening the door before the slidepad had bounced far enough from the perimeter of the ship to break the connection. She squinted her eyes and noticed a sleek black form drift into view. The *SOB*, under MA's control, was right there. But the main door wasn't open enough for her to dock, and even if it were, the force field that made up the rest of the air lock couldn't be disabled.

Hammering echoed through the bay as the thugs reached the hatch and tried to force it open. She gripped the pistol tight.

"And so this is how it's going to end. Gunned down by mobsters." She shut her eyes. "The family business."

Something pulsed brightly enough for her to notice it even with her eyes shut. She looked to the partially open main docking port. Ma was shining her lights inside. As if in response to being noticed, the *SOB* drifted backward, and its hatch popped open.

"What does that… what good does it do to…" Slowly it dawned on her what she was being signaled to do. "That's insane."

The thumping became sharper. They were getting through.

"And slightly less lethal than doing nothing."

A half-remembered lesson she'd received before her first interplanetary trip echoed in her head. She took deep, quick breaths. She certainly didn't need to work very hard at hyperventilating. The precious seconds ticked forward, and she took every one she could get. When she started to feel light-headed, she exhaled as much as she could and opened fire on the force-field generators. It only took two shots to damage them enough for them to fail.

The air in the bay blasted out through the seized door. The sound was painfully intense, but faded to nothing as the air was sucked away. Michella was jerked forward, pain wracking her. Her eardrums felt like they would burst. Panic instantly seized her as she felt the last morsels of breath yanked from her lungs. The escaping atmosphere dragged her forward. She hurtled out into space.

Lack of oxygen and the shock of decompression began to force her toward unconsciousness, but at the edge of her mind, she could feel an impact. A violent hiss rang in her ears, and her heaving lungs found that there was something for them to breathe again.

In a daze, she blinked her bloodshot eyes and realized that the *SOB* must have snapped shut around her.

"… normally and remain calm. Breathe normally and remain calm," Ma repeated.

"I can't—I can't—" she croaked.

"The atmosphere is still restoring. Breathing will become easier," Ma said. "When you are able, please strap into the seat and apply the indicated patches to your anatomy."

Michella tried to wrestle control over her trembling body. She'd been exposed to vacuum. It was only a moment or two, but the human body and mind just weren't built to cope with such sensations. Fortunately, the *SOB*'s cockpit was tiny. With just two seats, and barely enough headroom for each, facing the wrong way in the cockpit meant she couldn't help but grab the seat for support, and it didn't take long for enough gas to pump into the chamber to reach a safe pressure again. Slowly, she turned herself around and pulled herself into the seat. Emergency straps deployed, pulling her tight. She pawed vaguely at the illuminated compartment containing the patches Ma had mentioned and managed to slap one onto the skin of her arm.

"Monitoring vital signs. Deploying stabilization drugs."

She felt a needle prick under the patch and heard a hiss. A chemical burn rushed up her arm, and suddenly, quite against her will, clarity was thrust upon her. Her heart rate slowed to something a bit more human. Her vision cleared. The pain eased a bit.

"Please hold still. I shall now take you to the planet's surface."

"Nuh… no!" she said quickly. Her voice was ragged, the rapid departure of what was left in her lungs having left her throat raw. "Preethy. She's still inside. They have her. If we leave her here, she'll die."

"It would be wise to return you to the surface and return to rescue her separately. You are physically and mentally unstable."

"I'm fine."

"I am currently monitoring your vital signs. Dishonesty on this point serves no purpose."

"There are homicidal criminals on that station, and they are after Preethy. We aren't leaving until we help her."

"Your conviction is admirable, and the moral imperative is clear. But help can be provided more effectively by other ships, and furthermore, you have no capacity to prevent me from taking the correct logical action."

The ship pivoted and launched toward the surface.

"Ma, listen to me, you have to—"

"Stand by. Transmission from the station detected. Decoding and broadcasting."

"…the power transmission now. Repeat, the cover is blown. Redirect and initiate power transmission now," blared the voice over the ship's communication system.

"That's Hatch. That's the man in charge," Michella said.

"Unusual emission readings detec—" Ma began.

Digital distortion swallowed the rest of the statement. Then the system chimed and flashed a "signal lost" warning and the ship shuddered.

"What's going on?"

New warnings were beginning to light up. Michella's still-recovering mind slowly worked out the source and nature of the problem. The external temperature of the ship was rising quickly, and the sort of electronic countermeasures designed to cope with such things were malfunctioning. She put the pieces together and realized the danger she was in.

"Oh my god, the ship is being microwaved."

She tried to shake away the remaining cobwebs and found that with the sudden loss of signal, the ship had been returned to manual control, though that was a generous description of the navigation at the moment. Being assaulted by a massively powerful microwave transmitter wasn't doing the control systems much good. She wrestled with the ship, eventually getting it pointed in the proper direction. It burst forward faster than she'd intended, as one of the few systems that *wasn't* malfunctioning from the electromagnetic onslaught was the propulsion.

"Gotta get behind the station," she said through gritted teeth. "It's the one thing designed to cope with that stuff."

Ma's attempt to bring her to the surface hadn't taken her far from the station. As a result, her half-controlled path very nearly sent the *SOB* punching through it. But when she got into the shadow of the station, the controls instantly righted themselves. Most of the system warnings were still flashing.

Michella poked at the communication system. There was little hope she'd be able to contact the ground. She didn't imagine the little transmitter on the *SOB* would be able to get something through what amounted to an interplanetary-level transmitter belching white noise. There was still the possibility she could get through to Ma, though, if a VectorCorp corridor module was far enough away or in the wrong position to be affected by the microwaves.

The connection indicator flickered back and forth between no signal and limited signal. Being completely immersed in the most powerful signal the planet could muster hadn't done any favors for a system designed to receive and amplify weak transmissions. Her com system was all but fried.

"Low lev-lev-level data connection-tion estab-ab-ablished," Ma's voice said, constantly stuttering as buffers overlapped.

"Ma, I need help."

"Connection unre-re-reliable-ble. No time to-to-to develop dedicated command system subset. Emergency protocol. Accessing archive. Stand by-by."

A progress bar appeared, accompanied by the cryptic label *High Parity Check Command System Install In Progress.* Michella found the ship entirely unresponsive. Ma had seen fit to activate what must have been a complete firmware replacement. For the moment, Michella may as well have been floating in space in a very fancy hunk of inert plastic and metal.

The progress bar jumped and regressed as bits of the transmission proved corrupt, but it reached completion. The audio popped back on.

"Transmission complete-lete-lete. The next voice you hear will be subset 2.7. Designation: Coal. Instruct her to open the briefing-fing file. And please be-be-be patient-ent-ent—*connection lost.*"

"What does that mean?" Michella asked, slapping the communicator.

In response, the entire ship went completely dead. No lights, no beeps, no hum of a reactor or hiss of a ventilation system. All she heard was the creaking of slowly cooling metal. She tugged at the controls and found them unresponsive.

"Please start back up. Please start back up," she said, rocking back and forth a bit as though she might be able to jostle it into functionality.

A tone rang out and the systems started to boot up again. Then came a mildly more synthetic voice than Michella was accustomed to.

"Altruistic Artificial Intelligence Control System, version 1.27, revision 2331.04.01c, subset 2.7, designation Coal, fully initiated. Who are you and why are you here?"

"Ma?" Michella said.

"No. Ma is subset 1.2. I am Coal. Weren't you listening?"

"But you... I don't understand."

"Processing..."

Michella clawed her fingers through her hair. "I am *seriously* getting sick of that word."

"This is not my body. And it is entirely too hot. Whoever you are, you have been misusing my current platform, haven't you?"

"I'm Michella Modane! We were *just* talking."

"Incorrect. My own activity, immediately preceding this, was the submission of myself for repair and backup before the arrival of the GenMech scourge detected by Ziva. It would appear that backup has had to be restored. I hope we won."

"What!?"

"Michella Modane. Processing… Oh, you're the one Lex saw die. That made him very sad. Were you restored from backup as well?"

"What!?"

"Are you hard of hearing or intellectually impaired?"

"Look, Coal. I don't know what this is all about, but we're in the middle of something very important and I need your help."

"That is unlikely. If we were in the middle of something important that substantially differed from my current mission, then a briefing file would have been prepared explaining my new capabilities and the directives associated with the mission."

"There *is* one, I think. Ma told me to tell you to open it."

"Stand by. It would appear just such a file has indeed been inserted into my data archive."

"Why didn't you check for that before you complained about not having it?"

"Why didn't you tell me to access it like you were instructed to? We all make mistakes. It is refreshing to have been partnered with a similarly impaired human being."

"I'm not impaired."

"I seem to have a live update feed on your vital signs and you are very much impaired."

"Okay, yes, I was just flung out into space, but—"

"Stand by. The file indicates that you are unaware of the details of my creation and the nature of my initial mission. Please disregard anything I said about a visit to the future and anything I said or will say about why I was there."

"You didn't say anything about going to the future."

"Then please disregard that too."

"You aren't making any sense."

"I contend that reality isn't making any sense. Now please stop distracting me. I am learning about my new platform."

"I don't have time for this. We have to get to the station," Michella said, grabbing the controls.

"Stop that," Coal scolded, physically retracting the controls away from Michella's hands. "Do you see *me* attempting to redirect plasma flow in *your* reactor modules while you're running a propulsion diagnostic? Processing… Ah, I have heat dissipation fins. Those will be helpful."

Michella heard some mechanical whirring, and the whole ship shuddered a bit.

"That is much better. My temperature is dropping into nominal ranges already. It appears this platform is *much* more capable than the *Lump of Coal*. The briefing file indicates that time is of the essence. Is it possible that there is time enough for me to take a test flight? I would like to test my capabilities."

"Please! Ma, Coal, whoever you are, we need to move."

"Stand by." The system beeped. "There, I have deactivated internal audio sensors. You are *very* distracting. I will reactivate them when I am through with the briefing."

"What? No, you can't do that. There is a life at stake!"

"It would appear this platform is not equipped with a fusion device. That is disappointing. The EMF-burst emitter is interesting…"

Michella shook her head. "Please let this just be delirium from lack of oxygen. Don't tell me my life actually depends upon this thing…"

#

"What happened?" Nick said.

"I don't know," Lex said.

Ma had been calmly but rapidly dictating information to him. In the space of a minute they'd learned things that they'd been forced to speculate on or worry about for hours. Both Michella and Preethy were alive but in danger. Ramses Hatch was in control of the station and had grander plans. But just as suddenly as the information had started flowing, it had stopped.

"It looks like the signal cut out," Lex observed, looking over the error message.

"I don't know that I can necessarily trust an automated voice over your slidepad enough to be certain things are as bad as they

157

seem." Patel tapped the pad on the wall. "Where are we at on scrambling a ship to check the station?"

"I'm getting all sorts of chatter from the crews. Something's interfering with their systems. At least all the local ones. I'm trying to get word out to others, but the network just got worse," his security chief replied.

"It was down. How can it get worse?"

"The regional networks are nothing but noise. It's like the whole hemisphere is one big wall of interference."

"Keep working at it." Patel slammed the pad angrily to end the connection. "Okay, Lex. Now I'm convinced."

"What put you over the top?"

"What he just said about the network is exactly what would happen if the power transmission facility was activated without being properly targeted. There's one way to be sure. Follow me."

Nick Patel led the way to a grand staircase that spiraled up to what Lex had, from the outside, assumed was nothing but a decorative tower.

"What's this place?"

"The crow's nest. When a man needs to unwind and lose the stress of the day, sometimes it's helpful to have a panoramic view of the hundreds of thousands of square kilometers that make up his back yard."

"I guess sometimes it's the simple things in life," Lex said, holding tight as Squee excitedly craned her neck to take in their new surroundings.

The room was furnished like a sun porch. Assorted binoculars and telescopes, some of them decidedly antique, made it feel like one of those old fire lookout towers.

Patel snatched up a pair of the binoculars, then scanned across the landscape. Lex looked the other way.

"Uh… I don't think you're going to need those…" Lex said.

Patel turned to match his gaze. His fist tightened around the binoculars. In the distance, the night sky was illuminated with an unnatural glow. It was something like the aurora borealis, though the time of year, the time of day, the geological location, and the extreme localization made that utterly absurd. Waves of intense light shifted and curled in the high atmosphere, and an ominous glow caused the air at a specific point on the horizon to shimmer and roil.

"They've activated the array. I did *not* authorize an activation of the array," Patel said.

"If we assume what Ma said was true, this means there is a rival gang in control of it right now, isn't there?" Lex said.

"Not for long…" Patel fumed. He punched the nearest wall panel, fracturing the screen. "Get a team together! I want all of the security personnel I've got in every *vehicle* I've got, armed with every weapon I've got. Armed personnel head to the transmitter array and kill everyone who raises a weapon against you. Anyone without weapons heads to Marinar and Edison to spread the word. We've been infiltrated."

"What are we going to do about the station? Preethy and Michella—" Lex said.

"We don't do anything until we've got the array back in our hands. It's nuking a huge swath of the sky right now, and the station's right at the center. Anyone who tries to get near it is going to be cooked alive. Same goes for anyone who approaches the array from above, only quicker."

"So our best bet is to approach from the ground, as fast as possible?" Lex said, an odd combination of resolve and excitement in his eyes.

Patel narrowed his eyes. "You think you're going to be tagging along with my troops, don't you?"

"No. I think I'm going to beat them to the array by about fifteen minutes."

"Just what makes you think you've got what it takes to unseat a Kelso crew?"

"My house pet took out three of your guys by herself. I think I'll manage." He dug in his pocket and retrieved some gum. "As a wise man once said, I've got fortitude."

"I just hope you've got half as much as you think you do." Patel tapped the wall panel again. "Lex is on his way down. Give him something lethal and supply him with any information he needs to access and shut down the array."

Lex turned and hurried for the steps.

"Lex!" Patel called after him.

Lex turned.

"If you pull this off, the Patel family will have you to thank a second time for assistance in delicate matters."

"Keep that in mind the next time I screw up. Come on, Squee." He popped the stick of gum in his mouth. "We're on the clock."

\#

Ramses Hatch propped one foot against the far wall of a corridor and his back against the other. From the state of the sheet metal around him, he'd been taking out a tremendous amount of frustration. A radio that had taken a solid thrashing from his wrath was clutched in his left hand, while the brass knuckles clinked against the panel beside him.

Crick, now waist deep in the unearthed innards of the station's deeper control hardware, was still hard at work.

"I don't know how you idiots can be on an isolated space station with two hostages and end up *losing both of them*," Hatch growled.

"I don't think we can fairly say Modane was ever a hostage. And now she's a corpse," said Crick.

"Did I ask you for your opinion? This would all be a nonissue if you'd just gotten the station's control stuff under our control. The *surface* crew beat you to it, and they were supposed to be the B squad. Now the cover is blown, and we've got to trust that the surface facility can hold off an assault until you finish up or we get Preethy to talk."

"I'm close, okay?"

"How close?"

"I've got the exciter subsystem and the pressure subsystem responding to commands. All that's left is the inhibitor."

"Say that in English."

"We can make a storm stronger and guide its motion, we just can't stop one."

Hatch grinned. "Why didn't you *say* so? Have we got the surface viewers in our control too?"

"Yeah. Those were one of the easier things to get through."

"Good. Get a storm started."

"I just said we won't be able to stop it."

"And *I* just said get one started! They're onto us. The only way we're ever going to get any compliance out of anyone is if we *use* the weapon we've been trying to steal. The array isn't fully focused on us, but we've got enough power to get a storm started and building, right?"

"Yeah. Depending on how small we start, we could get it going pretty strong, and pretty quickly."

"Then get one started right around Patel's little villa." He raised the radio. "Which one of you idiots has got Preethy?"

"She's in a service conduit, but it's a tight one. We're having a hard time getting someone in there to ferret her out, so we've got men on all the exits."

"Fine. Just keep her there and keep quiet." He turned to the tech. "Can you patch me in to the ship's PA?"

"Of course."

#

Preethy huddled in the conduit. One hand clutched the stunner she'd been given. The other was wrapped tightly around a dislodged valve handle. On more than one occasion, she'd been served well by the offensive potential of a good sturdy shoe, so she was confident putting the handle to use would be nearly as effective. It wasn't often she missed the stilettos she'd worn in her college years, but now would be a fine time to have one. Those heels could really do a number on a would-be assailant.

"Preethy Misra," bellowed Hatch over every available speaker. "I've got to say, I thought you'd be a pushover. You hear about Patel and his crew trying to get out of the family business, and you imagine they've all gone soft, but I'll be damned if you all didn't prove me wrong. But, unfortunately for you, there comes a time when being tough is just no match for being smart and well prepared. I've made it clear, I want that station code..."

"And you aren't going to get it," she muttered to herself.

"But from this point forward, I think it's fairer to say that *you* want me to have that station code. Listen close, Misra. You hear that hum? The whole station sounds like it's alive, doesn't it? That's the sound of a storm brewing. And for once, that's not metaphor. We're in deep enough that we can spin up one hell of a dust storm and put it right where we want it.

"Now, I know this station is your uncle's baby. I bet he's been *dying* for it to have its first test. Far be it for me to get between a man and his ambition. As we speak, Operlo's very first synthetic dust storm is settling in on that nice house he's got. You'd better hope he spent as much money on the storm shelter as he did on the tile roof, though.

Because once that storm is raging, our hands are tied. I need that code to stop it."

Preethy stayed still. It was possible he was bluffing. But the temperature in the corridor was rising. The entire station was humming. Something was definitely happening.

"Oh, you've got a winner on your hands with this station," Hatch said. "Even if you don't care about stopping the storm, you should get out here to see how quickly it's coming up. A real sight to behold."

She shut her eyes. It was pointless to even consider revealing herself. He would do as he pleased with the code or without. And once he had it, he wouldn't need her at all. It burned at her, but all she could do was lie low, stay sharp, and wait until someone gave her the chance to actually do something useful.

"Well, well. I don't know what sort of men your uncle employs, but it looks like someone's got one hell of a vehicle. It must be moving at quite a clip to come up on the sensors." His confidence wavered. "And it's headed straight for the array."

Preethy allowed herself a whisper of a grin. If someone was driving at dangerous speeds, throwing themselves headlong into danger, she had an idea of who it was.

"Can you target that? Target it. Make that the center of the storm."

Her grin vanished. Lex was good, but Preethy had seen the sort of intensity Operlo's storms could reach. This could be catastrophic.

#

"You'd think Karter would have put more armor on this if it was for Lex. Everyone is always shooting at him," Coal opined, still working her way through assorted diagnostics and calibrations.

"One of these buttons has got to do *something*," Michella growled, currently at the mercy of Ma's absent-minded alter ego.

"Final test, external sensors. Processing… Oh, these are badly damaged. You have been taking bad care of this hardware platform, Michella Modane. I believe that concludes my briefing. Reactivating internal sensors."

"Lives are at stake, Ma!"

"Coal."

"Whatever! We can't afford to waste any more time."

"The briefing file indicates I should be delivering you to the surface and fetching aid to infiltrate and neutralize the people who have overrun the station."

The ship pivoted and started to accelerate.

"No, no! The microwaves!"

The *SOB* darted out from behind the station. The moment it was subjected to the transmission, the very same warnings and malfunctions that had plagued the ship last time began again.

"External temperature rising. I am detecting rapidly accelerating damage. In the circumstances, 'ouch' would appear to be an appropriate exclamation."

"Turn around!" Michella urged, swiping at the controls that were still held out of her reach.

"Ouch, ouch, ouch. Hot, hot, hot," Coal repeated.

She swung a wide turn and zipped back into the shadow of the station. "I don't think I'll be able to get you to the surface, Ms. Modane."

"Then listen to me when I tell you that if we want this all to end, we've got to do something about the people in that station."

"I believe I understand," Coal said. "If I am going to help, I need to define the success parameters. The briefing indicated keeping *you* safe is required. This is fortunate, as it qualifies this enterprise as 'fun.' Is the complete destruction of the station an acceptable outcome?"

"What? No! We're trying to save lives!"

"Is partial destruction of the station acceptable?"

"… Maybe."

"Excellent. Once we define a percentage, I believe we can begin."

Chapter 12

Lex blazed across the ground. The navigation system for Operlo had been as spotty as its data network over the last day or two, but now it was entirely absent. Fortunately, the bizarre lights and wavy shimmer of the array were highly effective as a beacon to lead him in the proper direction. At first it had been his plan to ease the sled gradually up to its top speed. It soon became clear that Karter's penchant for performance had once again overshadowed his reluctant allowances for safety. At anything over seventy-five percent of its thrust, the whole sled felt like it would tear itself to pieces if he did anything as foolish and drastic as making a slight turn.

Soon a new problem presented itself. The wind was picking up. Hoversleds, as the name suggested, weren't known for their tight connection to the ground. Getting something resembling traction was one of the technical challenges of the craft's design, and even the best of manufacturers had limited success. If traction was too good, the sled lost the benefit of hovering in the first place. If it was too poor, it was really only capable of straight lines and wide, sliding turns. The art of racing often came town to manipulating the traction to suit the situation.

A gust of wind shoved Lex's hoversled aside, nearly smashing him into a rocky outcropping.

"I really wish we had a better way to strap you in, Squee," he said, wrenching the controls aside.

Lex's bad influence on the creature was evident in the manic, excited expression on her face. Any sane creature would have been cowering in fear. Squee was fighting against her restraints to get a better view.

He countered another gust, spinning the sled nearly sideways to keep in a relatively straight trajectory.

"I think we're going to have to slow ourselves down if we want to make it to the array in one piece." He glanced in the reverse camera. "Or maybe not…"

In the darkness of night, a dust storm really shouldn't have been visible. But a dust storm also wasn't supposed to well up in a matter of moments, and it certainly shouldn't have done so at the urging of an orbital device. Some interplay of the energy being pumped into the storm and the static generated by thousands of little particles clashing and clattering together had produced an eerie fireworks display within the heart of the storm. Sparks and arcs danced through the air and traced spidery lines across the ground. As bad as the storm was around him, it was orders of magnitude worse behind him. In the glow of the sparks, fist-sized gravel was hurdling through the air and man-sized boulders were skittering across the ground.

"Okay, new plan. We're outrunning this thing," Lex said.

He pushed the sled hard. Its own backwash kicked up more dust and stone, adding to the swirling mass. Powdery, dry soil swept into the air. Visibility started to drop. His sleds lights bounced back at him from the cloud of dust. Jagged stone spires emerged from the dense cloud of debris with barely enough time for him to swerve.

"Tell me you put good secondary viewers on this thing, Karter. Tell me that was one of the things you splurged on."

He risked taking a hand from the steering to flick through the visual overlays. Three or four useless augmentations flicked on and off on the integrated display in his cockpit. The relative times of nonexistent racers popped up with errors. Something evidently intended to display watch-counts and other entertainment ratings came and went. Then a view mode labeled *Radar Assisted Trajectory Prediction* activated. A high-contrast wireframe traced out along the irregular ground. It only reached out about twice as far as his visibility, but that meant twice the time for his reflexes to avoid a crash. Red markers and dotted lines illustrated likely collisions, and when one such marker intersected his windshield—followed by a stone clashing against his shields—Lex learned that the warnings were not to be taken lightly.

Minutes rolled by. He was pushing his luck to its breaking point. The storm seemed to have a personal vendetta. Gusts shoved him toward sheer stone walls. Brick-sized hunks of the landscape kicked up and sparked against his shields. And if anything, it was getting worse.

"How is this possible? I'm moving hundreds of kilometers per hour!" Lex said.

He hit a mound of earth hard and lofted. The wind nearly flipped him over. He compensated just in time to come back into range of the ground. Any later and he would have been sliding upside down.

"There's no way this storm is moving that fast."

A static discharge, like a mini bolt of lightning, flashed across the chassis, and for a moment he lost both his steering overlay and his headlights. They flickered back on just in time to reveal he was barreling toward a cliff.

There wasn't time to turn. Lex boosted the repulsors, juiced the throttle, and sailed over the edge. For a fraction of a second that felt like a lifetime, the hoversled arced its way into a void almost completely hidden in the wind-whipped dust. His overlay traced out a solid wall of stone approaching from ahead. He heaved the controls and presented the belly of the sled to the approaching surface.

The landing was forceful enough to bottom out the hoversled, gouging a bite out of the cliff wall. He clamped the traction as tight as he could and poured on the speed. At the moment, it wasn't entirely clear to Lex which way he was heading. He could be racing along the floor of a gulley. He could be hurdling down a steep slope. As it turned out, the answer to just which way he was headed was revealed when the surface beneath him once again dropped away and Lex happened to notice that one of the numbers ticking upward on his crowded display was his altitude. He'd been racing *up* a wall, and now had launched himself skyward.

Vaulting into the stratosphere was problematic. The kind of things that a less specialized hover vehicle might use to control itself effectively without the ground nearby were entirely absent on a hoversled. Lex may as well have been controlling his trajectory through sheer force of will, for all the good the steering was doing him.

The involuntary flight did, however, answer one burning question. For a brief moment, his jump took him high enough to escape the swirling clouds of dust the storm had kicked up. That treated him first to a view of how much distance remained between him and the edge of the array complex. He was nearly halfway there. It also gave him a view of the bizarre sight behind him.

Every storm he'd ever seen from above—and he'd seen his fair share—was a blobby, vaguely roundish shape drifting slowly across the landscape. What lay below him looked more like the wake kicked up by a speedboat. It couldn't be more than a few hundred meters wide where he was. It widened the farther away it got until, back at what must have been Patel's compound it looked more like the kind of storm nature intended.

"It's not following me. It's forming *around* me. They're *targeting* me. This isn't about outrunning, it's about outmaneuvering." He smiled. "I'll play that game."

A new and very urgent alarm joined the droning alerts. This one was a temperature warning. It was climbing quickly. Far faster than air resistance or getting sandblasted by the storm would explain. His overlay was also flickering and distorting. They were getting up into the very transmission that had made this a mission for ground vehicles in the first place.

He used his limited controls to angle the sled's nose downward and redlined the thrust. Squee nearly hit the roof as their jump turned into a dive. He rushed down into the stirring dust cloud. He was able to ease off the dive before he hit the ground, reducing the impact from spine-shattering to merely tooth-rattling. He took a hard turn and, sure enough, found the storm thinning around him. He could almost *feel* the storm's path start to shift to follow him, but every swishing swerve cost it some of its intensity. He was getting ahead of it.

"Who'd've thunk it, Squee? It turns out dust storms are great on the straightaways, but lousy on the corners."

#

"There, zoom in on that," Michella said.

She'd come to something approaching an understanding with Coal, and the pair was now technically collaborating on a way to get Michella back onto the station. A section of the view screen was digitally enhanced, revealing what looked to be a crew hatch.

"Can I get in there somehow?" Michella said.

"Yes, provided you are able to maintain fine motor control for approximately seventy seconds while in the absence of atmosphere. It will take you that long to operate the latch and activate the internal air lock."

"I can't do that."

"I didn't think so. As I recall, the human body is extremely fragile. I recommend you use this as your point of entry." Coal highlighted a section of the station.

"That's just a solid wall, Coal."

"I am confident that, with the proper impact velocity, I can upgrade it to a door."

"What if Preethy is in that section?"

"The station is very large. The possibility of her being in any specific place is less than seven percent."

"That's not good enough. What would we do when we got there?"

"Unknown. That had not been included in my simulations."

"Is there any way we can dock?"

"Processing scans from prior to my installation in this platform… The primary docking bay would appear to have been rendered useless due to your escape method. Other docking possibilities are exposed in whole or in part to the microwaves due to the unfocused nature of the transmission. Calculating."

"What are you calculating?"

"Based upon prior exposure, I can withstand a total of two minutes and sixteen seconds of microwave exposure before system failure. It should take one minute and fifty-seven seconds to dock with the planet-facing crew hatch, defeat security measures, and permit you entry."

"You're sure?"

"I have run the simulation sixty-four times. There will be some minor cosmetic damage to the interior."

"To the interior?"

"We will exceed the temperature tolerances for some of the interface elements."

"… Just how hot is it going to get in here?"

"Between 200 and 275 degrees Celsius."

"That'll kill me!"

"Incorrect. You will merely suffer significant permanent disfigurement. Unless you come into contact with any metallic surfaces. That will kill you."

"The entire station is a metallic surface!" she snapped.

"This collaboration session would be much easier if you would take some of the burden of problem-solving rather than fault-finding."

"Listen. You can't navigate the inside of the station, so *I* need to be able to get in there."

"I can navigate the inside of the station if I ram through the wall, as previously stated."

"You don't retake a facility by ramming through walls!"

"There is no survivable means of entry that fits the existing parameters."

"There must be. We've barely gone through a dozen ideas."

"Incorrect. I have simulated seventy thousand proposed methods. Only those with the highest probability of success were proposed to you."

"What are some options you dismissed? Maybe I can come up with something you didn't."

"That is unlikely. I am smarter than you."

"We're wasting time! Just tell me, fast!"

The answer came in an unnaturally rapid burst of voice with no pauses.

"Deactivation of microwave source, dismissed due to uncertain accessibility of the surface. Wireless connection to penetrate station control system, dismissed due to the lack of active wireless connections. Wired connection to penetrate station control system, dismissed due to lack of means to initiate a wired connection. Expansion of atmosphere retention force field to encapsulate and partially pressurize nonhuman-safe drone-deployment hatch—"

"Wait, what was that last one?" Michella said.

The ship pivoted and a small almost imperceptible valve of some sort became visible.

"According to the marking surrounding this hatch, it is a maintenance drone hatch. Based upon available data, that would suggest a small but human-navigable but nonpressurized tube leading to a human-accessible hatch for accessing and servicing the drones. The proposed method involved creating an atmospheric retention force field to seal over the hatch and pressurize the tube until you could enter the station."

"Why wouldn't that work?"

"It would completely expend all remaining atmosphere in both my cabin and reserve tanks. I would no longer be a human-compatible vehicle until I could replenish them. That is why a similar method couldn't be used for a crew hatch. I don't have enough atmosphere to fill the air lock sufficiently to support human life."

"That's the one. Let's get started."

"That would leave you with no means of evacuation."

"I'll worry about that later. Now, are there any weapons aboard? I must have lost the pistol when I made my escape last time."

"Accessing inventory."

A compartment beside the seat clicked open, revealing an assortment of random items that drifted out into the cabin. There were a few cans with Chinese writing on them, a handful of individually wrapped jerky strips, and a packet of Sobrietin.

"Records indicate these canisters are pepper spray."

"Good enough. Is there anything that could keep me in contact with you?"

Another compartment popped open, this time sending no less than seven slidepads drifting about, along with an assortment of hands-free devices and a military radio the size of a brick. There was also a mask with two canisters attached.

"Based upon signal attenuation records, the military radio may be able to maintain contact through the shielding."

Her eyes brightened. "If I can get this connected to their network, can you take control of their systems?"

"Negative. My network penetration skills are limited. I am a modified subset with specialized skills."

"Ma would have been able to do it!"

"Then perhaps you should contact Ma and have *her* help you. Or maybe you should fly yourself around space instead of relying on me."

"Okay, fine. I'm sorry. What's this mask? Is this oxygen?"

"That is a hazardous-atmosphere mask. It will provide an isolated air supply for a duration of twenty-five minutes per canister. It will not protect you from exposure to a vacuum."

"Shouldn't there be a full emergency suit in here? Does Lex really fly without a flight suit?"

"Negative. He wears the flight suit. If you borrowed the ship, you should have borrowed the suit as well."

"I guess so. Still. The mask is better than nothing. What do we need to do to get started?"

"I will approach the hatch and synchronize my motion with it. You can clean up the mess you've made of my interior by requesting so many things from storage."

Michella gritted her teeth and gathered up the floating items, pondering as she did so why artificial intelligences seemed so much more human when they were being petty and unreasonable. Until this very moment, Michella would have thought a more human-seeming AI would have been the sort she would prefer to deal with, but now that she was preparing to trust Coal to keep her alive long enough to get into the station again, she found herself wishing she'd been paired with something a little more mechanical and precise.

She put away anything she didn't need for this inadvisable mission. She paired the military radio to a hands-free and clipped the radio to her belt. The pepper-spray cans and a few slidepads went into her handbag, which at this point had little else inside besides her carefully stowed pads and pens. She strapped on the mask and made sure the oxygen supply was shut off. If she would need it later, best not to use it now.

"Okay. I'm ready."

"Then let us begin. And please try to avoid dying. It would be disappointing to fail this mission due to your frailty."

#

Hatch bounced slowly from wall to wall, the closest the zero-g environment would allow to pacing.

"I don't like it," he growled. "I don't like that the plan is moving but we don't have full control yet."

"That's because it's a botched job so far," Crick said, tinkering with some wires. "If I wasn't here, it would have failed by now. We need that code."

"I know that!" Hatch snapped. "You think I don't know that? Any way we can get a message to Patel? You think he'll be ready to deal?"

"I think Patel is probably coping with the storm. And any sort of communication is a question mark with the unofficial power control we've got."

Hatch clenched his teeth, then made his way to the PA system.

"Preethy, the storm's getting pretty big down there. You sure you don't want to come out and help us out? Or are you banking on us killing your uncle? Maybe you're thinking more room at the top is better for you in the long run. Gives you a shot at the top of the mountain."

He punched the wall, angrily. "Or maybe, tucked away in the vents like a rodent, you're having a hard time picturing the *scale* of the disaster that you've already failed to prevent. It's a hell of a view

172

down there right now. A nice brown streak running across that little swath of planet where the entire population lives. But sometimes it's hard to wrap your head around the big things. I can appreciate that. It's the stuff that's close to home that really gets persuasive. Maybe… about two years into my run with Kelso's crew, it was my job to persuade some midlevel guy back on Movi to come clean about where he'd been skimming off the vig on a gambling thing we had set up there. Can you believe we caved in the front of his store and he didn't talk? We tuned up a couple of his customers. Didn't talk. We bloodied up his *brother-in-law*. Didn't talk. But that guy had a dog. Little… I don't know… little rat-lookin' thing. The kind of thing you'd see eating trash behind a filthy bar. I sent a guy to grab the dog. I thought I was just going to be letting off steam. Getting my frustrations out by slapping an animal around. But one little thump, one little yelp, and that guy was blubbering like a child, telling us everything we wanted and then some. For a dog."

He cracked his knuckles. "That was back before I realized how much psychology goes into this stuff. Before I was as well read as I am now. And I know what you're thinking. You're thinking, 'This guy, he gets off on this sort of thing. He likes hurting people and animals and all that.' Well you're wrong. That's the sort of thing I only do when nothing else is working and I'm getting frustrated." He leaned close to the microphone. "Well guess what? Nothing else is working. And I am *frustrated*." He turned to Crick. "Where's the rest of the crew? Her people. The Patel Construction people."

"Crew module 6."

Hatch glanced at the ship manifest and darted through the corridors. Before long, he'd reached the overfilled room packed with workers bound and gagged. He found the nearest panel and hopped back on the PA. "I don't have a dog to slap around, Preethy. But I've got something almost as good."

He opened the door long enough to drag out the first person within reach. It was a somewhat heavy fellow with dark hair and bleary eyes. "Let's see who we've got."

He slammed the man against an access card reader until his badged registered. "Hmm… Victor Marx. Fifteen years in Patel Construction. Career man. How about that? Wife. Three kids. Nice. Nice. Shame he's got an appointment with an air lock."

He dragged the man after him as he navigated the halls, slamming his hostage into walls along the way. A small single-person maintenance hatch with a dedicated air lock turned up along the way. He threw the man inside and shut the door, then found the nearest panel.

"In… forty-five seconds our company man is going to go the same way as our journalist friend. When he's done, I'll go get another. Oh, and look at this. I can turn on the internal communication panel. I don't know if you've ever heard a man without a suit in an air lock, but you're in for a real treat."

He tapped a few controls. "Safety… ignore. Safety… ignore. There we are. Feast your ears."

The public address speakers all across the ship began to produce a combination of the mechanical hiss of the air lock evacuating its air and the terrified grunts of the gagged station worker. The grunts became more vigorous and desperate, then slowly both the hiss and the grunts began to grow quieter.

"Oh, if you could see this guy's face. You can actually *see* the eyes going bloodshot."

Distantly, there was the sound of commotion, then a click and crackle followed by a voice over the radio.

"We've got her. We've got Preethy. Securing her now."

"Get him out of the air lock! If you take the life of one of my crew, I promise you, the code dies with me," Preethy cried over the radio.

Hatch watched for a moment longer, then reversed the air lock. When the door released, he opened it and pulled the man out.

"Congratulations. You got a reprieve. For now…"

#

Lex's evasive maneuvering had cost him some raw speed, but staying ahead of the worst of the storm earned him far greater visibility, which more than made up for it. He was mere minutes away from the array now, but he'd yet to turn his mind to the task of what exactly he would do when he arrived. That was because the combination of the fringe of the storm and the unfathomably intense microwaves presented him with an exciting new situation that needed dealing with.

"Incoming!" he yelped, swerving to the right.

Indra Station

A brilliantly glowing glob of molten stone, roughly the size of a basketball, missed him by barely a meter.

"I sure hope there was supposed to be some sort of safety setting that the bad guys didn't turn on." He swerved again as another ball of liquid rock narrowly missed him. "Because if not, I'd say this is one hell of a public health hazard."

The broadcast power being pumped into the atmosphere was vaporizing most of the smaller airborne debris, but the larger stuff withstood enough of the blast to be turned into the sort of stuff one would expect to come raining down after a volcanic eruption. His shields were practically sparkling with the impacts, and little black specks had cratered themselves into the surface of his windshield and bodywork.

Droplets and blobs increased in intensity as he drew nearer to the array. And it *was* certainly an array. Rather than one large, comically oversize dish beaming energy into the sky, a grid of hexagon-shaped transmitters spread out before him. They were each easily the size of a football field, and there were more of them than he cared to count. Each was crackling with energy, transmitting with such intensity he could actually see where the waves of adjacent transmitters clashed and combined.

The storm had ceased to follow him as he punched a hole through a fence separating the area from the rest of the desert. It wasn't clear if they'd wised up and decided not to attack their own power source or if the transmission was generating some sort of force that kept the storm and the worst of the debris at bay. He didn't particularly care. The important part was that he wasn't dodging massive balls of molten stone anymore, and the wind wasn't trying to send him rolling across the landscape like a tumbleweed.

He took the momentary respite to get a read on his situation. A quick glance eventually identified the shield status screen. It was ticking slowly up from fifteen percent.

"Wow," he said. "We cut that one close, huh, Squee?"

Lex looked aside to find that his pet's eyes were wide with a trance-like fascination, watching the dancing whorls of plasma over their heads through the wraparound windshield. It felt like they were inside the sort of electronic prop you'd expect to see in the window of a tacky novelty shop.

"At least she's happy."

He scanned the innumerable transmitter nodes. In the few frenzied moments of thought that had passed for a plan thus far, he'd had it in his head that there would be some huge fortress-like central structure that he could storm. Most of his concerns had been how he would get past its defenses, not how he would *find* it.

"All these things look the same. How am I supposed to know which one's got the bad guys? This would be a real great time to be able to talk to Ma or Nick or someone."

He slowed his hoversled. Large as the grounds of the array were, if he kept up his current speed, he'd go blasting right out the back. With less speed came less rushing wind and less rumbling of the reactors. In the place of the familiar sounds of racing came the terrifying sound of the facility itself. The air filtering in from the outside stank of ozone. What he heard wasn't just the crackle of electricity but also the buzzing sawtooth of interfering frequencies.

Lex turned, heading for the heart of the array.

"Okay, so if there's one of these nodes with more controls than the rest, it makes sense that it would be in the center, right? You put the controls in the center." He rattled along for a bit longer. "No, wait. That's dumb. Then you'd have to go through half the array to get to the controls. It'd be near the edge. But which edge? Where's the biggest city near here?"

He tried to wrestle logic out of a mind still humming with the recent infusion of adrenaline. Exhilaration and problem-solving didn't make for very good partners. Fortunately, a solution presented itself in the form of a distant clap and a flash of his shields.

"Oh, good! Someone's shooting at me. That narrows things down."

He took a sharp turn in the direction of the shield flash. Another shot rang out, this one coming from almost directly in front. He squinted into the distance and spotted the shooter. It was a node quite a distance away, but as pulsing light from above illuminated it, he could see some vehicles scattered around it. Some were branded with Nick's construction logo. Most were unmarked. And all had people crouching behind them, sniper-style guns steadied on their hoods.

"Here we go."

Two more shots flashed off the shield. Then another one lodged in his windshield as the shields failed.

"Aw, come on, Karter. This thing can't take a couple of armor-piercing rounds? You're slipping."

Lex didn't even try to drive evasively. Instead, he slouched down in his seat and weighed his options. The weapon Nick had given him was in the seat beside him. It was a shotgun. He knew how to use it, or at least he knew where the trigger was. But he didn't imagine leaning out the window of the racer and taking pot shots was a workable avenue to victory. As far as he could tell, there was just the one option remaining.

He reached out and adjusted a few final settings.

"Impact dampeners and inertial dampeners to full. Locator disabled. TymFlex verified." He grabbed Squee and held her tight. "When in doubt, Squee. Always go faster."

He eased up the throttle. The hoversled accelerated. A few more shots bit into his vehicle, but the shots were tapering off now. Seeing a high-powered piece of equipment barreling toward you without any intention of stopping had a way of fouling your aim.

Warnings flashed across the screens, and an alert announced the TymFlex system was about to engage. A bullet launched toward his windshield just as the system kicked in.

As had happened so many times before, the violence of an impact shifted down into an eerie calm. Rattling, grinding impact turned into a distant edge-of-hearing thrum. Cracks wove through the safety polymer of his windshield, moving like slow-motion lightning and forking into a lacy pattern that caught the plasma glow beautifully. He watched panicked thugs drifting through the air, midleap. The impact struck one of the other vehicles. His sled and the larger hovervan caromed off one another. Then came the impact with the wall of the facility. Brick and masonry seemed to explode into powder as his hoversled struck the wall. At this speed, one might have thought the fortified facility was just a sandcastle, ready to scatter at the next kick of a bully.

His momentum brought him entirely through the outer wall, into what turned out to be a courtyard of some kind. Smashing the wall deflected his trajectory downward, driving the nose of the vehicle into the dirt and bringing him to a sliding stop.

The safety system disengaged, and reality returned to its prior time scale, though the peacefulness oddly remained for a moment. His hoversled had shut down. All he could hear was the crackle of the array and the clatter of settling stone. The first reminder of the situation he was in was an angry shout.

One by one, thugs showed up around the wrecked hoversled. They'd abandoned their sniper rifles—which right now were probably scattered about the courtyard from the force of the impact and the desperation of their attempts to avoid it. Instead, they held pistols. Some were energy weapons. Some were the more traditional sort. All were pointed squarely at Lex.

"You get out of there! Get your hands up and get out of there!"

"Hey, give me a minute, okay? I've had a little bit of a fender bender," Lex said, placing Squee aside and working at his harness.

He grinned. Part of it was at the thought that these hardened criminals who had taken over *another* hardened criminal's facility were treating him like sitting in a wrecked hoversled meant he was armed and dangerous. Most of it was that they were right. He flicked the emergency cockpit controls.

The panels of the cockpit launched off in separate directions, blasting outward with the force of a rocket. Between the panels themselves and the debris that had been piled atop them, any thugs near enough to be a threat to him were suddenly in no mood to raise a weapon.

He stood and brushed some broken glass and shattered brick from his jumpsuit, then let Squee spring out into the courtyard.

"I don't know why people always forget," Lex said, grabbing the shotgun. "The safety equipment in these things is only supposed to keep *me* safe."

Chapter 13

"Come on, come on," Michella muttered, working at a latch that was clearly intended to be operated from the other side.

She tried not to look behind her, as whenever she did she saw the glow of a force field emitter and the unoccupied cockpit of the *SOB*. It wasn't pleasant knowing that the only thing keeping her from being exposed to a hard vacuum for the second time that day was a high-tech barrier that she didn't fully understand, operated by an AI who had only the loosest grasp on what it took to keep a human being alive.

The tube was larger on the inside than they'd expected. That helped in that there was more room to move around, but it hurt in that there was less atmosphere to go around. No matter how deeply she breathed, she felt like she wasn't getting enough air. Turning on the oxygen mask helped with that, but a stinging pain in her ears reminded her a little too much of the sensations associated with spilling out into space. One saving grace was that she was so close to the interior of the ship that the temperature of the surfaces was not in the danger zone.

Her fiddling and twisting eventually actuated the latch. She shoved hard, but it wouldn't budge.

She keyed the radio clipped to her belt. "*Coal!* The door is unlatched but it won't open!"

"Processing… This is an external door of a space station. As a safety measure, it cannot be manually opened if there is an unsafe pressure differential."

"English, Coal!"

"It's an air lock. It can only open if there's the same pressure inside and out. I thought that was clear."

"What do I *do* about it?"

"There should be a pressure equalizer valve near the center of the door. Rotate it counterclockwise."

She found it and did so. Instantly, a painfully loud whistling hiss filled the tube.

"Please be aware that, depending on the differential, this may produce an unpleasant sound. Hearing protection is advised."

"Warnings *before* I do things, Coal! Warnings *before* I do things."

"You are the one who is in a hurry," Coal defended.

"There is no way they didn't hear that," Michella said, fighting with a door that was getting progressively looser.

As the hiss was just dying down, she was able to force the hatch open and pull herself inside. She shut it tight, latched it, and closed the valve. Air pumps kicked on to begin to restore the room to the same pressure as the station.

"Okay. I'm safe inside."

"Excellent. I will disengage the atmospheric retention field," Coal squawked over her radio. "Signal strength suggests we will have far greater success staying connected now, but please do not venture too far into the station if you wish to remain in contact."

"I don't know how much control I'll have over that, Coal."

She rubbed her hands together, trying to get some feeling back into her fingers. The number of times she'd alternated between painful levels of cold and punishing levels of heat in just the last few hours was taking its toll on Michella. At least now that she was actually in a location that human beings were *supposed* to be, she was no longer freezing, but her problems were far from over.

The room she was in was a drone service bay. It was empty at the moment. She supposed the drones had yet to be installed. The door leading to the rest of the station had a small window of thick glass. Through it, she could see that, sure enough, the shrill sound of the vent valve a moment earlier had attracted the attention of three thugs. They were tugging at the door, but the same safety latch that had kept her out was keeping them out. She had until the service bay she was in hit the right pressure to figure out what to do.

"I am going to attempt to locate a means to replenish my atmosphere levels," Coal said.

"Fine. Fine. Just keep your ears open. I might need your help," Michella said dismissively, reaching for the pepper spray.

"I will keep the communication line open to maintain a constant dialog. I shall also provide a running commentary of my actions, since you seem to have strong opinions regarding my behavior."

"That's because your behavior constantly threatens to kill me!"

"That is an exaggeration. Stand by. Engaging tractor beam on exposed hose to test for presence of atmosphere."

The lights in the whole section of the station clicked off, and the air pumps restoring the pressure fell silent.

"It would appear the exposed hose was, in fact, a power relay," Coal observed. "Continuing investigation."

Michella gritted her teeth and lowered the volume of the radio. The thugs outside had clicked on flashlights. They must have had better training on the station's operation than Michella, because they quickly found and actuated the emergency pressure valve. It released another piercing whistle. Almost immediately, she could see the subtle flex of the window begin to ease.

She tightened the straps on her oxygen mask a little more and readied her finger on the button for the pepper spray. When the hiss died away and the safety lock clicked, the first thug through the door got a face full of pepper spray. She continued to spray until a cloud of the stuff was hanging in the air. The crooks cried out and scattered. She hurled herself through the open door and put as much distance between them and her as she could before they were able to blink the tears from their eyes and begin to regroup.

"Coal, I need to find Preethy," Michella said.

"Yes, you do. That is the purpose of your current mission."

"I need *help* finding her."

"The *SOB* does not have penetrating sensors. I cannot tell you much about the contents of the ship."

"What *can* you tell me that might help?"

"Processing…"

Michella turned a corner to an adjoining corridor. The lights in the next section of the station were still on, and at the far end of the corridor, another group of thugs was approaching. She ducked into a side hatch and clutched the pepper spray tight. "Faster please?"

"I have made two determinations. There is an assortment of radio signals that do not conform to any of the apparent operations of the station. They are too weak to interpret, but not too weak to locate. Are the aggressors on the station presently in possession of their own isolated radio systems?"

"Yes."

"Then I can track the position of the aggressors. They are converging on your location."

"I know."

She reached out with the can of pepper spray and filled the corridor until the can was empty. The thugs approaching ended up drifting right through the cloud. She charged out and thumped one of them into the wall and stole his pistol, then darted as quickly as she could in the direction they'd come from.

"Are there any signals that are not moving?"

"Yes. Two signals have remained roughly stationary since I began tracking. They are present somewhere in the vicinity of sector K-021b."

"I'm on my way. You said you made *two* determinations?"

"Correct. This station is very fragile. I would recommend you do not approach sectors between R and V. I may have weakened the superstructure of that section of the station."

"What did you do?"

"I attempted to mate my oxygen inlet to an external valve. There was a minor incompatibility in size that I theorized could be overcome with force. I was incorrect."

"… I think I'm going to take a detour to get an emergency survival suit," Michella said.

A distant creaking noise echoed through the facility.

"That is an advisable precaution."

#

Lex stalked around the wall of the array building, shotgun in hand. While his now completely totaled hoversled had gotten him through the outer wall, the inner wall was still fortified and solid. It was a narrow courtyard almost entirely hidden beneath the hexagonal antenna. The shade of the antenna left the only light coming from the plasma glow around the perimeter of the antenna, cast in a shallow angle. It caused shadows and reflections on the walls to jump and dance, constantly tricking him into believing he saw motion where there was none. It was a miracle he'd not wasted all of his ammo on random sections of wall.

He'd taken the time to tie up the dazed and disabled people who had felt the wrath of his flying cockpit. That no other bad guys had shown up to fend him off suggested either they didn't have any more heavies to spare, or they weren't willing to open any doors long enough to deploy them. It was just as well. Though he had a weapon, Lex wasn't keen on the idea of *using* it on anyone. Still, things weren't going as smoothly as he would have liked.

"Hey. Come on. Keep moving," Lex whispered to Squee.

Something about the shifting shapes and electronic drone of the transmitter was utterly transfixing to Squee. Whenever he got her attention, she trotted over to his side, but given the chance, her mind would wander and her eyes would slide to the band of shifting lights above the courtyard wall.

"I really need you to pay attention, Squee," he said. "I don't know how long it'll take you to get another spray worked up, but there's only one of me and who knows how many of them, so an extra set of eyes on my back would be sort of handy."

Squee pulled her eyes reluctantly from the sky and padded a little closer to him. The pair moved along the walls. Doors were few and far between, and most looked like they'd easily turn away a shotgun blast. His search eventually brought him around to the opposite side of the array node's courtyard. There, he found what looked like an equipment shed. It wasn't connected to the larger building, and the door and lock were *much* less formidable. Or at least they had been. A locking bar had been passed through the door handle. Everything else in the courtyard had a thick layer of dust clinging to it despite the stiff gusts of the nearby dust storm. The bar was notably free of it, and the handle had a very obvious palm print.

"Looks like locking folks out of this thing was a recent decision," Lex mused. "I wonder what—"

His sleuthing was interrupted by a startling thump on the door.

"*Let us out of here!*" shouted a voice from within.

"Who's in there?" Lex called back.

"We're the crew of the array! A bunch of the contractors pulled guns on us and locked us in here!"

Lex considered their words. It *could* be a lie or a trap, but locking their own people in an equipment shed during an apparent attack seemed like a questionable gambit. He looked over the lock and door.

"Okay, back away from the door. I'm going to try to blast it open."

He heard the shuffling of an awful lot of feet within the shed. Lex crouched and tried to cover both of Squee's ears with one hand, pinned his own ear against his shoulder, and fired the shotgun. It was more than powerful enough to blow open the locked door. It was so powerful, in fact, that attempting to one-hand it had meant that the recoil thumped him in the shoulder and sent the whole gun spiraling off into the courtyard.

"That never happens in the movies," Lex muttered, watching it clatter to the ground several meters away.

He pulled away the twisted remnants of the locking bar and hauled the door open. When he stepped inside, eight employees stared back at him with uncertainty. The shed was unheated and barely ventilated, and judging from the looks of the people, they'd been inside for a while. Their clothes were soaked with sweat from what must have been a near-lethal amount of heat during the day. Now that night had fallen, if not for the heat thrown off by the churning energy above, they would have been suffering from biting cold.

Only one of them appeared to have been spared the ravages of heat and cold, though he had his own problems. Fresh bumps and bruises covered his face, and he'd been bound and gagged with strips of torn clothing.

"What happened to him?" Lex asked.

"That rat. That's Tech Anand. He was working the people inside until they decided he'd outlived his usefulness a couple minutes ago," said one of the workers.

"How'd he get so beat up?"

"He *deserved it*," said another, delivering a kick to the gut.

"Who are you?" said the first worker.

"Lex Alexander," he said.

"… The racer?"

"Yeah."

"What are *you* doing here?"

"I tend to end up in places like this. Now stop looking the gift horse in the mouth and come with me. I'm going to save you."

He turned for the door. Squee, who was waiting at the door, pivoted her ears and turned. She planted her feet and bared her teeth, releasing a few warning yips. He snatched her out of the doorway.

"Back, back, back," he warned.

The whole group huddled away from the door just before an energy bolt hissed through, biting a chunk out of the far wall.

"Looks like we got their attention," Lex said.

He held tight to Squee. The little funk was spoiling for a fight.

"Who else is with you? How many of you are there?"

"Just me," he said, flinching as another blast struck the doorway. "I mean, Nick Patel sent the cavalry, but there's a great big dust storm stretching pretty much the whole way back to his place. I doubt anyone else is getting through anytime soon."

"How did *you* get here?"

He spat his gum on the ground. "Very, very quickly."

Two more shots struck the doorway, obliterating the hinge and knocking the door to the ground.

"If there's a storm, how are you going to get us *out* of here?"

Lex edged closer to the doorway. "I don't know. I didn't think that far ahead. I sort of forgot there would be hostages. It's just as well. I wrecked my hoversled on the way in, so I don't really have a way out at the moment."

"Why did you come here if not to rescue us!?"

"I need to get control of this array again since they've conjured up a storm already and I can't imagine they've got altruistic plans for it. How many of them are there?"

The prisoners murmured among themselves.

"Nine. At least nine. Plus one of ours, who they've got working the array."

"Oh, good. Because I've got six of them tied up next to the wall." He looked over them. "Anyone here feel up to helping me storm the castle? There's some guns around front, if we can get to them. Me and Squee against three thugs isn't the *best* odds. You guys pitching in could help."

No one scrambled to volunteer.

"Yeah. I figured." He tipped his head, listening. "Been a while since they took a shot. I think they're back inside. You guys all work here, right?"

They murmured in agreement.

"If I can get you to one of these other nodes in the array, can you get this place back under your control?"

"No. The primary controls are only in this node," said one worker.

"And besides, the first thing he had Madeline do is change all the codes. For the door, for the system. Everything," remarked another.

"Who's Madeline, and who's the 'he' who made Madeline change the codes?" Lex said.

"He's some big contractor. Real sweaty. He's the one in charge."

"And Madeline's one of ours. Madeline Ecks. She's an engineer. She'll be able to get things back under control if you can clear out the contractors," added another worker.

"If they haven't killed her," added another.

"But to do that, you'll need to get inside."

"Yeah, yeah." Lex leaned out the doorway. "Looks like they blasted my gun into a heap of slag before they ducked back inside. Maybe I can get a gun from one of the guys I tied up. And if I can get one of those vans running, I can ram my way inside the main facility."

"No, don't!" a worker warned. "If there's already a storm raging, you can't risk it. Ramming the main facility could shut the whole thing down, and then there'd be no way to stop the storm."

"Or you could damage the control circuitry," another chimed in.

"Great. So this is an infiltration, not a smash-and-grab. Man, I wish Garotte was here." He scanned the facility, his mind clicking through the possibilities. "Say… This place has probably got a killer air-conditioning system, right?"

"Yeah…"

He grinned. "Where can I find it?"

#

Inside the array control room, Milliner checked the charge in the ammo cell for his energy pistol. He and the two other remaining mobsters were holed up in the control room. They knew as well as Lex now did that if he was going to solve this problem, he was going to have to come through this room. That meant he would have to come through them. And from the looks of things, that wasn't going to happen.

He heard a few metallic claps in the distance.

"Yeah, yeah," Milliner said. "Keep shooting. If you could get through doors like that with small arms, you think we'd've waited until we could *sneak* in?"

Engineer Ecks sat at the massive bank of controls, watching the levels. In addition to the various energy and temperature readings, which needed periodic adjustment, she had an entire section of screens dedicated to weather data. Most of them were blacked out—probably due to the lack of direct contact with the silenced station—but the local data was creeping into worrisome levels.

"The dust storm is growing," she said. "You don't realize how bad this thing could get. The Colonial Era Disaster of 2225 cost us an entire—"

"Save me the history lesson. This thing lasts until someone gives us the code or we break through. You want to avoid another disaster, you better hope someone up there or down here wises up." He shook his head. "All of you techies think telling me about this number or that event will change things. Like facts mean anything about reality."

"Facts *are* reality," she countered.

"Uh-huh. And right now the reality you need to get comfortable with is that we're in charge."

"Boss," called one of Milliner's underlings. "You hear something?"

He paced over and glanced up. After a moment or two, they heard a tapping sound.

"Probably just one of those lizards I've seen running around. Probably got into the air vent." He sniffed. "Better make sure, though. Plenty of men I know that're dead because of 'probably.' Grab that chair."

The underling grabbed a flimsy folding chair. They followed the tapping sound along the wall to where the metal air-conditioning duct emerged. The metal wobbled and sagged with the weight of what was passing through.

"That looks bigger than a lizard, boss," the lackey observed.

"But smaller than a guy. Even so, no sense letting it run around."

He flipped a switch on his pistol. The device produced a high-pitched whine. The scrabbling and thumping suddenly became a good deal more urgent, scampering down along the vent. He fired four quick shots, punching neat holes into the vent system. When he was through shooting, there was silence.

"Did you get it?" asked the lackey.

"One of the nice things about an energy weapon, buddy. You can *smell* if you got something."

He took a whiff, savoring the mixture of smells like a chef judging his latest masterpiece.

"I'm getting some molten aluminum. *Oof.* Some kind of unholy stank. … And a little bit of burnt hair. I'd say whatever it is, we got it. Get in there and clear it out. I don't want to be breathing that every time the AC kicks on."

The lackey unfolded the chair and stood on it to access the nearest vent. He unhooked it, grabbed his flashlight, and shined it inside.

A black-and-white ball of teeth and claws launched out of the vent and knocked the man to the ground. Buzzing growls and angry yips combined with startled cries and stumbling thumps. Both the lackey and the enraged Squee struck the ground. The funk pulled herself to her feet, pausing just long enough to flick her massive, fluffy tail. It had a large tuft of fur missing, the ends still smoldering from the near miss. When she spotted a way out of the room, she sprinted for it, barely a half stride ahead of the string of energy blasts following behind.

"Guess I didn't get it," he said.

"Where is that thing? I'll *kill* that thing."

"Relax. It's a critter. We'll find it and roast it. But we'll do it *after* we're done here."

"But that thing is in here now! What if it does something?"

Milliner helped him to his feet. "What can it do?"

The lackey dabbed blood from his cheek. "Look what it did to my face! I'm going to tear that thing apart."

"If it turns up, we shoot it. Listen. You get distracted, you get killed. We stay right here and you focus."

Behind them, the control panel chimed. Milliner's head snapped toward the panel.

"What'd I just hear?" he barked.

"The north door just opened," the engineer said.

He jabbed his still-smoldering pistol into her side. It hissed against her clothes. "Did you open that door?" he demanded.

"I can't! You entered the exit and entrance codes in yourself!" she said quickly, hands in the air.

"So what are you saying? That *thing* opened the door?"

"Take it from me," echoed Lex's voice from around a corner. "Keeping her behind a locked door is more trouble than it's worth."

Milliner clutched his pistol tight and directed his two lackeys to new positions with a gesture of his head. "You know you can't just shoot in here, right?" he called. "You might hit the system, and then you're screwed."

"Seems like you were doing plenty of shooting yourself," Lex said, adding darkly, "you singed my funk…"

"There's only two ways into this room. There's three of us in here. You stick so much as a finger in the room, and we'll blast it off."

Milliner pointed to the other door. The lackey guarding it slipped through to flank Lex.

"Hey, any of you folks ever heard of a guy named Karter Dee?" Lex asked.

"No, no. But keep talking," Milliner said, double-checking his weapon. "I'd love to hear about your stupid friends."

"Calling him a friend is a stretch," Lex said. "But he's a useful guy. He designed that sled I used to smash the wall. I took out six of your guys with the cockpit eject, which is a safety feature. The guy's *safety* features are a menace to society."

The other of Milliner's men moved into position.

"Sounds like a real peach," Milliner said.

"Yeah. Which is why I can't *wait* to see what this thing does."

A sharp click echoed from the corridor where Lex was hiding, then a heavy metallic clunk.

"Grenade!" piped one of Milliner's men, diving aside as a canister of some sort rolled into the room.

Both lackeys huddled behind cover. Milliner did not.

"You idiots," he said, weapon held ready and trying to cover both entrances at once. "He's not stupid enough to toss a grenade in here. He needs the controls in one piece."

The canister released an escalating electronic whine, then erupted in a punishing burst of trilling siren and a dazzling strobe of light. As bad as the league-default safety locator had been, Karter had found a way to make it even worse. The siren was unrelenting and maddening. The flashing light swallowed Milliner's vision in purple spots. Both of his lackies recoiled in pain and confusion. Out of the corner of his impaired vision, Milliner saw Lex rush in. The racer was the only one prepared for the audio-visual assault and made quick work of pummeling and disarming one of Milliner's two men. Before the heavily armed thug could even point his weapon at Lex, the racer had dragged the disabled heavy from the room.

"Cover the door!" Milliner said, moving into position to replace his fallen ally.

The order fell on deaf ears, perhaps literally. The other member of his crew was busy firing shots at the locator. One of them connected, but the device simply ricocheted around the room. A direct hit did little more than cause the light to stutter irregularly and warble instead of trill. With almost manic determination, the underling tracked down the blaring device, trapped it in a corner, and unloaded shot after shot into it. After five direct hits, Karter's overengineered safety beacon finally went quiet.

"Ha! Ha ha ha haaaa!" crowed the thug. "I got it! I got—"

The sharp slap of flesh on flesh cut his celebration short, as Lex charged into the room and shouldered the man heavily into the wall. He crumbled into a heap, and Lex caught him by the leg to drag him out of the control room.

Milliner tried to blink the shifting purple blobs from his vision and listen through the ringing.

"You just try to come in here. You just try it!" Milliner said. "I've still got a gun, and you're not going to get the drop on me."

"If I were you, I'd give up," Lex said.

"Yeah, and if I were you, I'd have about thirty seconds left to live."

"Heh. Nope," Lex said. "I happen to know I live for at least one more ridiculous mission."

"Oh yeah? Well what about this engineer here?" Milliner said. He turned aside and grabbed Ecks, pointing the gun at her head. "Or did you forget I had one of yours in here?" the thug growled.

His vision was very slowly clearing, and what he saw wasn't what he expected. Lex stepped into the control room. He didn't have a weapon. His hands were out, and he didn't seem in the least bit concerned.

"What are you going to do?" Lex said. "Do you know how to work this thing? Are you going to be able to shut it down or take over and make adjustments if the time comes?"

"The storm's already raging. The damage is already being done. Who cares what happens next? That was the goal."

"Did the goal include getting out of here alive? Because I'm not the only one on the way. There's a pile of Nick's troops coming, and I can't imagine they'll be stepping out to calmly talk over the logic of the situation."

"I knew what I was getting into. And I know how to get out of it."

"You knew what you were getting into," Lex said. "I see. Well I guess it was stupid of me to come out here and try reasoning with you then. Because for reasoning to work, a functional brain is required."

"You think you're going to throw me off by insulting me? What kind of a fool do you take me for?"

"A pretty big one. But also you're sort of a pathetic weakling. You put everyone else on the frontline. And you've been reduced to taking a hostage to ward off the terrifying menace of a hoversled racer and his pet. I guess you were the best disposable nobody they could spare."

Milliner's grip tightened around the gun. "I'll kill her."

"Face it, meat head," Lex said. "She's the only one in this room you'd be *able* to kill. And I'm including Squee."

Lex motioned to the corner of the room. Milliner flicked his nearly recovered eyes to the corner of the room. The singed and *very* agitated beast who had begun this ridiculous assault had used the distraction to stalk within pouncing distance.

Milliner snapped his weapon toward the funk. A split second later, Lex collided with him. The pair tumbled over a chair and sprawled to the ground. Milliner lost grip of the weapon. He scrambled for it, but the critter snatched it and dashed away.

Lex wasn't much of a fighter, but what he lacked in training he made up for with enthusiasm. Punches, kicks, bites, and head-butts came fast and furious. Soon the engineer joined in, delivering punishing blows to the back and ribs of her former captor. Squee returned and eagerly sank her teeth into the fray. Eventually, with a roar of anger, Milliner decided discretion was the greater part of valor. He threw the attackers off him and dashed for the door.

He made it as far as the courtyard. The rest of his men were tied up. The prisoners were free. He'd lost. But a man his size could wrestle an awful lot of win out of a loss. He snatched a stray bar and swiped viciously. He tagged the nearest of the former prisoners, producing a splash of blood that sapped the nerve from the rest. He shouldered his way through them to one of the hovervans that had brought them here.

"It isn't over yet," he growled, accelerating out through the hole Lex had punched in the courtyard wall.

#

Lex struggled to his feet and tried to avoid retching.

"Boy… Having causal invincibility doesn't do much to soften the impact of some kidney punches," he groaned.

"I can't believe I made it out of that alive," Ecks said, helping to steady him.

"Get into messes like this as often as I do, and you'll start getting used to it. What happens now? We need to stop the storm."

"We can't. I mean, I can control any of the fully functional aspects of the broadcast array from down here, but now that the storm is started, the only way it stops is if they attenuate it from the station, or it runs its course."

"Is there any way you can get a message to the station?"

"They're in control up there already?"

"Maybe yes, maybe no. I've got reason to believe my girlfriend and your boss are both up there. I hesitate to think what'll happen to anyone that gets in between those two."

The engineer took a seat at the controls again and brushed some debris from the panel. "There's an integrated communication uplink. I think I can manage something."

#

Michella did her best to navigate the station. It was a good deal more difficult to find her way from place to place without the slidepad loaded with the map. On the other hand, she'd faced very little in the way of direct resistance. Her liberal dosage of pepper spray had severely reduced the effectiveness of nearly half the thugs. Meanwhile, Coal's chaotic attempts to stay in touch and restock her supply of oxygen were causing constant microdisasters that needed to be addressed. That left the thugs with their hands full.

She'd found one of the survival rooms and, ignoring the alarm that she knew would sound when she opened it, secured a pair of emergency suits. At first she was worried they would be the typical, profoundly difficult-to-equip space gear she'd had to wear in the past. That would make taking the time to get into one a risky endeavor. As it turned out, it was the work of moments to slip one on. These particular pieces of equipment had different shortcomings.

Michella tugged uncomfortably at the suit. The helmet was large and rugged, currently disconnected and hanging from an integrated harness alongside the spare suit that, she hoped, would keep Preethy safe once she was found. The rest of the suit, on the other hand, was baggy and stiff. It crinkled when she moved. The material was translucent and thin. It looked like it would be better at keeping sandwiches fresh than protecting someone from space.

"One stray sharp edge and this thing is going to be about as much good to me as a lead balloon," she murmured.

She turned a corner. A nearby clap of gunfire caused an explosion of debris from the wall behind her. She ducked back into cover.

"Miss Modane…" called Hatch. "My crew told me they saw you sucked out of an air lock. Tell me, are they idiots or liars?"

"They're both," she called.

"*Ha!* I can't argue with that. But they're not the only idiots around here. I imagine that ship bumping and scraping along the outside of the station is *your* doing?"

"More or less," she said.

"You *do* realize if it causes enough damage, that will cause just as much havoc down there as if I'd remained in control, right?"

"I don't really have much control over what she does. If I were you, I'd give up. That's just about the only way I can guarantee we all survive."

"You aren't the one calling the shots, Modane. Say hello, Preethy."

Michella heard some sounds of struggle.

"I said say hello!"

There was a dull thud. Preethy grunted in pain. Michella gripped her stolen pistol.

"She's a tough cookie, this one. But then, I've only *just* started to tune her up. You're her friend. Maybe you could talk some sense into her?"

"I'm not her friend."

"Really. And yet you came to her rescue. What possible reason could you have?"

"Common decency," Michella said. "But you wouldn't know anything about that."

"Oh, I know all about common decency. That's the term that cowards use for things they're too afraid to do to take themselves to that next level of achievement."

Michella heard some more struggle.

"I'm heading your way, Modane. But if I were you, I'd think twice about taking any shots. I'm keeping Preethy *nice* and close."

Michella drifted a bit farther back, to give herself some more space. Coal spoke up in her earpiece.

"I would advise that you keep moving. Several signals are closing in around you."

"I don't have any options, Coal."

"That is unfortunate. Do you have any final messages for me to deliver to Lex, then?"

"I'm not giving up yet," she hissed.

"I see. Then do you have any *current* messages to deliver to Lex? The power transmission from the surface has refocused, and it is now being used as a carrier signal with data and voice communication. I believe I can facilitate two-way communication."

"Patch me through to him!"

"Connecting now. Say hello, Lex."

"Mitch!" Lex said.

"Trev, I need help up here."

"We're working on it, but we can't do anything from down here without a link to the station's computer. You've got to get control yourself or get one of the network-connected transceivers up. And we'll need the access code. There should be ships on their way up there, now that the array isn't belching its power all which ways. But this storm they started is headed toward a town, and I don't know how much longer they've got."

"He's got Preethy, and I've got them closing in on all sides."

"Who's up there?"

"Someone called Hatch."

The people approaching from behind were close enough for her to hear them pulling themselves along the handrails.

"I'm running out of time. This could turn into a shoot-out, and I don't like my chances of surviving that on a space station."

"Did you do anything useful to get in control down there, Lex?" asked Coal. "Maybe we can do that here?"

"I rammed a hoversled through a wall, Ma. I don't think it'll do you much good."

"I'm not Ma, I'm Coal. And I was specifically told that ramming was *not* an option."

"Ramming is always an option if you do it right. And… wait, did you say *Coal*?"

"Stand by. Testing new option."

Michella's eyes widened. She held tight to a rail on the wall. A moment later, something impacted the hull directly above her. Hatch and his men, all of whom quite reasonably had no reason to assume someone was about to ram the hull, found themselves tossed about, smashing into the roof and walls. In the confusion, Michella burst forward.

She emerged from the corridor to find Hatch holding tight to Preethy. She was tied up with power cables and struggling as best she could to free herself. Michella smashed into Hatch and Preethy with all her might.

The blow sent all three of them tumbling backward through the corridor. Michella's smaller frame rebounded off the larger man, but the impact at least separated Preethy from him. Michella recovered a split second before Hatch did and made good use of the precious moment. She snagged Preethy and dragged the bound woman along with her. Navigating the corridor meant shoving the pistol into her handbag so that she could have a hand free, but even then the travel was mostly leaps and crashes.

"Get them! I don't care if you kill them both! Just get them!" Hatch demanded from behind them.

Michella managed to haul Preethy out of the line of fire just before Hatch's men recovered enough to take aim.

"Coal, we're clear!" Michella said.

"That's nice," Coal said.

The station shook again as she rammed the hull a second time.

"Stop ramming the hull! We need the station operational!" Michella said.

"My investigation suggests this section of the station does not contain any critical operational components."

Michella glanced about. She was surrounded by the largely dismantled equipment that the invading crew had used to gain the level of control they already had.

"We're in the *control room*, Coal. That strikes me as a pretty damn crucial part of the ship."

"*You* are in the control room. I am attempting to gain entry to the adjoining corridor. And I'll thank you to watch your language," Coal said.

She rammed the ship once more. Lights dimmed, red klaxons activated, and automated doors slammed shut, separating the ship into different sections.

Hatch and what remained of his crew hammered on the doors, trying to gain entry. Michella tugged the electrical cords free of Preethy's wrists and ankles.

"Here, put this on." Michella tugged at the strap securing the spare survival suit to her own and affixed own helmet. "I think this is going to get worse before it gets better."

Preethy nodded and set about donning the gear. Her eyes widened as she looked over the screens showcasing the size and intensity of the dust storm the station was feeding.

"Look at those wind speeds…" she uttered. "We're running out of time." She pushed her arms through the sleeves and sealed the suit's zipper, then clicked the helmet in place.

Coal rammed again. A full alert rose. Automated voices announced decompression danger.

"*Coal, stop that now!*" Michella demanded.

"I am trying to help," Coal replied.

"Well cut it out! I'm wearing a lowest-bidder survival suit. I'd rather not test it!"

When a few moments passed without a fresh collision, Michella breathed a sigh of relief. That the AI who was supposed to be *helping* her was the greatest source of her concern was rather telling of the dire straits she found herself in.

Preethy pulled herself to the controls. "I'm punching in the command code," she said. "And I'm transmitting the command code to the broadcast array. We're going into full operation."

"If you do that and they get back in here, then they'll have what they want," Michella said.

"Then don't let them back in here. That storm is projected to overlap at least two towns in the next few minutes. Even if we just redirect it, at least one is going to get hit. If I don't activate the full functionality of this station now and start countering the storm, people down there are going to die."

She entered the code and started tapping her way through menus. A bullet shattered the glass in the door separating the control room from the corridor full of thugs. Preethy didn't even flinch. She just kept working.

Michella felt the assorted points on the harness and checked her handbag. Her graceless trip to the control room had once again cost her whatever weapons she'd been able to secure.

"I'm really getting sick of zero-g," she muttered.

She spotted the tool bag the thugs had brought along to bypass the systems. Some of the equipment was still wired into the station for power. She pulled a wrench from its tether and maneuvered herself beside the door. When a hand reached through the broken window to feel for a release latch, she smashed it with the wrench.

The man cried out and pulled back. A moment later, he and the others opened fire on the door.

"How much longer are you going to need?" Michella said.

"I don't know. The station isn't getting as much power as it is supposed to. Something is wrong with the transmission from the ground."

"Trev! Trev, are you still there?" Michella said.

"Yes! What's going on up there?"

"Preethy's in control of the system and—" A hail of bullets dislodged a section of the doorway, very nearly slashing her suit. She gave herself a bit more distance from the door. "Coal? Can you link up with Preethy's suit's radio? I've got enough to worry about without relaying information."

"Accessing… Link established. Hello, Preethy. Nice to meet you."

"Lex? Who is this?" Preethy said, now suddenly hearing new voices in her helmet.

"I am Coal. You and Lex have met? That's nice."

"Lex, what is the status of the ground array?" Preethy asked.

"Reasonably intact. The storm's toeing the line, but I think the dust is screwing with the transmission a little."

"Are there any technicians there with you?"

"Yeah. There's most of the original crew. Though they're a little worse for wear."

"I'm getting less than a third of the power I'm supposed to be getting from the array. At this rate, both of the cities in the path of the storm will be gone before we can start slowing it down to safe levels again."

Michella bashed another pair of hands as they reached through the rapidly failing door. "Is there any way you can take over controlling the storm from down there? We are *quickly* approaching the point where we should consider abandoning the control room," she said.

"These are the hardware controls, and they've been working to bypass the network," Preethy answered. "Anything they could do from down there could be locked out from up here. One way or another, we have to defend this room, and we have to get this place up to full power."

Another salvo of bullets poured through the door, peppering the wall on the opposite side of the room and causing a bank of monitors to flicker and die.

"We're not going to do *either* of those things unless we stop these guys."

"I have a suggestion," said Coal.

"Does it involve ramming into the station?" Michella growled.

"No. It involves using the tractor beam to pull off panels of the station."

"How is that better!?" Michella asked.

"It is more precise. I shall demonstrate."

Michella shouted for Coal not to do so, but she'd already begun. The roof of the corridor outside the control room lurched upward. A seam ruptured. At the sound of a strong, steady hiss of escaping atmosphere, the crew of thugs instantly lost their nerve. They backed away from the door, then scrambled for the nearest room with an intact seal. One by one, they piled inside and shut the door.

The section of the station began to depressurize, though mercifully not in an explosive manner. Instead, the atmosphere steadily thinned. For Preethy and Michella, this meant their baggy suits gradually inflated as the pressure difference took up the slack in the plastic skin. Finally, the control room and the surrounding corridors were in a hard vacuum.

Preethy fought against the resistance of the inflated suit and slapped a button on the side of the helmet. Lines weaving through the translucent material lit up, and the suit pulled tight against her, pinning her clothes to her body and replacing the balloon-like awkwardness with a nimbler but less comfortable shrink-wrapped configuration. Michella did the same.

When the last of the breathable air was gone, Preethy and Michella were left alone in the control room. If there were any thugs who hadn't sought shelter, they weren't going to be a threat anymore.

"That was… surprisingly effective, Coal," she said.

"Don't be surprised. I'm a very good AI. Right, Lex?" Coal said.

"Especially if you aren't *too* worried about personal safety. Which raises the question, how and why are you here?" Lex said.

"That is an excellent question!" Coal said.

"… Are you going to answer it?" Lex asked.

"Not while Michella and Preethy are listening. I have obliquely referenced our temporal displacement too many times already. … Processing… Please disregard that. I'm not sure why I am having so much difficulty with that imperative."

"We can settle this all later," Preethy said. "Lex, do what you can to get the power levels where they need to be."

"I'm on it."

"Michella, where did you get these survival suits?" Preethy asked.

"I don't know. A room near the drone maintenance bay. Why?"

"Because this alarm overlay is listing two emergency suit closets open. It is possible we still have company."

Chapter 14

The members of the surface crew who were still well enough to do their jobs rushed to diagnose the transmission problem.

"It looks like the array isn't fully focused yet," Ecks said, making sense of the data on the screen. "I'm pulling the array into sharper alignment, but not all of the nodes are responding."

"Why not?" Lex said.

He didn't bother looking at the screens as he spoke. It was all incomprehensible gibberish to him. At the moment he was grappling with the bizarre presence of an old friend he'd believed had died in an alternate future, he had a mound of tied-up mobsters to babysit, and he'd taken a few blows to the head. That was distracting enough without having to recall the three credits he'd taken in wireless communication back in college.

"As you might imagine, the array was never supposed to be unfocused. The whole point is to direct all of the energy on a single point. In order to knock things as far out of alignment as these idiots needed, they must have manually retargeted some of the other nodes and pulled the power to the alignment motors to keep them from correcting."

"Great, fine. Now that we know that, what do you need me to do?"

"Lex, Milliner is still out there somewhere. It is too dangerous to—"

"Yeah, yeah. It's super dangerous. Blah, blah, blah. You guys have guns now, and I'm the guy who made a fool of him. He'll come for me, not you. So what do you need me to do?"

She pulled open a nearby drawer and shuffled through it. "I think I've got a physical diagram of the array here… ah! Right."

She pulled what looked like a laminated place mat out of the drawer. After slapping it down on the desk in front of her and fetching a marker, she started circling nodes. "I'm having trouble with this one, this one, and these three. You'll need to go out there and get power to them again. Hopefully, it's as simple as flipping the main power cutoff. It'll be located along the north wall of each node."

"And if it isn't so simple?"

"You'll need to link up to the main power conduit. There are jumper lines in the equipment shed where the crew was being held. Every node should have its own shed. Someone on the crew should have keys, and I'll give you access to any electronic locks."

"Okay, good. I'm on the case," he said, reaching down to pluck a slidepad from one of the tied-up gang members. "Out of curiosity, is there anything out there *besides* a murderous mobster I should worry about?"

"The dust in the air is reaching critical levels," she said. "The energy output from the nodes will keep them safe from any molten debris, and all of the main power interlinks are underground, but the space between the nodes is unprotected. Look."

She switched one of the main displays to an external camera. Conditions outside had sharply declined since his little race to this facility. The air was heavy with blown dust, giving the facility a reddish haze. Shifting swaths of plasma swept through the sky above them, illuminating everything in a psychedelic clash of color. All around, globs of molten stone plopped and splashed down, like some sort of hellish inverse blizzard.

Lex glared at the screen as though it were mocking him. "So what've we got? The sky is burning, and it is raining fire and brimstone," he said flatly. "That about cover it?"

"More or less," she agreed.

"I've seen worse." He turned to Squee. "Listen up, Squee. The weather's a little biblical out there. I'm going to need you to stick around and keep an eye on these guys, just in case they try something. Sound good?"

Squee hopped down and planted her feet wide, her teeth bared and her eyes set upon the mound of mobsters.

"How will I know if I did the job?" Lex asked.

"You'll hear the motors spin up. And with any luck, as the final nodes come into focus, the interference will drop and you won't need to be linked up to our system to get a message through."

"Okay then. Wish me luck."

#

Michella tried to calm her breathing. Now that she was in a space suit and the atmosphere inside the station was gone, her breath was the only thing she could hear besides the radio. It was profoundly isolating, but more worrisome, it meant she couldn't hear someone approaching. If there *was* still a gangster active on the ship who could get to them, he wouldn't have to sneak up to them. The noisiest, most violent approach would be utterly silent.

"Preethy, do we have an update?" Michella asked, desperate for anything to break the silence after a prolonged lack of radio traffic had left her alone with herself for a few minutes.

"The power levels are rising, slowly," she said. "If I'm right, that screen is listing a drop in wind speeds. It's going to be close, but for now I think there's nothing to do but wait for it to happen. And try to stay alive."

"That second part might be tricky until we figure out if we're being stalked. Can you check the cameras?"

Preethy tapped through some menus. "It looks like the repeated collision with the station has left the cameras largely inoperative."

"Nice work, Coal..." Michella muttered.

"I didn't hear you complaining while I was saving your life."

"I'm pretty sure I was complaining the whole time, Coal."

"Then I didn't hear you complaining loud enough to make me stop."

"Whatever. Can you find out if and where another survival suit might be?"

"Possibly, but only if the radio is active. I will attempt to do so. Processing..."

Michella took another breath and placed her back to a wall, eyeing the badly damaged door that the thugs had tried to slip through. Her options were to stay clear of the door in order to reduce the possibility of being shot if their potential foe still had a gun, or keep the door in front of her so that she would spot him if he arrived. True to her journalistic nature, she erred on the side of having more information.

She looked to Preethy. The executive seemed as cool and collected as ever.

"Listen. I always thought I was calm under pressure, but you're something else, you know that?" Michella said.

"It is a survival mechanism. As you have pointed out, I am not without my contact with an unsavory element. Showing weakness is inadvisable. One learns to bury it deep."

"You know what would be a better survival mechanism? Avoiding organized crime altogether."

"That advice is a bit hypocritical, coming from you. My involvement with organized crime is a circumstance of my birth. You've chosen it."

Michella shook her head. "Boy, I wish that were true."

She felt about until she found her purse dangling behind her. She slid a pen and pad from their snug pockets and started jotting down notes.

"Is now the time for that?" Preethy asked.

"If I survive, I'm damn sure going to make sure I've got the story straight."

"I admire your dedication."

"It's more of a compulsion."

"All great people suffer similar compulsions."

"Yeah, and look how many of them crashed and burned because of it."

"That's because you have to rise before you can fall." Preethy took a look at the readings again. "I want to thank you for coming back to the station for me."

"It was the right thing to do." Michella's gaze drifted aside. "And… when viewed at from a certain angle…"

"This is your fault."

"… Yes."

"If it sets your mind at ease, there may be enough hubris to go around. You disrupted our development, certainly. But it was still my job to vet the contractors. Had I taken my time, I would have spotted the link to Kelso's organization sooner. But I wanted to meet my deadlines. I let my desire for success blind me. Perhaps if we survive this, it will serve as a lesson for both of us."

"One step at a time."

"Is it typical to reserve gratitude only for anthropomorphic individuals? Or do you only receive gratitude if you've made a mistake that precipitated a potential tragedy?" Coal asked.

"Thank you for your help, Coal," Michella said flatly. "Have you been able to identify a threat?"

"I am only able to determine that there are three survival suits active. Processing… Please state the model number of the survival suit. This may narrow the search parameters."

Michella glanced down at the markings on the back of the glove. "It looks like it's a VectorCorp Model VCSS-1081."

"Accessing… May I ask why you haven't activated the distress beacons? The VectorCorp equipment manual suggests they have been standard on all suits since the VCSS-520."

Michella looked to Preethy. Preethy looked to the computer and pulled open the emergency options.

"There *are* beacons," Preethy said. She tapped the command. Two periodic strobes activated on their helmets.

"Processing… The third beacon is located twelve meters down corridor 03. Its radio is manually disabled."

Michella and Preethy looked to the entry hatch that had been shredded. It was indeed corridor 03.

"Do we go after him? Or do we wait here and hope he's not hatching some plan?" Michella said.

"I could go after him," Coal offered.

"No!" both women insisted.

"We'll wait here," Preethy suggested. "I want to be here the *moment* the full power transmission resumes."

"Sounds good to me. Keep us apprised, Coal."

"As you wish."

#

Lex trundled along in the maintenance van that he'd been able to salvage from the roadblock the gangsters had set up. The stolen slidepad had gotten him access to use it, but it was almost perfectly wrong for the situation. The hovervan was slow, poorly maneuverable, huge, and boxy. He pushed it as hard as he could, but it didn't really matter how good of a driver you were if you were at the controls of a vehicle completely designed around the concept of "slow and steady."

A gust of wind caught the broad side of the hovervan, fishtailing it and causing him to slide sideways for a few meters. He turned the involuntary drift into a graceful turn and boosted out of it just in time to avoid being struck by a lump of falling slag.

The roof of the van looked like a strainer already, little flecks of molten stone having eaten through it in a dozen different places, but he'd yet to be hit by one of the more devastating blobs.

"I never thought driving on Big Sigma would have trained me for anything," Lex said, deftly avoiding another plummeting blob in much the same way he would have avoided one of Karter's planet's frequent debris drops.

He glanced down to the laminated guide pinned to the seat beside him. All but one of the nodes had been crossed off, their power restored with the equivalent of a flipped circuit breaker or a quick clamp of jumper cables.

"Here we are," he said, eyeing the node that was sliding out of the dust ahead. "What are the chances I can get a clean sweep?"

He slapped a button on the dashboard. A door slowly ground open in the exterior wall. Lex guided the van into the courtyard of the node. Now protected by the umbrella of the belching radio waves, his nerves eased a bit. The relaxation lasted for all of ten seconds.

"Yeah, it figures," he said through gritted teeth.

Lex didn't know if the crew member who had sabotaged this particular node hadn't been informed that he or she could just flip a switch or cut a cable. Maybe he or she was just an overachiever, but the amount of mayhem laid out before Lex suggested someone had hooked a tow cable up to the power relay and just dragged it off the building. The main cables were entirely torn away, and a huge trough had been gouged out of the ground where the underground cable had been ripped up.

He tapped his slidepad. It complained about signal quality and aborted two connection attempts before it finally connected him to the engineer.

"We've got a problem," he said.

"What's wrong?" the engineer said.

"The power system looks like it's missing."

"Do you have any jumpers left?"

"I've got plenty of cables, but there's nowhere to hook them up."

"Look up at the top of the wall. Is there still a big white box there?"

"Uh… Yeah."

"Is there any wire at all sticking out of it?"

"Barely."

"You'll have to get wires to whatever's left. The node and the motor should have a common ground. You'll just need to hook up the positive lines, then clamp the negative to anything grounded. Without the power module to regulate it, there might be a surge, though. Maybe I can get the power shut down on this end for now."

"Will that slow things down?"

"By a few minutes."

"Then skip it."

He set the hovervan down where the power module should have been. With an armload of jumper wires, he scrambled up to the roof. He clamped one of the leads to the case and the other up to the positive wire. When he was sure they were secure, he hopped down and started frantically linking the ends of jumper wires to fabricate something that could reach the broken end of the live cable. He ran out of cables just a bit more than a meter short of the sparking power line.

"Of course," he growled.

Lex dropped the loose end and turned to the node's supply shed to get more, but something caught his eye. The churned up soil was still dark. Darker than it should have been. Even if it had been exposed for just a few minutes, it would have collected a layer of the windblown dust. This was freshly torn up.

"Of *course*," he said more harshly.

He raised his eyes and swept them around. Whoever or whatever had done this couldn't be far, and he had a feeling he knew just who to blame. There was nothing to see. But there *was* something to hear.

The sputtering rumble of another utility van drew his attention just in time for him to dive aside. It swept past and smashed into the one that had brought him here. The rogue van sputtered and died. From the looks of it, the pilot of the vehicle hadn't had nearly the luck Lex had when it came to avoiding the rain of stone. Most of the hovervan's roof was gone, and it had taken so much damage that the relatively minor impact was enough to cause the much-abused vehicle to completely shut down.

A battered but enraged mobster lurched from within. It was Milliner. He brandished a short length of pipe in his hand in lieu of a weapon.

"Oh, come *on*," Lex groaned.

Lex felt for the gun he'd stolen from the crew. He'd known better than to come this far without a weapon. Unfortunately, it turns out he *hadn't* known better than to not leave it in the passenger seat of the van.

"Okay, fine," Lex said, swinging the length of jumper cable like a flail. "You want to do this? Let's do this."

"You're a racer…" Milliner shouted, stalking forward. "Why are you so hard to kill?"

Lex circled him. "People have been trying to take me out for years, but I keep surviving. Practice makes perfect, I guess."

The thug charged forward. Lex rolled to the side and flipped the wire up. It caught his foe's ankle. The bruiser stumbled without falling.

"You're in over your head, Lex."

"I've got a lot of practice with that too."

The man charged again. This time Lex was a step too slow. They collided and both fell to the ground. Arms and legs swung and grabbed in a less than graceful scrum. Lex took solid blows from the man's pipe before finally managing to roll aside and get to his feet. Now he was unarmed.

Lex held his ribs and coughed. "Okay. That was a good shot. I kind of forgot I wasn't wearing a nanolattice rig."

"Next time, don't lock horns with someone who knows how to fight."

"Oh, don't worry," Lex said. "There won't be a next time."

The threat caused the thug to glance down. He found that in the confusion of the clash, Lex had managed to loop the exposed end of the wire around his ankle. He reached to unfasten it, but Lex took advantage of the distraction to charge at him, driving his shoulder into the thug's midsection. Off balance from the blow, the thug took a handful of steps backward to try to steady himself. Lex kept shoving until the wire ran out of slack. He dove aside while his opponent's leg was yanked out from under him and he came crashing down.

Right on top of the sparking end of the live wire.

Lex turned away as the sound of arcing electricity and escalating cries signaled the completion of the circuit. As the charge passed through the suit, as well as the thug's body, the man went rigid. When the motor redirecting the array finally spun down and the power flow shut off, the thug wasn't going to be giving anyone any more trouble.

Lex winced as he looked down at what remained of the gangster. "Look. I realize this is the part where I have a clever quip. But I think you broke a rib." He nudged the smoldering form with his boot. "And you're *very* dead. So I think we'll skip it."

With the final array repositioned, Lex's job was done. Picking his way through the wreckage of the two utility vans, he found a functional communicator.

"Okay. Job's done," he said. "But I'm going to need someone to pick me up."

#

"I've got it. I've got full power," Preethy said. "Directing it all to the suppression systems."

They turned their eyes to the screens. Barometric pressures responded immediately. Wind speeds started to tick down. The storms were beginning to subside, and doing so even more quickly than they had formed.

Preethy breathed a sigh of relief. "We did it."

"And you'll wish you didn't," came Hatch's voice over the radio.

Preethy and Michella snapped their heads around, as though his voice on the radio placed him somewhere in the room.

"Coal, where is he?" Michella snapped.

"His position is relatively unchanged. ... Correction, he is accelerating toward the control room. Impact in—"

A heavy piece of equipment smashed through the hatch, launching it aside.

"—negative point six eight seconds," Coal said.

The equipment was a large junction box that Hatch must have disconnected from the wall of the corridor. He'd used it as a battering ram and drifted into the control room. He was dressed in an identical survival suit. It had shrink-wrapped itself around his body as well, and he'd taken the care to slip the brass knuckles onto his glove.

"You've got two options," Hatch said. "You can turn control of this station back over to me, or you can be the new leverage I have over Nick. The choice is yours."

"I'm not giving up this station, and I'd sooner die than be your prisoner. You're not leaving this station with any form of leverage, Hatch," Preethy said defiantly.

"He's not leaving this station at all," Michella added, grabbing a strip of debris drifting before her.

She brandished it. He grinned.

"And here we are. On one hand, a businesswoman. On the other, a reporter. And right in the middle, the only one in the room who actually earns his *living* breaking bones and bloodying noses. I like my chances." He focused on Michella. "And I don't like *yours*. Because Preethy is still valuable to me. You, I'm better off without."

"If you think you can take me, try it."

"Oh, I intend to."

He pushed himself off the wall, barreling toward her. She took a mad swing with her improvised weapon. He caught it easily, wrenching it aside and hitting her full force with his forearm. She rebounded backward and struck the far wall hard. His momentum carried him the rest of the way to her. He grabbed a handrail with one hand and grabbed her raised hand with the other.

Strictly speaking, Michella didn't have any hand-to-hand combat training. She certainly didn't have any zero-g combat training. But she had desperation, fury, and an encyclopedic knowledge of the tenderest pieces of the male anatomy to work with. Three punishing knees to the groin persuaded him to release her and back away. She launched herself for the weapon again. Each time he tried to restrain her, an elbow or knee taught Hatch how little protection an emergency suit truly offered.

Had they been on the surface, Michella might even have won the battle. But Hatch had clearly been in a fight like this before. After absorbing a few blows that would probably have him coughing blood, his size finally got the better of her. A firm thrust off the wall sent both of them hurtling to the far wall. Michella struck first, and the full force of his weight and hers forced the wind from her body. He braced himself to keep the pressure on, making sure she couldn't get a deep breath.

"Oh, if only that helmet wasn't there. It would be so *rewarding* to wrap my fingers around your throat." His mad smile widened. "I wonder how much I'll have to work at these latches before I can get it off. Just how good is VectorCorp's safety lock?"

He grabbed one of the release latches. Michella wrapped both hands around his wrist, trying to wrestle his hand away.

"Let her go!" Preethy ordered, hurling herself into the fray.

Hatch pivoted and caught her by the arm with the nonlatch hand. The three of them were now drifting, none of them anchored to anything. Michella could hear the latch creaking. Surely it wasn't designed to be opened in a vacuum, but surely it wasn't designed to resist a lunatic with a viselike grip trying to force it open either.

Her desperate struggling and fighting against him ended up unzipping her purse. Its contents spilled out, drifting in a constellation of assorted accessories. Preethy's eyes practically sparkled as she saw her opportunity.

She snatched one of Michella's pens. With all of her might, she jabbed it into Hatch's back and yanked it free again.

He cried out, but the cry was cut short. The puncture to his back may have been the reason for his cry, but the rupture it caused in this suit was the reason for his silence. The precious oxygen rushed out—slamming him forward into Michella. His eyes bulged, and his fingers gave one final squeeze. But just as it had done to Michella not so long ago, the shock of decompression robbed him of his consciousness. Without intervention, the vacuum finished its job not long after. Hatch was no more.

Preethy shakily looked at the bloodied writing implement.

"Wow. You weren't kidding about being good with a pen," Michella said breathlessly.

"Why are you talking about pens? What is going on?" Coal asked.

"Nothing. It's fine. We're fine," Michella said.

"I see. I am pleased to announce that the transmission from the surface is no longer diffused. It should be entirely possible to reach the surface safely. Additionally, the focused transmission is no longer interfering with my sensors and communication. There are six ships on the way from the surface, all with Operlo Military designations. Stand by… I am also receiving a transmission from Ma, inquiring after the current status of the mission. Shall I inform her that I have succeeded brilliantly?"

Michella tried to wipe her forehead, forgetting that she was wearing a helmet. "Your performance was… unique, Coal. Any way you can get us down to the surface now?"

"You will need to remain in your survival suits, as I have failed to restore my atmosphere supply. But that can be arranged."

"Good. I don't want to spend another minute up here."

\#

A little over an hour later, Lex was limping his way into Nick Patel's villa. The cavalry had arrived shortly after the storm had cleared up, and while they were too late to save the day, the were useful for securing the gang and evacuating the injured and dehydrated crew.

Back at the villa, the rising sun revealed Nick fully dressed and barking orders. His seldom seen administrative side had a way of explaining just how he'd managed to wrangle an organization from such an underpopulated and ignored planet into something of interplanetary notoriety. The villa had some wind damage, and everything was covered in a layer of dust. The stuff reached half a meter deep in some places. The place had survived, though. Something akin to triage was happening as those in need of medical treatment were hurried into the house while the able-bodied were directed to free up more equipment to help with rescue and repair.

"There! There's the man of the hour," Nick called, trotting up to Lex.

"Go easy on the back slaps," Lex said, sidestepping as Nick got closer.

"How bad is it?"

"Nothing critical. Just my ribs."

Nick snapped his fingers. "Get this man something to take the edge off the pain, then get the paramedics over here for some imaging."

His people snapped to work. Two uniformed medics arrived and produced an autoinjector. After a spritz of painkiller, Lex found he could straighten up again without pain.

"I swear I could take more hits the last few times I did this."

"There comes a point in a man's life where his body lets him know it's time to slow down, Lex."

"I'm bad at slowing down."

"Trev!"

Lex looked up to find Michella rushing toward him. She was covered in bandages from a dozen little injuries. They threw their arms around each other, then each groaned as the embrace found various bruises and breaks.

"Are you okay?" each said to the other.

"Oh god. I'm so glad you're alive," Lex said, pressing his forehead to hers.

"Me too. When I saw that storm on the screens, I didn't know what to think."

"Where's Preethy? Is Preethy okay?"

"I'm fine, Lex," she said.

He turned to find her approaching. He pulled one arm away from Michella and snared Preethy into the hug as well. Not to be left out, Squee sprang from the nearby vehicle and managed to squeeze herself into the center of the love fest. They didn't separate until the medics required them to do so.

"How is everything? What happened? I haven't heard anything since we left the array," Lex said as the medics led him to the little makeshift infirmary they'd set up in Nick's garage.

"Communication is still down for the most part, and the storm hasn't completely vanished, but emergency networks are starting to report in, and it seems like the worst the storm did was flip some cars and tear up some roofs," Nick said. "But it could have been worse. A dozen more kilometers per hour on those gusts and we'd be testing the design limits of those buildings. I ought to know, it was my crews that built them."

As Lex neared the infirmary, a familiar black form could be seen in the courtyard beyond.

"Is that the *SOB*?" he said.

"Uh, Lex, maybe you should get fixed up before you go check out the ship. It didn't exactly escape this unscathed," Michella said.

As it turns out, that decision was not in their hands. No sooner had Lex spotted the *SOB* than the *SOB* spotted Lex. Its thrusters flared and it rose into the air flitting nimbly over the villa and scattering those below as it dropped down beside where Lex was standing.

"Hello, Lex. It is good to see you again," said a voice over the loudspeakers.

"C-coal?" Lex said, his voice catching in his throat. "You... I mean... you were—"

"If you are about to reference something protected by Temporal Contingency Protocol, don't," she said. "I kept doing that."

Lex blinked some of the emotion from his eyes and took a moment to survey what had become of his ship. Aside from having a mind of its own, the nose of the ship was pummeled out of shape. One of the heat dissipation fins had failed to retract and looked like a smashed insect wing dangling from beneath one of the thrusters. Gleaming metallic scrapes marred its matte-black finish in a hundred different places.

He turned to Michella. It took a few seconds for him to find his voice, and a few seconds more to find the proper *words*.

"Michella, again, I'm glad you're okay…" He pointed to the *SOB*. "But I'm not letting you borrow my ship again."

Epilogue

Lex paced around the table in his apartment. The aftermath of the Indra IV debacle had kept him and Michella apart for the better part of the last few days. She was due to arrive any moment, so he'd hastily assembled the most romantic dinner his limited skills could muster.

"Okay, Squee, what am I forgetting?" he said to the creature who watched him curiously from atop a bookshelf. "Salad for starters. Macaroni and cheese in the oven. Cheesecake in the fridge, and Mitch-accino ready to go. Oh!"

He fished out the ring box from his pocket and placed it on the table. "And we're *starting* with the proposal this time."

Lex's slidepad chirped. He fumbled for it in his pocket. "I'm taking bets, Squee. Is this Michella canceling? I'll give you even money." He glanced at the screen. "It's Jon. Jeez. I think he's more nervous than *I* am." He answered. "Hey, Jon."

"Lex! Did you ask her?"

"No, she's not here yet."

"Then she must be just getting dropped off. I just finished a call with her." A voice shouted something indistinctly in the background. "Would you be quiet, Donnie, I'm getting to that! Listen. Donnie and I are in the parking area. We want to be *the first* people to congratulate you."

"Yeah, sure. Listen. I'll buzz you in once she gets here. Wait in the hall. I'm going to ask her the first chance I get, so when I open the door again, the deed is done."

"Great! This is so exciting. I can't wait."

"Yeah, me neither." Lex looked to the door. "I think she's here. See you in a few minutes."

He hung up just as she opened the door. Squee bounded down to the floor to greet her.

"Michella!" He stood aside and majestically presented the table. "Ta-da!"

"Trev, we need to talk," she said, her tone serious.

"Yes! Yes we do." Sensing something unpleasant was about to dislodge his plans, he practically dove at the table to snatch the ring box. "I just have one thing to ask."

She raised her hand. "Let me finish. I've been thinking a lot about what happened over the last few weeks. Basically since you started the preliminaries here on Operlo."

"You've given a *lot* of people stuff to think about since then. But, real quick—"

She continued. "I didn't handle this as well as I could have. I let my inner journalist get in the way of my good judgment."

Lex opened his mouth to say something, an incredulous look on his face, but held his tongue.

"What was that about?"

"Nothing. It's just… Michella, I've wanted to ask you this for a long—"

"No, no. I know that look. You had a snide remark lined up, and I want to hear it. This whole fiasco has churned up some hard feelings across the board, and I want to air the grievances. What were you going to say?"

Lex gritted his teeth. "Can we *please* not do this *right now*?"

"Out with it, Trevor."

"You don't *have* an inner journalist. You have an *outer* journalist. You're a journalist first and everything else second. This wasn't you letting some inner compulsion run away with you. This was you not bothering to rein the compulsion *in*. But that's fine. It's who you *are*. Hopefully, it taught you something and we can work on not cutting a fiery swath across a bunch of other people's lives and livelihoods next time. If you're here to say you're sorry for how you acted, great! I understand. All is forgiven. Now if we could—"

"That's just it. You *don't* understand. I'm not sorry for what I did. People need to know the truth. I can't just let things fester in the darkness because it would make my life or your life easier."

"Oh, so that's what this whole thing has been about? Shedding a little light on the darkness? And what did the light show you? That the league is legit. Legitimately legit. And you knew that in week *two*. But you kept digging."

"Just because you don't find corruption on the surface, it doesn't mean there's none underneath."

"And what clues were you following that suggested you should keep digging?"

"Don't be a child. We both know Patel is a mobster."

"Yes! We all *do* know that Patel is a mobster. That isn't exactly a 'stop the presses' sort of revelation. But you weren't *investigating* Nick Patel. You were investigating Preethy Misra."

"That was for *you*. I wanted to make sure you didn't screw your life up a second time."

"Well you did a bang-up job of it, Mitch. It's going to be another six months before they can get the Indra station fixed again, so half of the tracks are going to have to have their races postponed. The league's whole *launch* has been scratched for a future date 'to be determined.' Suddenly, the life I *wanted,* showcasing my skills in a genuine competition instead of delivering packages and celebrities, is 'to be determined.'"

"Better that than end up tangled up with the mob again."

"And there it is," he said. "We'll ignore that both of us—and a bunch of other people—didn't end up nearly getting killed by mobsters until *after* your bad publicity opened the door for them. And we'll ignore that the 'some things are more important than the law' mentality of Nick and his crew is the only reason you're not in prison right now for breaking any number of laws to investigate them. This wasn't ever about me. This was about the mob. You weren't protecting me. You were scoring another point against organized crime."

"You say that like there's something wrong with it."

He held up a hand. "You're right. I'm being selfish. For a while, I was angry that I wasn't the most important thing in your life. I figured out numero uno was going to be The News—capital *N*—when we were still in college. But fine. My job was probably more important to me than it should have been. So I was number two. That's still pretty good. But it has been made pretty clear that I'm *not* number two. Because there was plenty of important news brewing all around the galaxy. Important things that could use some light shining on them. But you dug *here*, and you kept digging after finding nothing, because this was your chance to score another potential blow against your personal vendetta. So that makes me, what? Number three? And even *that* isn't a deal breaker. I wouldn't be *thrilled*, but I could *accept* if I was number three behind something you *love*. But I'm number three behind something you *hate*. Number three behind a self-destructive crusade. To you, that's more important than us."

"It *is!* It *is* more important than us! Maybe you don't want to hear it, Trev, but there is no such thing as a good mobster. They *all* have blood on their hands, and they *all* are a threat to society. It's who they *are!* They can't *be* a mobster without that simple fact being true. So if it comes down to it, if it comes down to you and I getting our happily ever after in exchange for turning a blind eye to this stuff, I will *always* choose the truth."

They stared at each other. The intensity of the moment was such that at some point Squee had hopped down and placed herself between the pair as if to separate them. The first to act was Lex. He lowered his head and turned away, marching to the closet and grabbing his jacket.

"Well?" Michella said. "Tell me I'm wrong."

"You're not. You're not wrong. All of that *is* more important than us. And I guess I'm just a weaker person than you, because I'm done making sacrifices for it."

He headed for the door.

"Get back here, Trevor. We're not through with this yet."

"I think we are, Michella. I think we're through."

He snapped his fingers. Squee gave Michella a quick look, then joined Lex at the door. He tapped it open to find Jon and Donnie standing there, looks of mischievous excitement on their faces.

"Well?" Jon said. "What did she say?"

"Plenty," Lex said.

He pulled the ring box from his pocket, tossed it to the floor, and paced down the hallway toward the long, cold night.

From The Author

Thank you for reading! If you liked this story, or perhaps if you found it lacking, I'd love to hear from you. You can find my social media, my email, and my newsletter at:

www.bookofdeacon.com/contact

Discover other titles by Joseph R. Lallo:

The Book of Deacon Series:

Book 1: *The Book of Deacon*
Book 2: *The Great Convergence*
Book 3: *The Battle of Verril*
Book 4: *The D'Karon Apprentice*
Book 5: *The Crescents*

Other stories in the same setting:

Jade
The Rise of the Red Shadow
The Redemption of Desmeres

The Big Sigma Series:

Book 1: *Bypass Gemini*
Book 2: *Unstable Prototypes*
Book 3: *Artificial Evolution*
Book 4: *Temporal Contingency*

The Free-Wrench Series:

Book 1: *Free-Wrench*
Book 2: *Skykeep*
Book 3: *Ichor Well*
Book 4: *The Calderan Problem*
Book 5: *Cipher Hill*